Valley Shadow

Jack R. Phillips

A Black Horse Western

ROBERT HALE · LONDON

© Philip Harbottle 2002
Based on a short story by John Russell Fearn
First published in Great Britain 2002

ISBN 0 7090 7160 4

Robert Hale Limited
Clerkenwell House
Clerkenwell Green
London EC1R 0HT

Typeset by
Derek Doyle & Associates, Liverpool.
Printed and bound in Great Britain by
Antony Rowe Limited, Wiltshire

1
WINNER TAKE ALL

To Diana Travers, daughter of Big Ben Travers of the Leaning H ranch, it was a hard task to make up her mind. In most things, as his secretary and assistant in connection with her father's cattle business, she was capable of making snap judgements, and more often than not they were right – but faced with the dilemma of two men who both wanted to marry her she was in a quandary.

This particular evening she was confronted with the problem again. She reclined in a basket chair in her usual red-silk shirt and riding-skirt, listening to Jeff Kelvin's impassioned appeals. Though she looked interested it was just a pose. She had heard the story too many times.

Jeff Kelvin, though, was undeterred. He studied her amber-bronzed face as he talked, noting every movement of her blue eyes, every stirring of her fair hair in the soft evening breeze.

'For the life of me, Diana, I don't see why you can't make up your mind,' he declared at last.

'What's so wrong with me? I've got my own spread – not as big as this one of your pop's, I reckon, but he's a lot older than me, and has had time to build up his business. I'm not without money – nor education, neither. It isn't as though I'm a rough cowpuncher . . . So what's holding things up?'

'I – don't know,' Diana said, hesitantly, regarding him – and she spoke truth.

She really *didn't* know. Jeff Kelvin fulfilled most of the qualifications of an outdoors man of the West. He was powerfully built with a fairly easy smile, and thick dark hair . . . He had a brown, lean face and level grey eyes. And yet . . .

'Look, Diana, there's something I have to tell you. I was waiting until you'd agreed to marry me, but since you're still hesitating, I'll tell you now. You know I've been away quite a bit these last few months?'

'Yes,' Diana said slowly, wondering what was coming. 'You told me you had business in Valley Shadow, a town about a hundred miles east of here . . .'

'That's right – I had. At least, business of a sort.' Jeff smiled enigmatically, and hesitated before continuing:

'I went out to Valley Shadow originally to visit my uncle, and help him with his business affairs. He was seriously ill. In fact, he died last month.'

'Oh. I'm sorry.'

'You needn't be,' Jeff said surprisingly. Then, as the girl looked at him in puzzlement, he added drily:

'In his will, he left me his property in Valley Shadow – his ranch, the Lazy Y, and the Double Dollar saloon, the biggest and best establishment in the town.' Jeff smiled expansively.

'I – I'm pleased for you, of course,' Diana said uncertainly. 'But why are you telling me this now?'

'Isn't it obvious? I wanted you to agree to marry me for myself, and not because I was newly rich! Of course, I'll have to sell up my small ranch here, and move to Valley Shadow. From what I saw in my visits there, it's a town with great potential for an ambitious guy like me. And every successful man has a good woman behind him. I'd like for you to come with me – as my wife.'

'I'm sorry, Jeff. I – I'd have to think about moving from my home town. And as for marriage to you . . .' her voice tailed off.

'This can't go on, Diana,' he insisted, becoming irritated. 'If there's another guy you're hankering after why don't you tell me?'

Diana laughed softly. 'And supposing there was? What would you do if I did tell you?'

'Shoot the boots off him!'

'There you are!' She spread her hands. 'That's what I don't like about you, Jeff. You're too ready with that iron of yours.'

'Why not?' he objected. 'I'm the fastest shooter in this town, and you know it. *Everybody* knows it. No reason why I should stand for some other guy wanting you. I've got all you need.'

'Doesn't it occur to you,' Diana asked deliberately, 'that I might have some say in it? Don't take too much for granted, Jeff.'

'What do you mean?' He looked at her levelly. 'You mean you're not taking me? That it?'

'The answer's the same tonight as it's been other nights. I'm not saying anything definite. Getting married isn't like branding cattle: you've got to think hard about it.'

Jeff got slowly to his feet, thumbs hooked in his pants belt. He shook his head as he looked down at the girl.

'I suppose it's just that I can't figure women,' he muttered, sighing. 'I'm offering you everything most normal women want and you still keep on turning me down. Look, just tell me one thing: *Is* there some other guy mixed up in this?'

Diana hesitated, then she nodded her fair head slowly.

'Yes, Jeff, there is – but since you aim to do some fancy shooting if I tell you about him I'm saying no more.'

Jeff's craggy face hardened. 'You know I've got more sense than to go about shooting up a feller; I was only joshing. Who is he? Let's be seeing what sort of opposition I've got.'

Diana uttered her next words in a very quiet voice. 'It's Art Cranley.'

There was no outburst from Jeff. Instead he began to grin widely; then he laughed outright.

The girl sat looking at him coldly.

'Is that so funny?' she asked at length.

'I'll say it's funny! *That* tenderfoot in opposition

to *me*! Why, I reckon he don't know which end of a gun to get hold of. Where'd you ever get the idea you liked him?'

Diana didn't answer. Her firm mouth set.

'Anyway,' Jeff added, his amusement subsiding, 'you don't have to worry about me blowing the dust from under him. It wouldn't be worth exercising my trigger-finger. You'll think again, Diana!' He looked at her seriously. 'And mighty soon! He's got nothing to offer you like I have, working in that small office in town —'

'He's the owner of it,' Diana retorted, getting to her feet. 'He's trying to build up his own business as an architect. I'm more interested in getting the man I want than in weighing up his prospects. I'm not ambitious – never was.'

'If you could be content with Art Cranley you can't be,' Jeff agreed heavily. 'Anyway, you've heard my proposition. I'll see you again when you've gotten yourself more sense.'

He put on his sombrero and went down the porch steps to his horse.

Diana watched him ride off the ranch land, his hand waving, and her eyes followed the trail of dust as it went back down land towards the nearby thriving town of Sycamore Halt.

'What's wrong, Di? Still a-tryin' to make up your mind?'

The girl turned sharply as her father's heavy footsteps sounded on the boards of the porch. There was a half-smile on his good-natured face as he closed the screen-door.

'I'm a-goin' into town,' he said. 'One or two things I want to attend to at Bart Thompson's concerning the cattle-drive this weekend . . .' He paused, contemplating the girl as he settled his hat on his grey hair. 'What's the matter, Di? That palooka Jeff talk outa turn?'

'No, Dad.' Diana shook her head slowly. 'He never does that. It's just that I'm trying to make up my mind between Jeff and Art Cranley. I like both of 'em, and Art best of all. Jeff's just a bit too proud of himself, though. Once I was married to him I mightn't be able to keep a rein on his ambitions.'

'Well . . .' Her father scratched his jaw reflectively. 'It ain't none of my business, of course, an' I'm not goin' to influence you either way because I'll lose you any road; but I will tell you this – In my day we acted *like* men, whether it were about women or a bonanza lode. We shot it out between us, an' there weren't nobody as dared interfere. I ain't ashamed to say there was another guy hankerin' after your mother – rest her soul – but when I'd gotten through with him —'

'This,' Diana interrupted, laying a gentle hand on his arm, 'is not your day, Dad! There's law and order now. We're not pioneers with only a gun for an answer. We're a settled community.'

Big Ben Travers nodded. 'Yep – you're right there, Di. Well, I'll leave it to you to decide. I must be on my way to make the arrangements for the weekend. You're still coming with us on the drive?'

'Of course I am, Dad.'

Travers went past her and down the steps. Long after he had gone from sight Diana stood by the porch rail, thinking, her eyes fixed on mighty grey peaks which reared defiantly into the sunset. The ranch, the mesa, the plains, the arid winds of summer and the relentless bite of winter: she had known nothing else in her entire twenty-three years.

If she married Jeff Kelvin the scene would be completely changed; she'd have to move to a different town entirely, and a new way of life. But if she took Arthur Cranley instead? Well, he too had ambitions of a sort, and chief amongst them loomed the desire to leave the changelessness of Sycamore Halt.

She turned away at last. There were accounts to be dealt with, some steers to be seen to – then she paused at the sight of a lone rider approaching through the violet mists of the twilight along the trail from Sycamore Halt.

He swept in at the ranch gates at last and resolved into Art Cranley himself, mounted on a powerful bay. In five seconds he'd tethered the horse to the tie rail below the ranch house steps and then came hurrying up them.

'Howdy, Diana.' He pulled off his hat quickly and stood looking at her half-apologetically in the dimming light. 'I don't want to interrupt anythin' if you're busy, but I met Jeff Kelvin in town —'

'And he told you that you're the other fellow, I suppose?'

'Yes. I thought I'd hop over and get things

straightened out.'

Diana shrugged and Arthur made an uneasy movement. He was tall, loose-limbed, with light-brown hair. To a man, his natural hesitating manner suggested nervousness; to a woman – of Diana's type anyway – it was an appealing fault, if fault it was. There was considerable sterling worth under the diffidence.

'I mean,' he went on, 'you've sort of led me to expect that you and I'd hit the trail together. I didn't know you felt that way about Jeff, 'specially as he seems to have been out of town a lot recently.'

'Listen, Art,' Diana gripped his sinewy arm, 'you two don't seem to realize the spot you're putting me in. I like the both of you – and if it's any consolation to you I like you a good bit more than I do Jeff. You're quieter, more my type. But I've got to be fair with each of you. I can't say "Yes" to either one without hurting, neither can I say "No", for the same reason. If you can find a way to turn Jeff's affections in some other direction you know what my answer will be.'

'Yes, but . . .' Arthur rubbed the lobe of his ear and shook his head doubtfully. 'That ain't so easy, Diana. Jeff's a feller who knows his way around far better than I do.'

'You're both men,' Diana told him quietly. 'Figure it out for yourselves. You can tell Jeff what I've said, if you want. Maybe you'll work it out in a poker-game or something – winner take all! If that's the way it is I shan't grumble.'

They stood regarding each other in the pale gloom for a moment, then Art drew a deep breath.

'I'll think of something!' he vowed. 'You see if I don't!'

Arthur Cranley returned to Sycamore Halt full of resolution but with no fixed plan in mind. In fact the only course seemed to be to tackle Jeff Kelvin himself. He found him at the bar of the Red Ace saloon, drinking alone, elbows on the counter and hat pushed up on his forehead.

'Seen her?' Jeff enquired briefly, then drained his glass and plonked it down.

'I saw her . . . Whiskey.' Arthur added, to the bartender.

'Same again,' Jeff ordered, and then he gave a grim smile. 'And what did she say? Plain, ornery, stubborn, I'll bet? Same as she is with me.'

'I don't reckon there's anything ornery about her,' Arthur retorted. 'We've got to remember that she's in the hard position of havin' to choose between us.'

'For which,' Jeff observed calmly, 'there ain't no necessity. No dame in her right senses would have you while I'm around.'

Arthur said nothing but he tightened his lips for a moment. Turning to the whiskey he drank it down.

'Mebby you've got me wrong,' he said presently. 'I —'

'Got you wrong?' Jeff shook his head. 'I know you're that tame you only wear that gun of yours to make you look like a man. How good can you shoot with it? Tell me that!'

'Not as fast or as well as you can, and I admit it. But a gun isn't everything, Jeff.'

'No?' Jeff considered this and gave a sardonic smile. 'Well, I sort of think it is – 'specially in this part of the world. And let me tell you something, Art . . .' He tapped him on the chest emphatically. 'You'll do yourself a whole lot of good if you steer clear of Diana Travers from now on. She's my especial prize . . . *Sabe?*'

'Supposin' I don't?'

Jeff whipped his gun out and levelled it.

'I might get around to using you for shooting practice – even though I don't want to. And in case you think I'm bluffing . . .'

He whipped the gun round, sighted briefly at the oil-lamp on the wall over the rattling tin-panny piano, and fired.

Cowpunchers and pianist jumped violently as the lamp exploded in a shattering of glass. Faces, malevolent and surprised, were turned from the tables.

'Okay, folks, don't let it throw you,' Jeff told them easily, holstering the gun again. 'I was just showing my pardner here that I'm no tenderfoot when it comes to shooting.'

'Nobody ever said you were, Jeff —'

'—and there's no call for cheap exhibitions!'

Jeff turned sharply and gave a start of surprise at beholding Diana Travers standing at the bar. She had changed now into blue Levis, and a broad-brimmed hat sat well back on her fair head.

'Well, if it ain't Diana!' Jeff gave a grin. 'Not often you come in here. What'll you have?'

'Nothing,' she answered briefly. 'I'm not in here to drink. I'm on my way to fetch Dad back from old man Thompson's. There's trouble with one of the steers that he ought to know about. But it's not so urgent that I couldn't drop in here and see how you two were making out.'

'We're making out all right, Diana,' Arthur told her levelly. 'Why shouldn't we be?'

'Then what was the gun play for?' she asked, her blue eyes darting back to Jeff. 'I saw and heard it as I came through the batwings.'

As Jeff made no answer she added, 'I'll make one guess: You were telling Art here what he'd get if he tried to stand in your way. Right?'

Jeff looked about him at the assembled men and women at the tables. None of them was paying any attention now. They were too busy drinking or playing their eternal card-games.

'Well?' Diana asked sharply.

Jeff turned back to look at her.

'Yeah – it's right,' he assented. Then he added coolly, 'And I meant it, Diana. When a gal doesn't know what's good for her it's time she was told! And I'm telling you, right now. You belong to me, and if this tenderfoot here gets in my way I'll bushwhack him and fix it so that I don't get the blame. I've gotten things in my life through taking them, and I'll go right on doing it!'

'Not while I'm here you won't,' Arthur said, hard lights in his eyes. 'I told you earlier – mebbe you've got me wrong. Diana's going to make a free choice, and —'

'If it comes to that,' Jeff interrupted. 'I'll be gosh-durned if I can see what all the fuss is about. It isn't as if we were asking to marry a princess or something. Your ideas are too big, Diana! You're a nice girl, I grant, and you sure looked pretty early on this evening when you were wearing that green shirt of yours, but right now in them Levis you're as plain and ornery as the rest of us.'

Arthur's hand dropped to the butt of his revolver and remained there.

'Take it easy, feller,' he cautioned. 'Any more insults like that an' I may show you just how good I am.'

Gradually Diana's face settled in firm lines.

'I'm putting an end to this bickering right now,' she declared. 'Some of the things you've just been saying, Jeff, make me see that you're pretty no-account anyway – but I'm still willing to play. Just as Dad left this evening he told me something that sounded like mighty good sense. He said that the men of his day shot it out between themselves, whether it was gold or women that was at stake. He married my mother because he was quicker on the draw than the other guy. I'm willing to be taken the same way.'

'Then I reckon you'd better think again, Miss Travers,' commented Sheriff Latham. He had just come up to the further end of the counter and had been listening to the conversation. Now he came

forward – immense, lumbering, a resolute tight-
ness about his mouth. He'd hammered law and
order into Sycamore Halt in a few months and he
meant it to stay that way.

'Suppose, Sheriff, you give me a chance to
finish?' Diana asked, looking at him. 'I'm not
saying that Jeff and Art here should try and
outshoot each other; that's primitive. But there
can't be any objections to some target practice,
can there?'

'Depends on the target,' Sheriff Latham
answered, pondering.

Diana thought for a moment or two, studying
the cowpunchers who were now watching the
gathering drama with interest. Then, going
forward, she took the scarves from the necks of
the two nearest men and spread them out four-
square, a green one and a red one.

'What's the idea of red and green scarves?' Jeff
demanded.

He was not answered. Holding a scarf in each
hand Diana walked across the saloon, asked for
some pins from a woman seated at one of the
further tables, and finally fastened both scarves,
folded into a square and flat to the opposite wall.
Then she returned to the counter.

'What kind of a crazy scheme is this?' Jeff
asked, puzzling. 'Why the folded scarves?'

'It's simple,' the girl told them quietly. Then she
turned and addressed the men and women at the
tables.

'You folks had better make a clear passage in

case a bullet goes astray!'

There was a momentary pause as the drinkers scrambled noisily to one side and there remained, half-seated or else standing, watching. Sheriff Latham rubbed his chin and frowned.

'Now,' Diana said, turning back to Jeff and Art as they stood side by side. 'There are two scarves spread out there. Whichever of you fires through the centre of the red scarf can have me – and no questions asked. First though, let's have a look at your guns. Better still, you have a look at them, Sheriff.'

Arthur and Jeff pulled their guns from their holsters and handed them over. Latham examined each in turn.

'Yours is a thirty-eight,' he said, handing Jeff's gun back; 'and yours, Art, is forty-four.'

Arthur took the revolver back into his hand. The sheriff looked at the girl questioningly.

'Well, what happens now?'

'Both of you boys will fire simultaneously at the red scarf,' the girl instructed. 'Whichever of you hits the dead centre, or nearest approach to it, has me. Is that understood?'

'Not quite,' Jeff said, thinking. 'How'll we know which of us is the winner if we both fire at once?'

'You get dumber every minute!' the girl told him frankly. 'I had the Sheriff here examine your guns so the bullets can be gouged out of the wall afterwards. They'll make holes in the scarves and plug the wall behind the holes. The bullets *must* correspond with the holes, and the guns that fired them. That's fair enough, isn't it?'

The two men nodded slowly and there was a murmur of assent from the gathered onlookers.

'And you, Sheriff, a man whose word's enough for all of us, will be the judge. All right?'

'Okay,' he agreed. 'Get started.'

'Wait a minute,' Arthur said quietly. 'If this is what is to be done I think you might as well take Jeff by the arm right now and lead him out of here, Diana. You know as well as I do that I'm no match for him when it comes to fast and fancy shootin'.'

Jeff grinned confidently as he weighed his gun gently up and down in his hand.

'You can try, can't you?' the girl demanded. 'It's the only way – and there'll be no bloodshed. Come on.'

'All right,' Sheriff Latham said. 'Let's go. When I count three. One . . .'

Set-faced, Arthur raised his revolver and sighted the distant red scarf across the saloon. It seemed about a hundred miles away.

'Two . . .'

Still grinning, Jeff continued to play with his .38, ready to snap it to the ready.

'Three!'

Both guns exploded and the arms of the two men jolted momentarily. Smoke coiled slowly in a plume towards the oil-lamps. In a surging tide, men and women – Jeff, Arthur, the girl, and Latham in the forefront – swept across the room and formed in a circle around the scarves.

Both of them had holes in them – the red one a good couple of inches from the centre and the green one practically dead in the centre.

'Never was anything easier,' Jeff said complacently. 'Mebby in a few years' time you'll find out what that iron of yours is for, Art.'

'Mebby,' he agreed. 'I felt sure I'd sighted pretty close to the mark, too . . .' He shrugged. 'Well, I'd better be on my way, I suppose. It was nice knowin' you, Diana, while it lasted.'

'Not so fast!' the girl exclaimed sharply. 'We want the results first!'

'Results? They're there – starin' us in the face.'

Nobody spoke for a moment as Latham dug into the rough wooden wall with his penknife. Finally he extracted the bullet that bored through the green scarf and looked at it

'It's a thirty-eight!' he exclaimed, surprised.

Jeff nodded calmly. ' 'Course it is – right through the red scarf.'

Latham looked at him. 'Now just a minute, Jeff! What sorta game are you tryin' to pull? The *green* scarf was here: I took it down afore I dug the bullet out.'

'Like heck you did!' Jeff hooted. 'And you can't —'

'Aw, quit it, Jeff!' somebody shouted. 'We all see that! You can't get away with a game like that . . .'

Jeff frowned bewilderedly, then stared as Latham dug out the other bullet. 'Forty-four,' he pronounced, nodding. 'Through the red scarf, but not dead centre —'

'Near enough for me,' Diana said briefly. 'Come on, Art.'

'Hey!' Jeff called. 'Wait a minute! There's some blasted monkey business going on around here . . .'

He tried to move towards the girl but his way was blocked completely by the crowd. 'Lay off, Jeff! You fired wide – straight into that green scarf!'

'I tell you I didn't . . .'

The shouts faded away for Arthur and the girl as they passed through the batwings on to the boardwalk outside.

'I can understand hitting the scarf,' Arthur said, musing. 'That couple of inches from the centre is about my usual style – but I sure can't understand what happened to Jeff's aim.'

Diana smiled as they walked together to where their horses were tied.

'It's simple,' she said. 'Otherwise I'd never have taken such a chance of losing you. A bit unfair, maybe, but that's justified after the things Jeff said about me. You see, I knew you'd hit the scarf *somewhere*, just as much as I knew Jeff would *never* hit it.'

'For Pete's sake, Diana, come into the open and explain, can't you?'

'All right. What colour of shirt had I on when you came to see me tonight?'

Arthur stared at her in the light of the lamps. 'Huh? I dunno. It was getting too dark to tell.'

'It was red silk. Jeff saw me in it when the light

was still good, but at the bar he talked about my *green* shirt. Now do you get it? He's suffering from something a lot of people have and don't know it, and there's sort of no way to cure it for them because you can't describe what's wrong.'

'You mean he can't tell red from green?' Arthur gasped, startled.

'That's it. Green looks red, and red looks green – in varying shades . . . He's colour blind!'

2
MURDER

'A distraction!' Diana's voice rose sharply. 'So *that*'s all I am to you, Art?'

The girl got to her feet, her face indignant: she was very close to tears. She stood staring at Arthur Cranley where he sat at what had become – of late – their usual table in the Red Ace saloon.

All around them, heads turned in their direction. Both men and women – especially the latter – halted their own conversations, and paused to listen.

That Diana and Arthur should be quarrelling in public was definitely intriguing. Ever since the memorable shooting-contest held in the saloon some four weeks earlier, the couple had become quite well known in the local community.

The local newspaper had featured a write-up of the story of the shooting-contest, and the following week had also carried an announcement of their engagement to marry. Since then they had been seen everywhere together, and had seemed the perfect couple.

Evidently something had now gone badly wrong. But what?

'Diana, for heaven's sake!' Arthur looked about him in obvious embarrassment. 'Keep your voice down! And sit down . . . please! Everyone's looking . . .'

Diana hesitated, evidently on the point of walking out. Then, flashing an indignant glance at the onlookers at their nearby tables, she thought better of it. Slowly she sat down in her seat again.

'Let me explain,' Arthur implored, reaching out his hand towards the girl's own, where it was gripping the edge of the table.

She withdrew her hand, and looked at him uncompromisingly. 'All right. I'm listening,' she whispered.

'You know I'm studying to be an architect,' Arthur said earnestly. 'The spread of the locomotive is really opening up our country. Towns are beginning to grow. More and more people are no longer content to live in wooden houses and ramshackle communities —'

'You mean like my Dad's Leaning H ranch, and Sycamore Halt of course?' the girl snapped, and compressed her lips.

'Of course not,' Arthur said. 'I don't mean that at all, Diana. All I'm saying is that, as towns and cities grow, there'll be a tremendous demand for new and more substantial buildings – especially in places like New York. It means great opportunities for a qualified architect. And that's where I see my future . . . *our* future,' he corrected hastily, as he saw the girl's frown deepening.

'You know I only want the very best for you. Surely you can understand that?'

Diana's expression softened. 'Of course I can,' she whispered. 'But why can't we get married now, then I can come with you to New York? I can get work there too, and —'

'I've already explained that,' Arthur said miserably. 'I've had this offer to join a firm of New York architects, but it's just for a trial period . . . a sort of apprenticeship, whilst I complete my studies and qualifications. I won't be earning much above a subsistence rate initially, certainly not enough to buy a house and get married on . . . but that will soon change! I know it will. Then, once I've established myself, I can send for you – or rather, come back here for you – and we can be married.'

'But if I came with you and found work – maybe as a secretary – we *would* have enough to get by on,' the girl insisted, her colour rising. 'What's wrong with that idea?'

'Everythin'.' Arthur shook his head, his expression pained. 'If we were married, I'd have our home to fix, and I'd have to give you —'

'Your full attention,' the girl finished coldly, her voice hardening. 'As I said: you see me simply as a distraction to your precious studies!'

'But Diana —'

'I'm sorry, Art.' The girl's voice rose again, as she got to her feet decisively. Once again the background hubbub in the saloon dropped as heads once more turned in their direction.

'You obviously have no intention of marrying me now, and I certainly don't intend to hang around for months, maybe years, on the off chance that you *might* want to get married eventually. So I'm finishing things right now. *Goodbye!*'

Arthur sat stunned for a moment, then he got to his feet, bewildered by the turn of events.

'Diana – come back!'

But the girl had gone. Only her engagement ring remained on the table.

For the past week Arthur Cranley had not been able to show his face in the Red Ace saloon, the scene of his earlier humiliation when Diana had publicly walked out on him. But now . . . Now all that had changed – thanks to one simple letter. The very next day after breaking off the engagement, Diana had ridden away with her father on a week-long cattle drive, delivering 400 head of cattle to Austin.

It had given her time to think, and on her arrival at Austin, during her first night at the hotel where she and her father were staying, she had written Arthur a letter.

In the letter she had expressed contrition for her hasty decision, and asked him to take her back. On reflection, she had decided that he was right – and promised to wait for him, and back him in his plans. The letter explained that she and her father would be away for the rest of that week – but she had promised to call on him at his home on the following Monday evening, when she and her father's outfit were due to return to Sycamore Halt after the completion of their business.

Receiving the letter on the morning of the day Diana was due to return, Arthur had promptly celebrated the turn in his fortune by calling in at the Red Ace to celebrate. He had taken the letter with him, flourishing it to anyone who doubted his news. Word that the engagement was back on soon spread amongst the habitués in the saloon, and, as chance had it, thay included Jeff Kelvin.

Kelvin had himself been extremely busy in recent weeks. Immediately after losing Diana in the shooting-contest, Jeff had put matters in train for the sale of his ranch to his foreman, Sam Oakes, and made good his decision to move to Valley Shadow.

During the past weeks he had made several journeys back and forth, and today was his last visit. His buckboard, with two horses, was loaded with his last few personal possessions outside of the Red Ace saloon. Earlier that day, he had signed the conveyance of his ranch, completing its transfer to his old foreman, who had bought it as a going concern.

Now, inside the saloon, his affairs completed, and about to drive back to Valley Shadow, he was having a farewell drink with Oakes. Jeff aimed a sour look at his ex-foreman as Oakes returned to their table with two drinks.

'What's going on over at the bar, Sam?' he

asked, nodding to the counter some yards distant.
'Seems a lot of hollering and back-slapping going
on since that jigger Cranley waltzed in twenty
minutes back. Surely he can't *still* be celebrating
his engagement to Diana? That was about a
month ago!'

Oakes stared blankly, then his leathery face
creased into a somewhat embarrassed smile. 'Of
course you don't know anythin', do you?'

'Know what?' Jeff snapped, irritated at the
sound of merriment at the bar and the fuss being
made of his hated rival. 'Out with it, man!'

Oakes took a long drink, then: 'Last week
whilst you've been away in Valley Shadow –
Diana Travers threw over young Art Cranley –
right here in this saloon. She gave him back his
ring and stormed out. I was here, an' saw – an'
heard too – the whole thing myself.'

Jeff opened then closed his mouth in astonishment. Anger suffused his swarthy, handsome face.
He glared at Oakes.

'Why the hell didn't you mention this earlier,
Sam – when I was out at the ranch with you, sign-
ing the transfer deed?'

Oakes looked uncomfortable. He picked up his
glass, not meeting his former employer's eyes. 'I
was goin' to tell you afore you left, Jeff. I guess it
just slipped my mind earlier.'

'What you mean,' said Jeff deliberately, 'is that
you didn't mention it, in case it made me change
my mind about selling my ranch to you! You know
I was set on marrying Diana myself! Well?'

'I – I'm sorry, Jeff. I guess that might have had a little to do with it, but,' his slightly hang-dog expression changed and brightened considerably, 'that don't matter no more. No sirree! The engagement's right back *on* again! That's what the celebration at the bar's all about.'

Jeff expelled his breath, and sat back in his chair, his tenseness relaxing. 'I get it.' He smiled faintly. 'Mebbe just as well you didn't tell me, Sam. Would have made these present shenanigans a lot harder to take . . .' He looked at the bar counter in the middle distance, and took a long drink from his glass.

'What's that piece of paper he keeps waving about? Did you pick up any details when you were at the bar getting these drinks in?'

'Sure I did. That's the cause o' the whole thing. It's a letter Cranley's just received from Diana Travers this mornin' —'

'Letter?' Jeff frowned. 'Ain't the gal in town?'

'No – she and her old man, and a bunch of his boys have been over in Austin completin' a cattle deal. Guess she must have sent the letter from there.'

'And the letter told him their affair was back on? All lovey-dovey again?' Jeff spoke quietly.

Oakes took another drink, relieved that he was now apparently off the hook again.

'That's it. Cranley was a-readin' bits o' the letter out. She's due back this evenin' – goin' to visit him at that house of his on the edge of town . . .' he broke off with a leer. Then his grin vanished abruptly as he noticed the expression on Jeff's face.

'What *time* is he expecting her to call on him?' Jeff asked peremptorily, his voice like ice. 'Be late when she gets back from Austin . . .'

'Huh?' Oakes gave him a puzzled look. 'Around nine o'clock tonight . . . Cranley was readin' that bit out, when —'

'Nine o'clock!' Jeff breathed, his eyes slitting. 'Be dark, then . . .' Abruptly he got to his feet, picked up his glass and drained it quickly.

He held out his hand to the startled Oakes.

'Guess I'll say goodbye right now, Sam. I've a long ride ahead of me, back to Valley Shadow. Good luck with the ranch.'

Before the surprised Oakes could reply, Jeff was striding away from the table. But he did not head for the batwings. Instead, he turned towards the bar. As he neared the group clustered around Arthur Cranley, his face assumed a genial smile as he saw Sheriff Latham was amongst the group at the bar.

Catching sight of Jeff approaching, Arthur suddenly stopped talking. His listeners turned their heads to follow his gaze.

'Howdy, Jeff,' Arthur said carefully. 'Haven't seen you in some time. What do you want?'

The habitués in the bar tensed, and fell silent, expecting some imminent altercation between the two rivals. But then they received a shock.

Smiling broadly, Jeff clapped Arthur on the shoulder. 'I don't want anything, Art – 'cept to wish you and Diana all the best!'

Thereafter, to everyone's complete astonishment, he insisted on buying a round of drinks, and commenced chatting amiably to the astonished Arthur. When at length Arthur tried to buy him a drink, Jeff straightened up from the bar rail, and shook his head.

'No thanks, Art. I want to be hitting the trail back to Valley Shadow, and I need a clear head. I guess I'm late setting out already – so I'm leaving right this instant.' As he spoke, he had raised his voice, so that practically everyone in the bar heard him. Heads turned in his direction as he strode to the batwings. Reaching them, he turned, and gave a wave to the sea of faces watching him . . . then he was gone.

Back at the bar counter, Arthur looked about him, and smiled at Sheriff Latham.

'That sure was swell of Jeff, I reckon. I'm glad we buried the hatchet before he left town. Guess Diana'll be surprised when I tell her tonight – and pleased, too.'

He picked up his half-full glass, then smiled and put it down on the counter again.

'No more for me! Guess I'll follow Jeff's example, and get back home. Wouldn't do for Diana to find me drunk when she comes to see me at nine tonight, now would it?'

Towards 8.30 in the evening a shadow appeared in the dim light at the back of the house that was isolated from the rest of Sycamore Halt by nearly a mile. Arthur Cranley's house had been designed by his late grandfather – also an architect – and had been his parents' home. Now they too were dead, and Arthur lived in the house alone.

The shadow paused and looked about him, gun in his gloved hand. In the deepening twilight it was just possible to make out the features of Jeff Kelvin. A few hundred yards away, his buckboard was hidden in the hollow of a grove of trees, where his horses waited patiently, nibbling roots.

Cautiously Jeff ducked through the wire fence – not wishing to open the possibly creaking gate – and walked slowly up the smooth stones forming the pathway to the porch. He was careful not to leave footprints in the garden to either side.

Silently Kelvin reached the porch, where he stood surveying and weighing up the best means of entry. To one side was the main downstairs living-room window, where thin slats of light gleamed through the small gaps in the shutters. Inside, Jeff knew, was Arthur Cranley – impatiently awaiting the arrival of Diana Travers. 'Probably still reading that letter of hers,' Jeff murmured to himself. 'Right – here I go.'

He commenced a swift ascent of the trellis-work over the front porch, finally poising himself outside the bedroom which looked out frontwards. The curtains were not drawn and Kelvin could see that the room was empty. It was not likely to be locked, either.

He felt at the window and to his satisfaction it was not latched. Presumably the top sash had been left a little open to admit fresh air — a normal enough procedure for any bedroom. In another moment the bottom sash glided up and Kelvin slipped into the room beyond. Here he stopped for a moment, listening intently.

There was complete silence, so evidently Arthur was still downstairs, waiting for the girl's knock on the front door. Catlike, Kelvin glided across the room, and cautiously opened the door, looking out on to the stair landing. It was only in semi-darkness, some illumination being provided from the occupied lounge below, where the door was slightly open.

His lips compressed as he controlled his breathing, Kelvin descended the carpeted stairs slowly, one step at a time. Ever and again he froze as a slight creak sounded, his right hand firmly gripping the gun he kept pointed at the slightly opened doorway from which the light was spilling.

Reaching the foot of the stairs without mishap, Kelvin edged along the short length of hallway towards the closed front door. He thudded on it heavily with his gloved left hand, then fell into a slight crouch as he turned to face back along the short passage, his fingers tightening around the trigger of his right-hand gun.

Abruptly light flooded the passage as the door flew open, and Arthur Cranley came striding out to open the front door and admit — so he thought — Diana Travers. Kelvin fired directly at Arthur's chest at point-blank range. Once, twice, the noise sounding shattering loud in the confined space and silence of the night.

It was doubtful if Arthur even had time to recognize his assailant. He uttered only a faint groan as he staggered backwards and collapsed in a heap. He was dead before he hit the floor.

Kelvin smiled to himself – a cold, sadistic smile. He considered that he had just committed the perfect murder: everyone in the Red Ace saloon had seen him leave earlier that day, headed in his buckboard back to Valley Shadow. They had no reason to doubt that that was where he had headed. But instead, Kelvin had left the trail and hidden himself several miles outside of town, and had returned now – but only to Cranley's isolated house on the very outskirts – under cover of darkness.

When he did get back to Valley Shadow he would fix it for his manager at the Double Dollar to alibi for him, should any enquiry be made – but such an enquiry was not even remotely likely at the far-distant town. There was no reason why any suspicion should fall on him. Besides, he and Cranley had been seen to part on the friendliest of terms . . . and by the sheriff too. Yes, that had been a nice touch . . . But such was not the limit of Kelvin's devious planning. He still had other moves to make.

He did not reholster his weapon. Still wearing his gloves, he laid the gun that had killed Cranley carefully on the floor of the hallway, just outside the open lounge door. The bright illumination of the large oil-lamp on the lounge table spilled out through the doorway and showed the gun clearly.

Stooping, Kelvin gripped the dead body of Arthur Cranley by reaching under the armpits from behind, and dragged him back into the lounge. He laid him, face down, on the carpet in the centre of the room.

Then he opened the front door and went upstairs to hide himself in the bedroom through which he had gained entry.

Smiling grimly, he stood waiting in the darkness. Waiting for the imminent arrival of Diana Travers . . . .

3

LEGAL EAGLE

Dave Norton hummed softly to himself as his sorrel plodded gently through the soft darkness of the night, picking his way with unwavering certainty around hummocks and unexpected thickets, across small ravines and along arroyos.

Overhead, from horizon to horizon, loomed the vast upturned bowl of the stars, arching and vaulting until it was lost in immeasurable distances. Only where, to the west, the mountains reared up in crag and peak and buttress, were the stars blotted out by a darkness deeper than the night itself.

It was not far now to the end of the journey. Dave Norton, though somewhat saddle-weary from his trip, was nevertheless in a cheerful mood.

His trip to Farnworth Bend, the next nearest cattle-trading town to the south, had been successful. He had sold 500 head of cattle at a good price.

There was no doubt any more that he was the

best salesman his friend Will Pilkington had ever had, just as there was no longer any doubt that the Double J, which Pilkington had bought as a broken-down spread, was now definitely paying for itself. Between them, Dave Norton and Will Pilkington had built a cattle ranch worthy of the name.

In the morning the movement of the herd for the journey would begin – up Barren Sand Valley, along the foothills of Greycrag Mountains, and then by the short overland route to Farnworth Bend. It would be tough going all the way under the burning Arizona sun, but not half as tough as it had been to build the Double J into a profitable proposition.

The smile of contentment went suddenly from Dave Norton's face. His idle, pleasant speculations came to a dead end. He had just rounded the bend in the trail which after a further two miles across rolling pasture land, ended at the sweeping reaches of the Double J. He drew the reins taut on his mount and stared into the starlight, narrowing his eyes.

There was nothing sharply visible – only a vast, spreading blur of dark moving in the greyness, and moving in the general direction of Barren Sand Valley. Cattle, by the hundred, filled the still night air with their lowing and the scrape and beat of their innumerable hoofs. And here and there sounded the crack of a stockwhip and a man's sharp word of command.

It took Dave Norton about ten seconds to grasp

the situation. Certainly his friend could not be responsible for this sudden mass movement of steers from the corrals. The only other answer was – rustlers. The same vicious gang, no doubt, which had already denuded several well-stocked ranches in the region and had mysteriously evaded the clutch of the law.

'On your way, Loco,' Dave breathed to his horse, and dug in the spurs momentarily.

In a thunder of hoofs and dust the sorrel hurtled Dave down the remaining two miles of pastureland. As he went he drew his right-hand .45. He had half-completed the journey when he saw a blazing torch suddenly whirl through the air like a flaming serpent and land, he knew, on the tinder-dry roof of the big ranch house. Instantly there was a spurt of flame, and a second torch made disaster a certainty.

Dave swung the horse. His face was grim. The cattle no longer concerned him. It was Will Pilkington who counted. It was an even chance that the desperadoes had tied him up in the ranch house so he'd fry.

Urging his sorrel to even greater speed and skirting the perimeter of the shoving, moaning, butting cattle, Dave headed straight for the yard gates, dismounted at a flying run and raced into the already doomed log structure.

He came upon his friend in the living-room, flat on the floor with arms outflung. From the look of the place there had been no struggle; perhaps there had been no need of one. A second's examination showed Dave that Will Pilkington was dead – shot through the heart.

A look of murderous fury on his face, he hauled the limp body on to his broad shoulders – the body was still warm, he noticed – and went outside again, coughing now in the belching smoke. At a safe distance from the devouring fire he lowered his dead friend to the ground, looked at him for a moment, then, a .45 in each hand, Dave returned to the scene of the surging cattle.

But now the night was no longer cloaking him. The blazing ranch had become a positive glare and it illumined his figure for the two men standing on the edge of the swarming cattle and directing operations. They swung and caught sight of Dave, neckerchiefs up to their eyes and hats drawn well down.

Realizing he was not in any way connected with them they did not ask questions. Their guns exploded – split seconds after Dave had sized up the situation. He dropped flat and heard a bullet whang past his face and bury itself in the dirt. He took aim and fired. One of the men dropped. The other hesitated, half-turned, and then at a second bullet he too dropped, a victim of Dave's deadly marksmanship. Whatever other men there were directing the cattle were somewhere in the dust and starlight and impossible to reach. Dave got to his feet and tried vainly to locate them, looking left and right amidst the swirling animals . . .

'Drop your guns!' ordered a voice. 'Drop 'em, I say!'

Astonished, Dave twirled round. In the brightness of light from the flames he recognized Sheriff Tim Carson standing only a couple of yards away, his own guns levelled.

'You're not gettin' any more men if I can help it, Norton,' the sheriff added, walking forward. 'Two's enough for one night, I reckon.'

Dave did not drop his guns: he holstered them instead. He looked – and felt – like a man who has heard something incredible.

'Have you gone crazy, Sheriff?' he demanded. 'Don't you realize what's goin' on around here? The ranch is on fire, the cattle are being driven off by rustlers – a man's a right to shoot down thieves, and that's just what I did.'

Sheriff Tim Carson did not answer for a moment. He was a tall raw-boned man, tanned like leather, and, according to the inhabitants of the nearby town of Valley Shadow, was one of the best sheriffs the place had ever had. Personal sentiment never got mixed up with his unenviable calling.

'Thieves?' he repeated at last, his voice grim. 'You're talkin' outa turn, Norton, ain't you? This isn't your ranch; it's Will Pilkington's.'

'That's just it! He was my best friend. I found him shot through the heart. I've just come in from Farnworth Bend from a business trip. Being back sooner than I expected I happened on this. These rustlers figured I wouldn't be here until tomorrow, I reckon.'

'An' what *are* you doin' here when it isn't your spread?'

'I haven't the time to go into all that now. Give me a hand to stop these cattle being —'

'They won't get far; I'll see to that. They can't anyway – not with the ringleader fixed nice an' pretty.'

'Now wait a minute!' Dave set his jaw. 'Are you saying that I —'

'Yeah.' The sheriff's voice was level. 'Any reason why I shouldn't? How do I know Will Pilkington was your best friend? Since he's dead I've only your say-so for it, and I don't know anythin' about you beyond seein' you about the town now and again and knowin' your name's Norton. What I *do* know is that there's a whole lot o' cattle-rustlin' goin' on in this territory and nobody seems to know who's back of it. I also know that you don't seem to have no home of your own – and I saw you shoot down two men in cold blood. Don't ask me why you did it; you know better than me. Mebbe you figured they were better kept quiet. Norton,' the sheriff finished; 'you're coming with me.'

Dave tightened his lips. He could have said a good deal, argued about the utter wrongness of the situation. Only with twin guns trained on him it would not have been much use. He glanced towards the cattle moving away in the starlight.

'Where's Will Pilkington's body?' the sheriff asked abruptly. 'Frying in the blaze back there, eh?'

'I dragged the body out,' Dave retorted, swinging back to look at him. 'And that body will prove you're all wrong about me. An examination of the bullet will soon show it didn't come from my gun.'

'I'll take a look at the body anyway,' the sheriff said curtly. 'Start movin'.' Dave could do nothing else. The blaze from the ranch house was dying down now into a skeleton of glowing sparks and kindled wood, but it still cast sufficient illumination for the two men to see the dead body of Pilkington quite clearly. The sheriff looked at the wound over the heart and set his mouth.

'I suppose, with so many murders accountin' to you up and down the district, you figured that one more wouldn't make much difference, eh?' he asked, rising up from beside the corpse. 'I'm mighty glad I caught up with you as I did – and I shouldn't have done but for seeing the blaze from the ranch and wonderin' what was wrong. I rode out straight away.'

'You've got everything cockeyed,' Dave snapped. 'As you'll find out before you're much older.'

The sheriff studied the tall, whipcorded figure for a moment, the grim grey eyes and beak of a nose. Then he motioned with his guns.

'Pick the body up,' he ordered. 'Where's your cayuse?'

'Back of the ranch house —'

'Get on it – and put this body on it too. We're ridin' back into town. The body's goin' to be examined by Doc Walters and you are goin' to jail. As for those cattle – I'll stop 'em gettin' too far away. Later, I'll have those two men you shot brought in for examination as well. All right – move!'

Thrown into the adobe jail in the centre of Valley Shadow, and with a jailer on guard in the little lean-to office at the back of it, Dave Norton could do nothing – except think, and this he did most of the night.

Being fair-minded, he could see just how things must have looked to the sheriff, and in fact how they still must look.

It had been part of Dave's bargain with Will Pilkington that their friendship should be kept secret. At one time – before Dave had known him – Will Pilkington had been convicted for cattle-stealing and though he had served his sentence and thereafter gone straight, the taint remained. No reputable cattle-dealer felt inclined to transact business with him. Hence Dave, his best friend since he had gone straight, had always acted as the go-between.

Now things had recoiled in the strangest way. Without proof of his friendship with Will Pilkington it simply counted for nothing as far as Dave was concerned. He had been present at the very time of the rustling, and had been seen shooting down two men.

Dave shook his head moodily. But at least there was one thing that the sheriff could not stop, and that was the granting of legal aid. The moment morning came, and the sheriff himself was back on duty, Dave awakened from a troubled sleep and insisted that Ezra Munro be sent to him. Ezra was wily, one of the oldest and smartest lawyers in Valley Shadow, and more than once

Dave had sought his advice on a legal point and sailed cheerfully through a sticky situation in consequence.

Just after Dave had finished his meagre breakfast Ezra Munro arrived. He was grizzle-haired, stout, perpetually bland, with a face so creaseless it might have belonged to a month-old baby. As usual his battered black Stetson was perched on the back of his head, his shoestring tie was cockeyed, and his hands were deep in his trousers pockets.

'Mornin', Dave,' he grunted, as he was admitted into the cell. 'An' what sort of a mess have you gotten yourself into this time?'

'Nothing worse than cattle-rustling and three murders thrown in,' Dave answered drily, smoothing back his dishevelled black hair.

'Huh? Kinda wholesale, ain't you?' Munro lighted a black cheroot and smoked it pensively for a moment. Then, wheezing a little, he squatted down on the bunk at Dave's side. Musingly his keen little eyes went over the young, brown face and troubled grey eyes.

'Who says you done all this?' he asked presently. 'You – or that big palooka outside?'

'I can't blame the sheriff Ezra. I reckon I'd have done the same thing in his place, things being as they were.'

'You would, huh? Tell me about it. What happened? I'm no mindreader.'

In detail Dave outlined the events of the previous night. Ezra Munro sat in silence, listening, his eyes either fixed on the floor or studying the glowing end of his cheroot as he held it between his fingers.

'So, then, you rode in ahead of time from Farnworth Bend and happened on these jiggers cleaning out the cattle, eh? You also found Will Pilkington's dead body, shot down two of the rustlers, and the sheriff jumped to conclusions?'

'That's it,' Dave confirmed, nodding. 'The sheriff thinks he's got the head of the rustling gang which has been cleanin' up this territory pretty thoroughly the last few months. You must have heard of what they've been doing.'

'Yeah, I heard.' Munro gave a heavy grin. 'Well-organized raids they are too, as a rule. Nobody knows who's back of them, and I'll stake my best pair of half-boots that it ain't you! Look, tell me something. Who saw you shoot down those two rustlers, outside of the sheriff?'

'Nobody – far as I know. What other men there were there were mixed up with the cattle.'

Ezra Munro grinned again and patted Dave's knee. 'You just leave this to me, son,' he murmured, and got to his feet.

Smoking pensively, he called to be let out of the cell, and then followed the sheriff into his little office inside the lean-to. Carson threw himself in the swivel-chair in front of his roll-top desk and aimed sharp eyes at the paunchy lawyer.

'Well, not much can be done about Norton, can there?' he asked shortly. 'Nailed red-handed, I reckon.'

'You want to start polishin' up on legal procedure,' Ezra Munro said heavily, sitting down and puffing. 'You can't hold Dave Norton, Sheriff – and I ain't so sure neither but what he can't put in a claim for wrongful arrest.'

The sheriff sat up with a jerk. 'What in the blue thunder are you talkin' about?'

The lawyer smoked with exasperating calm for a while, his shrewd little eyes never leaving Carson's face.

'What's he charged with?' he asked at length.

'Cattle-thievin', arson, and murder. That's enough for one man.'

'Not quite. Where are the witnesses to support the charges?'

'Witnesses!' Carson exploded. 'I don't *need* witnesses! I *saw* him shoot those two men and—'

'I don't care if you saw him shoot *fifty* men; you're not carryin' out the law unless you got *witnesses*. You didn't see him directin' the rustling, and you didn't see him set fire to the ranch house. Find witnesses to those incidents, *and* witnesses to the shootin' of those two men, and then you can hold him for trial, but not until. I know the law, Carson, and in your capacity as sheriff you should too. Better knock the dust from your textbooks and start in readin'.'

Carson swallowed something and breathed hard. He seemed about to burst forth in protests and then controlled himself. In the end he gave a gloomy nod.

'I suppose you're right,' he muttered, knowing

better than to argue the law with an expert like Ezra Munro. 'All right, I'll release him – but I'll find witnesses, somehow. I'm not goin' to let the head of a cattle-rustling gang walk out from under my nose.'

'What about the cattle that was set movin' last night? And the men handling them? What happened?'

Carson tightened his lips. 'I got some of the boys to help me and between us we got the cattle back to the corrals of the Double J. Now Pilkington is dead there's only his ranch foreman in charge and he'll look after the beasts until things are straightened out. The men in charge of the rustling escaped, and in the dark we hadn't a chance of gettin' 'em. At least it was one thievin' plan that didn't come off, anyhow.'

'Then the men who could have proved Norton to be the ringleader got away?'

'Yeah.' Sheriff Carson sighed. 'And I've not the vaguest idea who they are. Be owl-hooters dug up from some place, I reckon. Naturally they'll be leery from now on so I'm not likely to find out much about 'em.'

'Which is just too bad for you,' Ezra Munro observed drily. 'Without proof one way or the other Dave Norton's story of being a friend of Will Pilkington's is just as good as yourn that he's a rustler.'

'And what about the bodies? Pilkington's and those two rustlers? No doubt that he killed the two men because I saw him. They've been identified as cowpunchers, but it doesn't seem that they belonged to any particular outfit in this territory. Not as far as I could find out, leastways. Just drifters mebbe – lyin' low some place during the day and comin' out at night when there's work to be done. I've checked the bullets in the two men with Norton's guns. No doubt he fired the shots, and since I saw him do it I've got him nailed there.'

'When you have witnesses, sure,' Munro agreed implacably. 'What about the slug in Pilkington? How does that match up?'

'It's a forty-five slug – and Norton uses forty-fives, but I ain't sayin' about the bullets matching up until I've had some expert advice.'

'Meanin' you can't be sure that it was one of Norton's guns which shot Pilkington?'

'There seem to be differences,' the sheriff admitted, shrugging. 'But if he didn't do that he certainly did the other two, so once I got my witnesses I'll fix him. If he didn't shoot Pilkington I'll find out who did when I've got the entire rustling-gang sized up.'

'That's in the future,' Ezra Munro said briefly. 'What you're goin' to do right now is release that lad. I'll see he don't skip the district while you start huntin' for witnesses. Better get your key, sheriff.'

Grim-faced, not liking the situation a bit, Carson got to his feet and went out of the office. In a moment or two he reappeared with Dave following him.

'How did you manage to swing it, Ezra?' Dave

asked, glancing at him gratefully.

'Never mind that, son. Just collect your belongings and thank your stars for Ezra Munro.'

Dave turned to the sheriff, and from him took his twin gun belts and buckled them on. Then he took up his hat.

'Your horse is at the livery stable,' the sheriff said sourly. 'You can pick it up when you want.'

'Thanks,' Dave acknowledged. Ezra Munro got to his feet and glanced at the sheriff.

'We'll be on our way then, Sheriff, and when you've got something worth while to talk about let me know. I'll be interested.'

With that the portly lawyer led the way outside into the burning morning sunlight. He walked in silence for a while along the boardwalk, thinking, then at length he turned a narrowed, questioning eye at Dave as he strode beside him.

'Well, son, you're out of that spot. What do you aim to do next?'

'That depends. I don't know how long I can count on being free. What have I got – a sort of parole?'

'Parole nothin'!' Munro answered, spitting. 'Carson can't put you back behind bars until he finds witnesses, and I reckon he won't manage to do that in a hurry.'

'Those two rustlers I killed were trespassers and killers,' Dave snapped. 'I did as any man's entitled to do who finds an intruder. Witnesses, eh?' Dave's grimness gave way to a grin. 'So *that*'s how you did it!'

'Yeah! And unless I'm plumb crazy he'll never

prove that you shot Will Pilkington either. The bullet in him was a forty-five, sure, but that doesn't mean a thing unless it checks detail for detail. For the time being, son, you're as free as air. So I'm askin' you again – what do you intend doin'?'

'It's hard to say.' Dave rubbed his craggy chin. 'While Will was alive I was a sort of go-between for him. Travelling around arranging cattle-deals on his behalf and living at his ranch house between whiles. Since I've had a passable education I could manage business affairs better than him. Now all that is busted up, I'm sort of nowhere. I might skip town and try my luck elsewhere, I suppose.'

'You'll not do that.' Munro shook his head. 'I have given Carson my word that you'll stay around – and you will because I'm responsible for you.' He came to a stop, lighted a fresh cheroot, and for a while contemplated the busy main street. Then he went on:

'I know what *I'd* be doin' in your place, son. I'd be findin' out who *did* kill Will Pilkington and who's back of this rustlin'. I can't guarantee how long it'll take the sheriff to spring some legal trick which will land you back under lock and key, so I'd start movin' while you've the chance, if I were you. Your one *real* chance of freedom lies in findin' the culprit – or culprits.'

'Yeah. I suppose it does.' Dave reflected, rolled a cigarette for himself and lighted it. He thought it out for a moment or two, the lines tautening on his lean, bronzed face. 'That won't be so easy if I can't leave town,' he said at last.

'What d'you want to leave town for?'

'Because I don't expect to find anything worthwhile in this one-eyed place. I don't expect to find the head of a gang of rustlers in Valley Shadow of all places!'

'There's no harm in tryin', is there? There's bits and pieces of all sorts here – saddle-tramps, cattle-dealers, cowpunchers, and plain hoboes. You mightn't find the head of the gang but you might get a lead on where he is just by keepin' your ears and eyes open. If you do that and the man you want should be out of town we'll talk again about you leaving. You don't know much about Valley Shadow, huh?'

'Very little. I've spent more time in Farnworth Bend than I have here. You are about the only man I know to call a friend. With the sheriff I've just a nodding acquaintance.'

The lawyer mused again and then popped out a question. 'How's about money? Got any?'

'A little. I've some left over from my expenses in Farnworth Bend. I was goin' to turn it over to Will until things happened the way they did.'

'And outside the sheriff the only two men who saw you last night were the two you rubbed out.' Munro gave a shrug. 'The whole thing looks plain and simple to me.'

Dave nodded and tossed his cigarette under the wheels of a passing buckboard. 'I'll settle at Ma Whittaker's rooming-house across the road,' he decided. 'There's stables at the back so I can put my horse there too. Then I'll see what information I can dig up, particularly at the Double Dollar.' He nodded to the gaming-saloon further down the street. 'No better place to hear things. Soon as I get hold of anything worthwhile I'll let you know.'

'That's good enough for me,' Ezra Munro agreed, nodding. 'You'll find something, son, or I'm plumb mistaken in you.'

4
FRIGHTENED LADY

That same evening, as on any other evening, the Double Dollar saloon was at full pressure when Dave Norton walked in through the batwing doors.

He had spent the day orientating himself with the little town, becoming more familiar with details which so far he had not had the time to study. There had been little to learn at Ma Whittaker's rooming-house, so his next obvious move had been to come here.

Silent, just inside the batwings, his thumbs hanging on his pants belt, and white sombrero pushed up on his forehead, he stood looking about him.

After the clean fresh air of the outdoors the atmosphere in here just plain stank. It was the hour when business in the Double Dollar was rapidly climbing to its peak, and the air was choked with the smell of liquor, burning kerosene, tobacco, and perspiration.

The roulette- and faro-tables had their usual habitués and at the ordinary tables there was the usual complement of cowpunchers, traders, saddle tramps, Mexicans, and overpainted and underdressed women. There came a hum of conversation, the rattle of poker-chips, and the clink of glasses.

Dave glanced across the crowded room to the far end of the big hall, where a striking blonde girl had just appeared on a crudely painted rostrum. In her black evening gown, relieved only by sequins, she certainly had everything. The creamy white of arms and shoulders brought forth a chorus of whistles and shouts, but they subsided the moment she began to sing as well as she could with an indifferent tin-panny piano accompaniment.

Surprisingly, the girl could hit a high C with the best of them, and the inhabitants of Valley Shadow, though by no means musical experts, realized the fact and applauded with deafening claps.

Dave Norton's eyes rested on her for a moment and he wondered vaguely how she came to be in such a set-up. She had looks, talent and personality, and a refinement that made her stand out a mile from the talkative rabble to which she was singing. She met his glance through the haze and went on singing.

Dave gave a shrug to himself and strolled over to the bar. The barkeep gave him a questioning look.

'Howdy,' he greeted affably. 'Stranger, huh?'

'Right,' Dave acknowledged. 'Make it whiskey.'

He waited until it had been given him, then he paid his money and stood with one elbow supporting him on the counter and his fingers playing with the glass. 'Ain't seen you around before,' remarked a scrubby-jawed puncher beside him. 'Any particklar outfit?'

'No. Just passin' through.' Dave glanced at his interrogator. He was an ordinary cowhand, copper-skinned, purely curious. He had a rough kind of friendliness, which might be turned to account in the matter of imparting information.

'Who runs this place?' Dave asked after a while. 'It isn't half bad.'

'Jeff Kelvin.' The puncher turned and jerked his head. 'That's him over yonder at the tables.'

Dave gazed through the furry atmosphere and presently picked out a tall man with a gleaming shield of shirt-front and a black suit. His hair, black and heavily oiled, gleamed in the light of the lamps. Swarthy-skinned, remarkably fastidious in his dress and actions, he looked more like a city dweller than the owner of a prosperous gambling saloon – until Dave came to noticing the squareness of the man's jaw. There was iron resolution there, even naked cruelty.

'Don't never play no tricks with him, stranger,' the puncher added, downing his drink. 'He's got a quicker draw than any other man in this town. See that girl doin' the singin'?' he asked.

Dave nodded. 'I've been wonderin' what she's doing in this bed of polecats.'

'That's Nina Voles. They say she came from back East. An' she's got class.' The puncher paused to have a gulp of his drink, then continued:

'Jeff Kelvin brought her here a while back, to sing. Dunno why. He ain't free with his information. But she's *his*, if you get me. Every guy around here knows it or should if he wants to stay healthy. I reckon that's one reason why she ain't never been mauled.'

'There's one man over there who doesn't seem to know the rules' Dave commented, nodding – and the puncher beside him gave a gasp at what he saw.

The girl, at the end of her song, had just bowed gracefully to the clapping hands and stamping feet when a square giant of a cattleman suddenly leapt up from his table and dived across at her.

The man was obviously liquored to the eyebrows from the way he lurched, and desperately though the girl tried to dodge out of his way she was not quick enough. His long, powerful arms closed about her bare shoulders and forced her face towards his.

At the same instant Jeff Kelvin glanced up and saw what was happening. His gun flashed up but a well-aimed chair from one of the cattleman's table acquaintances sailed through the air and hit Kelvin across the head and shoulders. He staggered backwards and dropped his gun.

' 'Scuse *me*!' Dave breathed, and in one bound he dived through the midst of the men and women who were now jumping up from the tables excitedly. In three huge strides he had crossed the saloon, seized the cattleman by the shoulder and whirled him round.

Drunk though he was the man was not too drunk to realize that he had a smaller man to deal with and that his playfulness had been interrupted. His massive hand blurred down to his gun but at the same instant a battering ram struck him clean in the jaw. At least that was what it felt like.

A second later another smashing blow followed it, breaking in living fire over the bridge of his nose. Gasping, he staggered backwards, collided with the table behind him, slewed over it and fell on the other side amidst a litter of broken glass and spilled beer.

'Next time you want to talk to a lady get an introduction first!' Dave breathed, standing over him and flexing his tingling knuckles. Then he glanced round at the men and women watching.

'You'd better get him out of here. Night air will sober him up a bit mebbe.'

There were one or two responsive nods, and looks of wonder were exchanged; then the man who had thrown the chair and a hefty cowpuncher hauled the dazed giant to his feet and dragged him through the interested crowd. With a faint grin Dave turned to the girl and took off his hat.

'Sorry I didn't arrive quicker, ma'am,' he apologized. 'I would have if I'd seen what was comin'.'

The girl was looking at him in something like astonishment. He also was looking – but in interest, not astonishment. At close quarters she was even prettier than he had imagined – oval-faced, nearly flaxen-haired, and with eyes so deeply blue they were heliotrope. In build she was slender; in height, perhaps five feet three.

'At least you're not lacking in nerve, stranger,' she commented at length, with the refined accent of an educated woman. 'Do you know who that man is?'

'No.' Dave shrugged. 'And I don't want to, I reckon.'

'He's Black Joe.' The girl's look of astonishment deepened. 'I never saw anybody knock him out before; in fact I don't think anybody ever did.'

'That's right, nobody ever did,' remarked a quiet voice. 'Fists are something new. The only language Black Joe understands as a rule is the business end of a shootin' iron.'

Dave and the girl turned their heads to look at Jeff Kelvin as he pushed his way through the little crowd.

There was a blood-smear down his swarthy cheek where the chair had struck him, but he was smiling – in a fixed kind of way – as though he realized he had to look hospitable even if his heart was not in it.

'I'm Jeff Kelvin,' he added. 'And that was a nice bit of work you put in, stranger. Have a drink?'

'Er . . .' Dave hesitated briefly and then nodded. 'Sure I will. Whiskey.'

Jeff Kelvin indicated an empty table, called his order to the barkeep, then drew out a chair for Nina Voles. The three of them sat down, and in the few moments that elapsed before the drink arrived, Dave took the opportunity to study the saloon-owner more intently.

He was handsome enough, obviously with a dash of Latin blood in him somewhere. Kelvin's manner, too, was polished, with none of the faulty pronunciation so common among the leather-necks around him.

'This is my place,' he said, suddenly becoming conscious of the fact that Dave was studying him. 'Nothing to boast about, mebbe, but it turns in the money. And this is Miss Voles. She's from out East. The one bright attraction in a den of iniquity.'

'So I've heard,' Dave murmured, and considered his drink as it was put before him.

'Heard?' Kelvin's dark eyes were suddenly questioning. 'Who told you? I thought you were a stranger around here? I've never seen you before that I recall.'

Dave shrugged. 'I *am* a stranger, sure – but I get to talking. A puncher told me over at the bar.' He gave a faint smile. 'In fact he went further and warned me to lay off looking at Miss Voles in case I got a bellyful of lead!'

Kelvin grinned widely and glanced at the girl. She was sitting looking at her drink, her face curiously fixed and expressionless, as though she were listening to a conversation decidedly distasteful.

'That sort of warning only applies to the Black Joe variety,' Kelvin explained. 'Different with you. You've got more culture than a dozen of these rats put together. What are you anyway? A rancher?'

'Just passin' through,' Dave answered, and he thought he caught an earnest glance from the girl's dark-blue eyes. 'I hope to be on my way again before long. If the sheriff should come in for a drink he'll recognize me quick enough. I got hamstrung by accident last night as a rustler. Since he couldn't hold me he let me go this morning.'

Dave had not wanted to say this but he knew it was necessary. It was highly probable the sheriff would turn up at some time for a drink and give things away – so the cards were better on the table face up to begin with.

'You don't look much like a rustler to me,' Kelvin shrugged.

'That's because I'm not one. Dave Norton's the name.'

Kelvin nodded slowly, then he glanced up sharply as the barkeep suddenly appeared and leaned over his shoulder. He listened as the man muttered something and then he nodded.

'Okay – I'll see him in my office upstairs.' Kelvin got to his feet and gave an apologetic glance.

'You'll have to excuse me. Some business has come up. You and Miss Voles had better get yourselves acquainted, eh? But not *too* acquainted,' he added drily; then he turned and went off across the saloon.

Dave watched him go up the little staircase at the back of the saloon which led to his office, then he finished off his drink and looked at the girl. Her eyes rose from a preoccupied study of the table top.

'When do you think you'll be going on your way?' she asked quietly.

'Day or two mebbe. Why?'

Nina Voles hesitated and looked about her, then she edged forward across the table and lowered her voice slightly.

'Would you take me with you?' she asked, and it took all of Dave's control not to blink with amazement.

'*With* me? But what on earth for?' Dave paused, puzzled by the look of entreaty on the girl's face.

'You're grown up. What's to stop you movin' about by yourself?'

'Jeff Kelvin,' she answered, and her painted mouth set in sullen resentment. The girl went on, 'I realize that I'm taking a chance in telling you this but as a rule I'm a pretty good judge of the people I meet. I – I know whom I can trust.' She looked at Dave earnestly, then added:

'You wouldn't have knocked out Black Joe tonight unless you'd got a pretty good sense of chivalry.'

'Well – could be,' Dave admitted, with a faint smile; then he became serious again. 'Look here, Miss Voles, are you in trouble, or what? I've been watching your expressions. For a girl as pretty as you are you look mighty unhappy.'

'With good reason,' she muttered. 'I can't explain it; it's too involved. All I want is to get out of Valley Shadow and go away as far as possible.' The girl clenched her fingers. 'Yes, I know what you're thinking. That I could ride out; that I could take the stage or the railroad. That's just it; I can't! Or rather I'd be afraid to without a man to help me.'

'I've heard that you're Kelvin's girl,' Dave said slowly. 'Do you mean to tell me that he loves you so much he'd shoot you rather than let you get away from him?'

'No, it isn't that — but if I tried to leave unescorted he'd move heaven and earth to stop me. With a man to help me he'd think twice — especially a man like you who isn't afraid of him or of a hulking roughneck like Black Joe.'

Dave picked up his whiskey glass, examined it absently, and then put it down again.

'What have you done?' he asked bluntly. 'Do you mean that Kelvin has some sort of a hold over you?'

'That's just what I mean — but I can't tell you what it is. All that I ask for is help.'

For a moment or two Dave did not speak. His eyes went over the girl's face. There was no gainsaying the intensity of her expression, the air of almost desperate anticipation about her.

He reflected that it certainly must be something pretty urgent for her to pick on the first man she felt she trusted — or so she had said.

'It'll be a day or two before I can leave town,' Dave said at length, 'An' even when I do go I'm none too sure which way I'll head. It may be to Farnworth Bend – or even to Tucson, and that's two hundred miles away across the desert.'

'I don't care where you go as long as it's away from here,' the girl broke in urgently. 'Once I'm free of this place I can soon work my way back to – to civilization. I just can't stop here. And it's not just because I hate the place, either.' A shadow crossed her face. 'The longer I delay the stronger becomes the possibility that I may have to marry Jeff Kelvin, and I'd do anything to prevent that.'

'You mean that's one of the reasons for going?' Dave asked.

'Yes – but not the *only* one.'

The girl turned and motioned to the waiter, and did not speak again until fresh drinks had been brought. She drank down a whiskey with a completeness that secretly astonished Dave. She saw and interpreted his look.

'I don't usually drink like this,' she explained, again with that little half-smile. 'Just pepping up my courage, I suppose. I've decided you're entitled to know the whole story instead of half of it.' She paused, then evidently making up her mind, she plunged:

'I'll be completely frank with you, then maybe you can help me.'

'Uh-huh – that's the way I like it,' Dave agreed.

'The issue's fairly simple,' she said. 'Kelvin knows I murdered a man back in Sycamore Halt, which is where I come from. He saw me do it, but he's the only man who did. As long as he remains silent I'm safe.' She sipped her drink. 'But you can see what that entails. I have to do everything he tells me. I daren't step out of line for a moment in case he talks. If I could only get out of Valley Shadow I could just – well, disappear, change my name, and it wouldn't matter how much he talked. Within grasping distance of him or his trigger-men I'm never really safe.'

Dave frowned. 'You don't look like a killer to me, Miss Voles!'

She started, her violet eyes fixed on him. 'Oh, I'm not! I didn't really kill the man I'm supposed to have killed – if you know what I mean, but things look as if I did, and I just can't prove otherwise. Kelvin knows that, too.'

'Who was it that got killed, anyway?' Dave asked, by now thoroughly intrigued with the girl's story.

The girl hesitated, then before she found time to answer Jeff Kelvin suddenly became visible again through the crowd. Dave caught sight of him approaching and whispered swiftly to the girl.

'Meet me outside Parker's General Store tomorrow morning at ten and we'll talk further . . .'

'Well, get acquainted?' Kelvin asked, coming forward and settling down at the table again.

'Yeah, but not too much so,' Dave answered, with a wide grin.

'You don't have to read more into my remarks

than you want,' Kelvin told him levelly; then he turned to the girl.

'You're due to give another song, Nina. How about it?'

'Yes,' she assented. 'Yes – of course.'

Set-faced, the rouge on her cheeks vivid against the pallor of her skin, she went over to where the pianist was waiting for her, a glass of beer on one end of the keyboard and a smouldering cigarette on the other.

'Nice kid,' Kelvin said, turning back to Dave. 'Only thing is she doesn't take kindly to this town or this kind of life.'

Dave drank some of his whiskey. 'I'm sort of wondering how she ever got into it anyway. From somewhere East, isn't she? How come she's here? Done somethin' she shouldn't and she's hiding out mebbe?'

'Not that I know of.' The calm gaze of the dark eyes gave nothing away, but judging between the girl and this emotionless owner of a questionable saloon was not a difficult task for Dave.

Kelvin, he decided, was a man who would never give anything away. With the girl it was a matter of almost tragic importance that she escape. Dave made up his mind to himself.

'Think you could find work around here for a jigger like me?' he asked presently.

'I might.' Kelvin contemplated him. 'What's your line?'

'Cowpunching chiefly. I was a foreman once with the Grey Z outfit at Dry Gulch. You probably won't know of it.'

Kelvin shook his head and idly knocked the ash from his cigar to the floor. 'I've no use for a cowpuncher, Norton: they're a dime a dozen – and you're much too smart a man for the job. But I might be able to use you if you're quick on the draw.'

'A trigger-man, eh?' Dave grinned. 'Okay, how's this . . .?'

His hand flashed down, up, and fired in the space of seconds. Half-way across the saloon a fancy art-pot containing a plant and suspended by a thin chain fell splintering to the floor. The snapped half of chain hung forlornly from the ceiling beam.

'Good enough?' Dave enquired, blowing the smoke from the barrel of his .45.

Kelvin raised a hand to quiet the murmurs of alarm.

'Nothing to worry about, folks – just a bit of target practice. That was fancy shootin', Norton,' he added, eyeing Dave seriously. 'Where'd you pick a draw like that?'

'Just practice, I reckon.'

They measured each other for a moment and Dave wondered if his plan was going to work.

He was willing to fall in with any scheme that would keep him beside Kelvin. Apart from the fact that in that capacity he might learn the truth about the circumstantial evidence with which Nina Voles was being blackmailed, he might also gain some inkling concerning the cattle-rustlings and the brains behind them.

'Yes, nice work,' Kelvin repeated, nodding. 'And you've got a mighty powerful fist, too. I'll give you seventy-five a month to work beside me.'

'Doin' what?' Dave questioned.

'As you're told. Later, I might find something else for you. See how much I trust you first.'

Dave reflected. On the one hand taking the job would mean he would not be able to get the girl out of town – which he was fully determined to do – but on the other hand accepting it might lead him into useful channels of information.

'I'd like time to think it over,' he said. 'Say until tomorrow evening. Can I find you here then?'

'You can find me here 'most any night – and any day at the Lazy Y spread out at Sunny Point. That's a couple of miles from here going south.'

'Good enough,' Dave nodded. 'I'll not come to your ranch, though: I'll see you here tomorrow evening and tell you my answer.' He got to his feet. 'You might tell the lady I had to go.'

'Why should I?' Kelvin asked, glancing towards her as she stood singing beside the distant piano. 'She doesn't mean anything to you.'

Dave put his hat on. 'Sure she does to you?' he asked – then with a nod he turned and went across the crowded saloon.

5

THE FLYING HORSEMAN

Ten minutes later Dave was in the unpretentious home of Ezra Munro at the opposite end of the town.

Since the lawyer ran his business and home together the main living-room at the back of the now closed office had something of the appearance of an office itself.

The only thing missing was a desk, a table being in its stead. Otherwise the law books and deeds scattered about in various parts of the room were an immediate pointer to Munro's profession.

When he had let Dave in he motioned to a chair and then resumed his seat at the table beside the reading-lamp. He lighted a cheroot slowly and peered at Dave from under his bushy brows.

'Well, son?' he enquired. 'Found anything?'

'I'm not sure, Ezra, and that's why I'm here. What do you think about Jeff Kelvin, the owner of the Double Dollar?'

'Kelvin? There ain't nothin' irregular far as I know. He came here about six months back, when he inherited the saloon and the Lazy Y ranch. Seems to be making a pretty good fist of both, too. Why?'

'I've been talkin' to him. He's a downy one, and no doubt of it. I'm wonderin' if he might know something about the cattle-rustlin'.'

Ezra Munro drew at his cheroot pensively. 'I can't answer that one, son. He's wealthy, I know that, and runs one of the best spreads around these parts. As for cattle rustling . . . Well, I dunno. Never gave it much thought.' He knitted his brows, then asked: 'Why? Got some particular suspicions?'

'Only an insight as to his character,' Dave answered vaguely, then added, 'Seems to me that a man who keeps a hold over a girl by what amounts to blackmail would not blink at murder or cattle-stealin'.'

The lawyer scowled. 'What in tarnation are you talking about?'

Briefly Dave sketched the events of the evening. When he had heard the story of how Kelvin was blackmailing Nina Voles, Munro chewed his cheroot to the other side of his large mouth.

'That's the way it is, huh? Yeah, I see your point. Unscrupulous in one direction and could be in another. Well, you've got your chance. Take this job an' see what you can dig out.' He looked at Dave thoughtfully. 'As for this girl – you struck on her, or what?'

Dave grinned. 'She's mighty pretty, Ezra, take it from me.'

'Yeah, she's got what it takes,' Munro admitted, reflecting. 'Seen her myself singing at the Double Dollar, but I never figured she stops there because Kelvin makes her. Obviously Kelvin's got circumstantial evidence over her. It can't be just the evidence of his word alone because that wouldn't hold in any court of law, and Kelvin's smart enough to know it. It must be written evidence of some sort – mebbe photographs. And he'd keep stuff like that either at his ranch or in the safe in his office at the saloon. Hmmm!'

Munro fell to musing, massaging his square chin, and Dave wondered what was going on inside that wily old brain.

'As I see it,' the lawyer said at length, 'there's one thing holding you out from saying "Yes" right away to this job with Kelvin – and that's because you know if you take it that you won't be able to give the gal a break. Right?'

'Right enough,' Dave agreed. 'I'd like to help her get out – but I can't do that and do myself some good at the same time.'

'And young men being what they are you'll chuck your own chances overboard to help the gal,' Munro commented, with a sly grin. 'Just can't go against nature, I reckon. But it's more important that you clear yourself, son, than help her!' Munro gave a serious smile. 'That being so you ought to look – and being a law-abiding citizen I ain't saying how – if there's some evidence put away somewhere, which if removed would draw Kelvin's sting completely and leave the gal free to do as she likes. Get me?'

'What you mean is that I should turn into a burglar and take a look in Kelvin's office, or his ranch house, and see if there's anythin' worth while?'

'I didn't hear a word,' Munro said calmly, his eyes on the ceiling. Dave grinned and got to his feet.

'I'll do just that – starting with the saloon. The thought of a man like Kelvin havin' his claws in that girl is making my trigger-finger itch. Okay, Ezra, I'll do that. See you again.'

His mind made up, Dave left the lawyer at his desk grinning ambiguously to himself. Dave went out into the main street and strolled slowly back towards the other end of town, disregarding the men and women who were now beginning to turn homewards after their evening's pleasure.

In time he reached a narrow alleyway between two roughboard buildings facing the Double Dollar. Into this narrow space he drifted, propped himself against the wall, and watched the batwings of the saloon across the street.

Gradually, as time passed, the place emptied, the men and women coming out into the cool night wind and the glow of the street's kerosene lamps.

Some people remained in little groups to discuss; others engaged in alcoholic quarrels and finished up with fisticuffs, but little by little the

street began to quieten and at length the lighted
top windows of the saloon became dark, and then
the lower ones.

Through the swing doors Jeff Kelvin himself
presently appeared, holding the arm of Nina
Voles. Dave watched, his eyes narrowed in earnest
concentration. Kelvin and the girl talked for a
while, then came down the three wooden steps
together and finally parted in opposite directions.

Kelvin untied his horse from the hitch rail,
mounted it, and went off towards the end of the
street that joined the valley trail. The girl for her
part crossed the street and finally vanished in the
Desert View hotel.

Dave would have liked nothing better than to
have followed her up and talked with her again –
but since he had made arrangements to see her in
the morning that would have to suffice. In the
meantime he had important work to do.

Satisfied after another ten minutes that the
Double Dollar was deserted he slipped across the
street, went round the side of the big building and
approached it from the rear.

The window of a washroom proved to be the
easiest means of entry and with his penknife
blade he had it open in a few minutes.

Silently he slid into the gloom beyond, opened
the door, and found himself in a dark passage.
Though he could not see where he was going the
change in the noise of his footsteps and the smell
of stale air and spent tobacco told him when he
had reached the saloon itself. By degrees, as his

eyes accustomed themselves, he could make out the dim details of the big room.

And Kelvin's office was up the stairs. He had seen that for himself when Kelvin had been called away earlier in the evening.

Easing one of his guns into his right hand just in case, Dave went silently across the expanse to the staircase and sped to the top.

The office door, as he had fully expected, was locked. He considered for a moment and then searched to either side of him for other doors that might give easier entry – and then through a window into the office. But the office door was the only one.

Finally, Dave pulled out a box of matches and struck one, holding the flame to the lock. The brief examination he was able to make satisfied him.

The lock was one of the self-fastening kind, like a Yale, in which case things might not be so difficult. Stepping back a pace he slammed his broad shoulder into the door. It creaked, but held. Three more shoves and a kick finished the job and he stumbled into the office as the door flew open.

Turning back to the lock he struck another match and examined the damage, which was as he had expected it would be. The clamp had been torn free of its screws. Neatly, with his penknife blade, he forced them back into place, removed all trace of damage as near as he could, picked up the spent matches, then closed the door and found it operating perfectly.

'More ways of killing a polecat than scaring it to

death,' he murmured, going over to the window to make sure the shade was drawn. Satisfied on this, he lighted the oil-lamp on top of the roll-top desk and then looked about him.

The office had no unusual features about it. There was a desk, a swivel-chair in front of it, two wooden filing cabinets, a water-cooler, a small table in a corner piled high with all manner of papers and odds and ends – and a safe, small but invincible, standing by the wall.

Dave looked at the papers on the table and then went no further as he realized there was nothing of value, otherwise they would not have been left open for anybody to see. Besides, time was short, so he turned his attention to the safe.

A moment's study satisfied him. Jeff Kelvin was evidently not a man accustomed to taking chances. Without the combination nothing could open that safe of forged steel. Dave compressed his lips as he squatted and looked at it, his hat cuffed up on his forehead.

'Think again, feller,' he muttered. 'You'll never . . .'

He broke off, intent and listening. There were sounds from somewhere in the saloon.

For a second or so he could not be sure – then when the sounds resolved into footsteps coming along the short landing at the top of the stairs he got to his feet quickly, blew out the lamp-flame and in two strides reached a point behind the office door. Gun cocked, his nerves tense, he waited.

The footsteps ceased outside the door and not a moment afterwards a key grated in the lock and the door opened. Dave waited until the dim figure had come into the office and gone over to the lamp to light it – then he glided to the door, opened it silently and slipped outside.

'Hey there . . .!' He heard a shout behind him from the office, in the familiar voice of Jeff Kelvin.

Regardless of the darkness, thankful indeed for its cover, Dave sped down the staircase, across the saloon towards the passage along which he had entered. At the top of the stairs a match spluttered and flared into life but its light was too feeble to be of any use.

'Come back there!' Kelvin roared, and simultaneously his gun exploded, hurtling a bullet aimlessly into blackness.

Dave grinned to himself, finished his journey down the passage and through the washroom, and left the way he had come.

Once outside in the night things were easy. He melted into its midst, slowed his pace and came to a stop. He was suddenly conscious of the fact that he had accomplished exactly nothing – but there was one other factor.

Jeff Kelvin could not be in two places at once, therefore this might be the ideal time to ride out to his ranch, find a way to enter, and see if there was anything simpler to break open than a forged-steel safe.

Decision and action were simultaneous in Dave's mind. In under five minutes he had got his horse from the stable back of Ma Whittaker's rooming-house, saddled it, and mounted.

Keeping well to the back of the town he rode out over the pastureland until he came to the trail which led south and, presumably, to Kelvin's Lazy Y spread at Sunny Point. Before he actually reached the trail, however, the growing thunder of a horse's hoofs made him draw rein and wait, hidden by a tall spur of rock.

From this higher position Dave could just make out the white track of the trail in the rising moonlight.

It was not long before the horse and rider became visible. Though at his present distance Dave could not distinguish real details he had little doubt that it was Jeff Kelvin riding back home from Valley Shadow. If this were a fact there was no point to be gained in going on to the Lazy Y.

Then Dave gave a start. Unexpectedly the rider had left the trail and was speeding his mount across the pastureland towards him.

For a split second Dave wondered if he had attracted attention by being silhouetted against the stars and moonrise – then he realized this could not be so. For some reason the horseman was taking a short cut.

Gently Dave drew his horse further into the shadow of the rock spur, and waited. In a few seconds the hollow beat of horse's hoofs on the earth became louder – and louder still. Then the rider came speeding by.

Dave had one clear look at him in the dim light, and satisfied himself. It was Jeff Kelvin all right, but the last objective he seemed to have in mind was his ranch. The direction he was taking led straight away from it.

'Somethin' queer here, Loco,' Dave murmured to his horse. 'I think we'd better see what our friend is up to.'

The horse flicked his ears, felt the prod of the spurs and began moving. At a respectful distance, but riding hard just the same, Dave kept up with the speeding Kelvin.

It was highly improbable that he suspected he was being followed. The noise of his own horse's hoofs would be sufficient to drown those of a pursuer. The further he travelled the more puzzled Dave became. Very shortly they were quite a distance from the normal trail, speeding across the desert in the general direction of the mountain foothills.

In the mountains themselves there were no trails, or at least not any which afforded safe usage. The trail through the valley was a good two miles from the base of the mountains, and this fact made Kelvin's spectacular dash through the night all the more peculiar. He was, in fact heading into wild and rocky land where nothing normal could be taking him.

Dave's interest sharpened. His original suspicion, that Jeff Kelvin might have definite connections with the rustlers, was born anew.

Still at a good distance he kept track of the

flying horseman, following him through the penetrating cold of the night.

Below the horse's hoofs the yuccas thrust up like javelins, surrounded by their prickly leaves. Here and there a giant cactus loomed like a fantastic signpost pointing to God knew where. Even the sage was invisible in the soft cotton wool of mist that clothed the desert; and this was only the edge of it.

To the east it stretched to the far horizon where the stars came down to its very edge. To the west, the direction they were taking, the mountain range loomed, blotting out the stars with its saw-toothed immensity of utter dark.

Presently the desert ended and Kelvin still rode on. Dave followed, more warily now, the horse picking its way over the stony ground. They were following a twisting arroyo that came down from the mountains and led . . .? It was not possible to guess.

Then, only a few minutes after they had entered this arid, unexplored region, Dave's luck failed him. His horse stumbled suddenly and fell headlong.

Instantly he jumped clear and helped the sweating beast up again and his chance had gone. There was no longer any sign of Kelvin anywhere.

Here, with the mountains imprisoning the starshine and growing moonlight it was not easy to follow a rider's movements.

'Too bad, Loco,' Dave murmured, patting the horse's nose. 'You let me down there, old-timer.'

The horse gave a snort and pawed the rough earth gently. Dave stood looking about him. He was in some kind of a canyon leading through the mountains, the existence of which he had never even known of before.

Ahead of him the stars seemed to descend in one vast glittering shower in the shape of a giant V cut in darkness. He realized after a moment that there must be a huge cleft ahead, a split in the mountains, which led through to . . . where?

Open cattle-country, as far as he knew. In that direction, across mesa, plain, and desert lay Tucson, the nearest town of any size – and even before the mesa could be reached there were miles of rough mountain country.

Puzzled and thoughtful Dave climbed back into the saddle and turned his horse's head. He had not discovered half as much as he would have liked, but the conviction that Kelvin was far more than just a rancher and saloon-owner insisted on being noticed.

Somehow the truth had to be unearthed.

6
THE GIRL'S STORY

At exactly ten o'clock the following morning Dave
was outside Parker's General Store, smoking idly
as he leaned against the hitch rail to which his
horse was tethered.

If, as he hoped, Nina Voles kept her appointment, he had no intention of talking with her
amidst the comings and goings of the townsfolk of
Valley Shadow.

The peace of the surrounding country was the
place for conversation, even if they had to share
the same horse.

It came as a pleasant surprise to him, therefore, when at five past ten the girl came into view,
mounted on a bright little pinto, her appearance
of the night before completely transformed by the
check shirt, riding-skirt, and half-boots she was
wearing.

Her flaxen hair, which the previous night had
been piled up on her head, was now flowing loose.
To Dave, watching her approach, it looked as

though she had slipped back some ten years into highly delectable girlhood.

'Hello, there!' she greeted, as presently she came up.

Dave touched the brim of his hat and squinted up at her in the blaze of sunlight.

'Mornin', Miss Voles. Glad you could make it – and I'm glad you came on a horse, too. I figured we'd be better able to talk while riding instead of where everybody's around us.'

'My idea exactly,' she told him, smiling, and waited while he swung up into the saddle of his sorrel.

'Where do we go? The valley trail?'

'Good as anything,' he replied, and drew his horse beside her own.

Side by side they jog-trotted their mounts out of the main streets at a leisurely pace, gradually leaving behind them the cramped, rickety confines of Valley Shadow.

'You don't mind taking the chance of being seen with me, then?' Dave asked at length.

'Chance?' The girl's dark-blue eyes glanced at him. 'I wouldn't call it that, Mr Norton. You're the only person who can help me, so as far as I'm concerned the risk's worth it.' She glanced about her and smiled.

'In any case I go for a ride like this every morning. It's the only way I can clear the filthy air of the saloon out of my lungs.' Catching sight of Dave's pensive expression, she added:

'Jeff Kelvin won't see us, if that's what you're

thinking. He's too busy on his ranch every day –
and we'll give his place a wide berth. If any of his
gunhawks have seen us . . . Well, we can risk
that.' She glanced at him in sudden urgency. 'You
will help me, of course?' she asked.

'Mind if I call you "Nina"?' Dave said. 'It cramps
my style to keep sayin' "Miss Voles" every time.
I'm Dave.'

'Actually, Dave, my real name isn't Nina Voles –
it's Diana Travers. But no one in the town must
ever know!' The girl flashed him an anxious
glance.

'Okay. I'll take care to use your assumed name
whenever we're not alone,' Dave assured her. 'I'm
sure you have your reasons, Diana.'

'I most definitely have. But when we're alone –
as we are now – I like "Diana" much better. But
you haven't answered my question. I asked if you
were willing to help me.' Dave was silent for a
while, his eyes on the lonely, dusty trail in front of
them as they jogged along.

'There's nothing I'd rather do than help you,
Diana,' he said presently, 'but as I told you it may
be a day or two before I leave town. Depends on
how long my business takes.'

'Business?' the girl repeated, surprised. 'What
business? I thought you were just passing through?'

'In a sense I am – but there's another reason for
my staying in Valley Shadow. You've been mighty
frank with me so far, so I'll be frank with you. You
remember me saying last night I had been
arrested as a rustler?'

'Uh-huh. By mistake.'

'It wasn't so much a mistake. I'm *not* a rustler, but I've got to *prove* that I'm not. I'm only out of jail because of a legal technicality that makes it I can't be held. My sole reason for stickin' around this district is to find out who is back of the rustling and so free my own name.'

'Oh!' The girl's voice was quiet. 'I see.'

'It occurred to me,' Dave added, 'that if we could find the evidence by which Kelvin keeps a hold over you we might free you from his clutches entirely, then you could move freely as and when you please.'

'You don't know Jeff Kelvin very well,' she answered, with a serious smile. 'If he caught you attempting anything like that he'd shoot you down – or one of his trigger men would. I wouldn't have you take that risk for anything.'

'There *is* some evidence, then?' Dave persisted.

'Yes.'

The girl seemed to have made up her mind to explain everything.

'The man who was murdered was Arthur Cranley. He used to be an architect back in my home town of Sycamore Halt, and was planning on taking up an appointment in New York. I was engaged to him. On the night he was shot I had an appointment to see him, by letter. I wrote the letter myself. Jeff Kelvin has that letter now.

'Since I was found in Art's home with the revolver in my hand and the letter on the table in front of his dead body, you can see how it would look if the law got the facts. What makes it worse is that it was common knowledge amongst our friends in Sycamore Halt that Art and I had quarrelled. That would provide the motive for my having shot him. I went to see him that night with the sole intention of trying to patch things up, as I said in my letter.'

'Why do you consider the letter to be incriminating?' Dave asked, puzzled.

'Because in the letter I named the time I was to meet him – and that was the time Art was killed. The authorities would say that what I said in the letter about a reconciliation was just a pretence, so I could get to see him without arousing his suspicion.'

'And where does Kelvin fit in?' Dave asked, listening to every word. 'Give me all the facts exactly as they happened. It's the only way I can help you.'

'I knew Kelvin before I got to know Art,' the girl went on. 'We'd been going out for a while, and I think Kelvin assumed that he and I would eventually get engaged. However, I was never really as keen as he was, and when I got to know Art Cranley, I realized that I cared for him a good deal more than I did Kelvin. I began, too, to notice a side to Kelvin that I hadn't seen clearly to begin with. He was ambitious, with a ruthless streak.' The girl brooded for a while before continuing:

'Kelvin began making long trips to Valley Shadow, when his uncle became ill. I don't think he really cared about him, but presumably he was ingratiating himself, because when his uncle died, Kelvin inherited his estate here.'

'Meaning that he took over the Double Dollar and the Lazy Y ranch?' Dave queried, and the girl nodded.

'He told me he was planning to move here, and he asked me to marry him and come with him. It was then that I told him I'd been seeing Art Cranley, especially when he'd been away – and that I needed time to decide between them. I was actually worried that if their rivalry intensified, then Art might get hurt. Kelvin fancied himself as a gunslinger, but Art only wore his gun for protection. So I devised a stratagem, that played on Kelvin's self-confidence and ability with guns . . . .'

As they jogged along in the blazing sunlight, Dave listened with astonishment, mingled with admiration, as the girl described how she had rigged a shooting-contest between the two men, knowing that Cranley was bound to win because of his opponent's colour blindness.

'Kelvin was humiliated, and he left town, selling his own small ranch, and making good his promise to make a new life for himself here in Valley Shadow,' Diana Travers continued, her mouth setting as she came to describe more recent – and tragic – events. 'On the evening I went to see Art at his house, in accordance with my letter appointment, I found the door slightly open, much to my surprise. Inside, there was a revolver lying on the floor just outside his living-room door. Hardly realizing what I was doing I picked up the revolver, and went into the room . . .' The girl paused, obviously finding the memory distressing.

Dave glanced at her sympathetically, and was about to speak when the girl recovered herself and resumed her story in a firm voice.

'Art was lying on the floor of the living-room. When I turned him over, I . . . I discovered that he'd been shot in the chest. He was dead! On the table beside him was the letter I'd written . . . and then Jeff Kelvin walked in. Imagine how it looked!'

The girl paused and gave a little shudder at the painful memory. 'Go on,' Dave encouraged. 'What happened next?'

'I was scared to death. As Kelvin pointed out, the law would say that I had committed the murder – and the law would still say that if Kelvin ever speaks. He said we should both get out right away – he offered to take me with him to Valley Shadow – and so, glad of his protection, I came here with him. I changed my appearance by dyeing my hair a lighter colour, and also took another name – "Nina Voles" – so that nobody would know who I really was, in case any one came looking for Diana Travers. That occurred six months ago, and since nothing has happened I presume the police have not got any further.'

'And the revolver with which Cranley was shot? What happened to that?'

'Kelvin took it with him, as he did my letter.

The revolver will have my fingerprints on it, of course. I noticed that Kelvin raised it by keeping his finger in the barrel to save smudging the butt. He put it, and my letter, in an envelope – and I've never seen them since. He's got them hidden somewhere.'

Dave gave a grim smile and glanced at the girl's troubled face in the bright sunlight. 'You realize, of course, that the whole thing was a plant?' he asked. 'That the real culprit – the real murderer – is probably Jeff Kelvin himself!'

'I only guessed it afterwards,' she admitted, sighing. 'I think he shot Art because he was the one rival in the way of him getting me. Somehow he must have found out that I had written saying I was going to visit him that night. Art always was free with his information. Jeff Kelvin must also have known of our quarrel. He fixed things up, I suppose, knowing I'd pick up the gun – or at any rate feeling pretty sure I would. Anyway, I can't prove he is the murderer: the only proof there is points right at *me*. That's why Kelvin has such a hold over me. As I told you, his main wish is to marry me. So far I've managed to hold him off. That's why I want to get out of town with some-body's help. Once I've done that successfully he can say what he likes to the law, because I'll disappear – and take care that I'm never found. If I try to leave on my own he'll stop me somehow and bring me back, make my life a bigger hell than it is already.'

There was a long silence as the horses ambled

on lazily, their tails swishing. Then Dave called a halt, lifted the girl down from the saddle, and together they went over to the shady relief of the trees at the side of the trail. Together they relaxed in the grass, side by side.

'Actually, Diana, I think Kelvin is playing a game of bluff,' Dave said at length. 'If the worst came to the worst I don't think he'd bring out his evidence. He's smart enough to know that the law would question where he got his facts and how he happened on the murder as he did. In a word, I think the whole set-up would be too mighty unhealthy for him to risk diggin' it up. It's the kind of game I'd never try on a man. Being a woman, and not very experienced at that, he risked it on you.'

'That may be,' the girl said, 'but as long as he holds that evidence I'll never feel safe.'

'He won't go on holding it,' Dave snapped. 'Rest easy on that, Diana. But, obviously, I've got to work carefully, and it may take some time. Meanwhile, don't be so anxious to get out of town. Try and find out from him where he keeps his evidence. Get all the information you can out of him and leave the rest to me. For myself I want if possible to hogtie him for something equally important – cattle-rustling. And the murder of Will Pilkington, mebbe. He was my best friend, and some dirty skunk left his dead body to fry.'

The girl gave a little start. 'You think that Jeff Kelvin might be connected with it?'

'I sure do – and why not? He seems to have a

finger in most of the pies in this territory. As for murder, if our guess about Art Cranley is right he obviously wouldn't stop at one murder. I've got to find out the truth, Diana, before I get nailed down myself for murder.'

'But I – I thought you said rustling?'

'*And* murder. You must know about that ranch fire the other night – Will Pilkington's?'

'Yes, of course I heard, but —'

'I was arrested for cattle-thievin' and murder, but legal hocus-pocus on the part of my lawyer friend Ezra Munro got me out. But I may get back in the hoosegow before I know it.' Dave smiled faintly. 'So you see, we're both in the same saddle, Diana – sharing each other's secrets, and both of us equally innocent of any crime. In the same fashion we're both the victims of one person – so I think – and that's Jeff Kelvin. And it's against him that I'm figuring to act somehow.'

'Which won't be so easy,' Diana said moodily.

'Don't be too sure of that – I got Kelvin to offer me a job with him. I'm to give him my answer at the Double Dollar this evenin'.'

The girl's expression changed. For the first time the worry on her features seemed to dissipate.

'Work for him! But – but that would be a wonderful opportunity to try and find things out . . .'

'I intend to. My life and your safety depends on it.' Dave patted the girl's slender arm. 'Don't worry yourself, Diana, I'll work things out in my own way for the benefit of both of us. If I get too stuck I've got Ezra Munro in the background who'll straighten things out for me. So you just carry on as though nothing had happened and help me all you can. Between us we'll get Jeff Kelvin where we want him.'

The girl relaxed a little, looking absently before her towards the horses nibbling at the roots beside the trail.

'About these cattle-thievings,' she said presently. 'You've no guarantee that Kelvin is mixed up in them, have you?'

'No legal proof, if that's what you mean, but I've a whole load of suspicions, which I'm aimin' to try and confirm. Apart from Kelvin's character – which I judge to be as pleasant as that of a skunk – there was his peculiar behaviour last night when I trailed him making a lone ride into the mountains.'

Dave gave the details of what he had seen, first describing how he had earlier broken into Kelvin's office at the Double Dollar. As the girl glanced at him wonderingly, he added:

'I've no proof that he was going to keep some kind of rendezvous with rustlers, but he certainly didn't make a hard ride like that just because he was hankerin' for the exercise. I've got to find out what there is in that mountain canyon which fascinates him. Your part in the set-up will be to wheedle out of him all the information you can. You'll have to play up to him.'

'I'll do it,' she said. 'Though I'd sooner play up to a sidewinder.'

She looked at him in sudden alarm. 'You actually broke into his office, then? Didn't he recognize you?'

'He couldn't. The place was in darkness.'

'But he must know that *somebody* is trying to find things out.'

Dave grinned. 'That's right enough, but I don't think he'll suspect me because I've given him no cause to. I've also let him think I'm prepared to let you well alone.'

'And if he should see us together this morning?'

'In that case, it was just chance that we met. Nothing unnatural about that, is there?'

Diana smiled. 'Not the way you put it – but I know Jeff Kelvin so much better than you do!'

7

ARRESTED FOR MURDER

When Diana Travers – alias Nina Voles – arrived at the Double Dollar that evening, half an hour before the place was due to open, she was surprised to find Jeff Kelvin in her dressing-room, his taut, powerful body sprawled in a chair by the window.

'Jeff!' Diana gave a little start and threw off the light coat she was wearing. 'Not often you wait for me coming.'

'Not often I've reason to,' he answered, his face set.

'Where's Ella?' Diana glanced about for the middle-aged woman who acted as her dresser.

'I told her to step out for fifteen minutes. She'll be back in time for you to dress, don't worry. Meantime, Diana, you and I've got things to talk about.'

Kelvin got to his feet and the girl gave him a brief, startled look. There was something menacing in the set of his jaw and the hard glitter in his eyes. Suddenly he gripped her arm so fiercely she cried out.

'Jeff!' she complained. 'That hurts!'

'It's meant to,' he breathed, his voice low. 'Think yourself lucky I don't break it! And your damned neck as well!'

As she stared at him he released her so violently that she staggered and dropped heavily in the chair at the dressing-table.

'What's the idea of spending the morning with that footloose *hombre* Dave Norton?' Kelvin demanded. 'Answer me – and quick!'

'You – you know about that, then?' Diana straightened up, a defiant fire creeping into her dark-blue eyes.

'You're darned right I know! Or have you forgotten I've got men scattered all round Valley Shadow looking out for my interests? You know I won't have anybody around you 'cept me. If it comes to that you should have more sense than risk it, anyway. For all you know this Dave Norton, as he calls himself, may be a marshal in disguise – or a law officer, tracing your connections with that Art Cranley murder.'

Diana said nothing, but her mind was working fast. Jeff Kelvin was in an ugly mood and one word in the wrong place might ruin the plan of co-operation she had agreed upon with Dave.

'What did he want?' Kelvin asked, after a heavy pause.

Still Diana did not answer, and Kelvin's fury

exploded. Once more gripping her arm, he whirled her out of the chair and shook her violently.

'I'm *talking* to you! What did he *want*? If it was about that murder you committed and you told him anything I'll . . .'

'Well, you'll what?' the girl demanded. 'I've been thinking, Jeff – maybe there's a lot of things about that murder which you *wouldn't* talk about if it came to it! Maybe I'm not alone in bearing the responsibility, after all.'

'The evidence is all against *you*, and you know it!' Jeff snapped, his lips twisting into a sneer.

'And suppose the law asked how you came on the scene so easily?'

'So you *did* talk about the murder to Norton,' Kelvin muttered. 'Ten to one he's a law official trying to squeeze information out of you and you're too dumb to see it.'

'He's not even interested in the murder,' Diana replied curtly, wrenching her arm free. 'All that interests him is getting a job with you. We didn't even talk about the murder,' she added, seeking a lie as the best way out. 'In fact, the most important thing we talked about was the cattle-rustling.'

The hard gleam came back into Kelvin's eyes. 'You did, eh?'

'Why not, when he was wrongfully arrested because of it?' Kelvin studied the girl for a moment, then he set his mouth.

'I'm giving you fair warning, Diana – you're to have no more talks with Dave Norton unless I'm in on them, too —'

'How am I supposed to prevent it?' she demanded. 'You introduced him to me last night; what more natural than us talking when we happened to meet this morning?'

'I don't trust him,' Kelvin muttered. 'Right from the first I suspected he might be a law officer. That's one reason why I offered him a job when he asked me for one. That way I can keep an eye on him.'

Diana went to the chair before the dressing-table and began to pull a comb through her flaxen hair.

'He's no more a law officer than I am, Jeff.'

'No? Then what was he doing in my office last night? No stranger in town would need to do that.'

Diana, though she knew of the fact from Dave himself, simulated complete surprise as she turned her head.

'In your office? But . . . Why, did you see him?'

'No. I didn't see who it was, but there was certainly somebody, and afterwards I found that the door-lock hasp had been removed and rescrewed in place.'

Diana shrugged. 'Might have been anybody.'

'There's nobody in this town who knows me who'd be fool enough to try a thing like that,' Jeff said, his voice hard. 'They know what they'd get. No, I'm convinced it was Dave Norton. I only happened to find out because I came back for some papers I wanted. And you know more than you're telling!' Kelvin added, suddenly seizing the girl and forcing her from the chair.

She staggered back against the wall, against which Kelvin's left hand on her shoulder held her immovably.

'You and this Dave Norton are up to something,' he told her slowly. 'I'm going to find out what it is, Diana, even if I have to beat it out of you. So, start talking!'

Diana set her mouth and glared, then she recoiled with a sharp gasp as the flat of Kelvin's right hand struck her a stinging blow across the face.

'Talk!' he snapped. 'I won't have things going on behind my back . . .'

The girl's courage began to desert her as Kelvin began to raise his hand threateningly, his expression merciless. Then,

'Who says you won't?' demanded a curt voice. 'Reach for the ceiling, Kelvin – quick!'

Breathing hard, tears in her eyes from the blow she had received, Diana stared through a mist. The dressing-room door had opened and Dave was standing there, his right-hand .45 levelled steadily. Kelvin half-turned his head.

'I said *reach!*' Dave roared at him. 'Don't think I can't aim straight either, Kelvin. I showed you last night that I can.'

Kelvin's hands rose upwards reluctantly. Diana seized her chance to escape and hurried over to Dave's side.

'Who told you to interfere in a private argument?' Kelvin demanded, swinging round. 'What are you doing here, anyway?'

'Doing?' Dave raised his eyebrows. 'I came to see you about that job you offered me. The barkeep told me you were in here. What's wrong between you and Miss Voles? Your temper gettin' out of hand?'

Kelvin hesitated and then gave a slow, crooked smile.

'Yeah, I reckon so. I shouldn't have done that, Nina,' he added, looking at the girl.

'What were you hitting her for?' Dave demanded. 'Was she holding out about something?'

'He's got the idea that you and I are up to something,' the girl said bitterly. 'He wouldn't believe me when I said we weren't. I told him that the only thing we talked about this morning was cattle-rustling, which is right.'

'Right enough,' Dave agreed, eyeing Kelvin narrowly. 'What do you figure is so odd about that, Kelvin?'

'Nothing.' Kelvin gave a shrug. 'I'm just naturally suspicious. I'm sorry for what I did, Nina. I should have known better.'

Somewhat taken aback by the sudden change in his manner the girl clearly did not quite know how to act. Dave glanced at her, then at Kelvin and finally holstered his gun.

'I've no wish to butt in on a private quarrel,' he said, 'but you can't blame me for protecting a woman, Kelvin. It's sort of natural to me. I don't like to see a man trying to take advantage. Remember Black Joe last night?'

Kelvin lowered his hands. 'I remember – and I'm not blaming you for it. It's just that that stubborn filly infuriates me. I guess she got under my skin. It won't happen again though, Nina,' he said, patting her arm. 'And you'd better be getting dressed for your songs. Ella ought to be here soon.'

The girl still hesitated, then she caught Dave's almost imperceptible nod.

'All right,' she said quietly, and returned to the dressing-table. 'But one more bust up like that, Jeff Kelvin, and I quit – no matter *what* you do,' she added significantly.

Kelvin looked at her for a moment, then with a jerk of his head he motioned Dave to follow him out of the room. Dave did so, after a final meaningful glance at the girl, and walked beside Kelvin into the saloon where the lights were up and the first scattering of customers were lounging at the bar.

'Sit down, Norton,' Kelvin said briefly, nodding to a table. 'What are you having – whiskey?'

'Uh-huh.'

Kelvin called his order to the barkeep and then sat down opposite Dave and contemplated him.

'So you came about the job? Well – what's the answer?'

Dave could not keep the surprise out of his expression.

'Let me get this straight, Kelvin. Are you still offering me that job after what happened tonight?'

'I am.' Kelvin's face was expressionless. 'Any objection?'

'I reckon not. But I don't understand it ... quite.'

The barkeep brought the drinks and Kelvin played with his glass for a moment or two.

'I like one thing about you, Norton – your courage,' he said, with a touch of cynicism in his voice. 'I guess there aren't many men who'd hold up their prospective boss with a forty-five and make a play for his girl, too. It's original!'

'If you're talking about Nina Voles, I'm not making a play for her.'

'You're not?' Kelvin downed his drink and tossed a cigarette packet across the table. 'You spent this morning with her.'

'Chance! Nothing else.' Dave pulled out a cigarette and held a burning match. He met dark, sinister eyes over the flame.

'See it stays that way,' Kelvin said. 'You'll be a good man for me, Norton, if you know your place. Otherwise you might get hurt. That being understood, do you still want the job?'

'Why not? I'll start whenever you like.'

'Okay then, tomorrow morning. And for the last time, have nothing more to do with Nina Voles. Nothing! Savvy?'

'You make it sort of clear,' Dave acknowledged with a grim smile, and back of his mind he wanted nothing so much as a chance to think quietly and figure out just what the man was driving at.

'Be at my ranch tomorrow at eight,' Kelvin said, getting to his feet. 'The foreman will tell you what to do. Play straight with me and I'll play straight with you.' Dave nodded but said nothing. He remained seated at the table, watching the saloon-owner's strong figure go stalking away amidst the gathering crowd. Somewhere, something was decidedly peculiar. Jeff Kelvin was not the kind of man to act with even a trace of pleasantness towards a man who had held him at the business end of a .45, much less offer him a job.

'Better watch yourself, feller,' Dave muttered to himself. 'The dice are loaded against you some place . . .'

For most of the evening he stayed in the saloon, watching Diana at intervals as she sang in her persona as 'Nina Voles', spending the rest of his time thinking. Towards half past nine he left and went for what he considered to be a much-needed walk in the fresh night air. As he walked he pondered and gradually felt that he had knocked some possible sense into Kelvin's quite unexpected behaviour.

It was late when he returned to town, late enough for the Double Dollar to be closing. Keeping to the back of the town he stopped eventually at the side opening beside the girl's hotel. Here he remained in the shadows, and waited.

At last, after what seemed an interminable time, Diana made her appearance. Silently Dave glided out of the shadows and intercepted her movement towards the hotel steps.

'Dave! she exclaimed, and glanced quickly up and down the almost deserted street. 'If we're seen . . .'

He drew her gently into the shadows at the side of the building.

'Not likely to be here,' he said quietly. 'I had to talk to you. How much did you tell Kelvin – about us, I mean?'

'I simply said that we met by chance but he jumped to the conclusion that you're a marshal or something in disguise. I was sort of goaded into telling him that he wouldn't reveal anything about the murder of Art Cranley for fear of involving himself.' The girl gave a shrug, then went on:

'From that he guessed we'd talked about the murder. I think that's what makes him think you're a law officer. To switch the topic I told him the only thing we discussed was rustling.'

'You did, eh?' Dave observed.

'There was no use in my trying to cover up for you too much, Dave. He knows it was you who broke into his office last night, chiefly because his egotism makes him think it couldn't have been anybody else. He believes everyone in the town is afraid of him.'

'Then as I see it he can only have one reason for offering me that job with him – to figure out some way of tripping me up and perhaps disposing of me.'

'That is his idea,' the girl assented. 'I was going to try and warn you about it somehow. He told me as much. And I suppose that's why he tried to stop us meeting each other, in case I warned you and put you on your guard.'

'Evidently. All right then, just as long as we

know which way the wind's blowing. Since his suspicions of me go as deep as they do he'll go to any lengths to get me dry-gulched – and I'll be ready for him.'

'And you mean to stay and risk it?' Diana questioned.

'I'll be ready for him if he tries anything. He's out to get me and I'm out to get him. One scrap of evidence in the right direction and I'll put him where he ought to be. In the meantime we both obey orders and don't see each other from now on. Let him think he's scared us into doing it.'

The girl nodded as Dave clasped her hand.

'I'm willing. Now I'd better go, in case we're seen.'

The following morning Dave rode out to the Lazy Y at Sunny Point and found Jeff Kelvin neither cordial nor unpleasant. He merely exchanged a brief greeting and then handed matters over to Rod Shepway, the ranch foreman, a lean, taciturn being who made no secret of the fact that he did not like Dave.

In the first day he found for Dave all the worst jobs he could, and used though he was to ranching and the handling of cattle Dave had never worked harder in his life – but he did it all uncomplainingly in the hope that it would bring him nearer his objective.

At sundown he rode back into town, somewhat weary, to find a letter waiting for him in his room when he reached Ma Whittaker's boarding-house. Puzzled, he picked up the envelope and looked at it. It said simply: *Mr Dave Norton, Personal*. Tearing the flap he pulled the letter from inside.

Dear Dave,
I must see you concerning an important development which may help our plans considerably. Make it tonight, any time.
Ezra Munro.

Dave reflected, then he went downstairs and sought out his landlady.

'Dunno who brought it, Mr Norton,' she answered, in reply to his question. 'I just found it in the hall this evening.'

'I see.' Dave gave a shrug. 'All right. Thanks.'

Leaving the rooming-house he went down the street in the gathering darkness to Ezra Munro's place on the edge of the town. In five minutes he had arrived and knocked forcibly on the frame of the screen-door. There was no response.

He knocked again, and still got no answer. Puzzled, he grasped the screen-door and, to his surprise, it opened easily – as did the inner door that led directly into Ezra Munro's offices.

'Asleep, I reckon,' Dave muttered, and walked through the dark office into the living-room.

The oil-lamp was burning brightly, but Dave's expectancy of finding Ezra Munro dozing in his chair by the table was instantly dashed. The old lawyer lay flat on his back on the floor near the fireplace, red staining the front of his white shirt, dead eyes staring up at the ceiling.

Dave dropped on one knee, and though he knew it was futile he took hold of a pulse that had stopped. He glanced about the room sharply. There was no sign of there having been a struggle . . .

There were sudden sounds. Dave got up, his hand flying to his holster, but before he could whip out his .45 a figure with levelled gun appeared in the doorway that led into the office.

'Get your hands up, Norton!'

It was Jeff Kelvin who stood there, and behind him was the leaned-faced Rod Shepway, the Lazy Y foreman. Dave obeyed slowly, and stood silent while his guns were taken from him.

'Not much mistake this time, Norton, is there?' Kelvin asked calmly. 'Murder – and caught in the act! Okay, Rod, go and get the sheriff'

'Why, you dirty —'

'Easy!' Kelvin snapped, as Dave took a pace forward. 'This is one time you can't wriggle out, Norton. It's too well planned for that!'

'And you planned it!' Dave retorted, as Rod Shepway departed to get the sheriff. To Dave had come the sick realization that Kelvin was framing him in exactly the same way as he had Diana – even down to the use of a letter. To his surprise, Kelvin admitted it with his next words.

'Sure. Rather well, too.' Kelvin seated himself on the edge of the table but his guns never wavered. 'I don't like you, Norton, and I want you out of my way. I only took you to work for me so I could keep my eye on your activities until I'd worked out a plan. I managed it quicker than I expected. I had another little talk with Nina during today and got a few interesting facts out of her . . .'

'What facts?' Dave snapped.

'In particular I learned that Ezra Munro was a big friend of yours, and I got more details about you being arrested for cattle-rustling and murder the other night. The rest was easy.'

'Nothing easier than to kill an old man in cold blood, sure,' Dave agreed bitterly.

'Before he died I made him tell me everything and write the letter you got, so the law can testify that it's his writing. Then, I freely admit, I shot him dead.'

'But your bullet won't match those on my guns,' Dave snapped.

'But it will!' Kelvin gave a grim smile. 'Remember that pot you fired at last night in the Double Dollar? The bullet hit the ceiling and I dug it out. At the moment it is in our late lamented friend down here, the actual bullet that killed him having been extracted. Pretty good, eh?'

'Of all the filthy, underhand schemes —'

'Naturally,' Kelvin interrupted, 'Rod Shepway and I will both swear that we heard the shot which killed Munro. That will be sufficient when the bullet is found to have come from your gun and that you got an invitation, in Ezra's own handwriting, to come here. Glad you did that fancy shootin' last night, though I didn't realize at the time how useful that slug was going to be to me.' Kelvin grinned coldly. 'So you thought you'd work for me and find out all about me, did you? Thought you'd work hand in glove to break me? Thought you'd bust into my office and steal my girl? I'm not such an all-fired fool as that, Norton! I never did like rivals, and where convenient I dispose of them. I only kept my temper with you last evening because it paid me to do so and keep you beside me.'

Dave said nothing because there was nothing he could think of to say. Presently there came sounds from outside, preceding Sheriff Carson's arrival in the room. He looked down at the body and then at Dave.

'Once a murderer, Sheriff, always a murderer,' Kelvin said drily. 'Shepway and I will testify to everything. We saw Norton come in here and we heard the shot.'

'Yeah?' The sheriff gave the saloon-owner a quick look. 'I reckon you're usually in your Double Dollar at this time, Kelvin. How come you heard a shot ways out at this end o' town?'

'Shepway and I were coming to see Munro on legal business – and this is what we found.'

The sheriff nodded slowly. 'OK. I've got Doc Walters on his way over. You'd better come with me, Norton. I'm takin' you in for murder.' He grinned malevolently. 'And this time it looks as though there ain't no mistake about it!'

8
THE FUGITIVES

Bereft of his guns and with only the hard bunk of the cell in the adobe jail on which to rest, Dave passed a wearying, uncomfortable night, the jailer coming at intervals to look in on him and then go back into the little lean-to office.

Most of the time between uneasy dozing Dave spent in trying to figure out just how much he was involved – and the more he pondered it the more he realized the completeness of Kelvin's scheme.

There was not, as far as Dave could see, a single point in his own favour.

A .45 from one of his own guns in the lawyer's body, a letter written by the lawyer's own hand asking him to call, two witnesses who would be prepared to swear on a stack of Bibles that they heard the shot – and finally the fact that Dave was already a supposedly unconvicted murderer and rustler with no proof of his friendship with Will Pilkington.

The outlook was definitely black and Dave was left wondering upon whom he could call to defend him. With Ezra Munro gone there was not another lawyer in all Valley Shadow whom he trusted. Dawn found him grim, unrefreshed, pacing about his little cell.

He was given breakfast, ate it moodily, and then sat down on the bunk to see what developed. Towards nine o'clock Sheriff Carson came on duty and made it his first job to take a look at him. In spite of himself the sheriff could not hide the look of triumph on his leathery face.

'Didn't do much good for Ezra Munro to try and spring you, did it, Norton?' he asked drily. 'You're back behind these bars in the finish – and in case y'don't know it you're headin' straight for a neck-tie party.'

Dave swung on him. 'By what right do you assume that? You're only the sheriff. It's for judge and jury to decide what'll be done. You don't think I'm going to be framed like this, do you?'

'OK, OK,' Carson responded soothingly. 'But there's such a thing as bein' able to see the obvious, I reckon . . .' He turned sharply as somebody came into the adjoining office, and then he frowned.

It was Diana, dressed in her riding-skirt and silk shirt.

'Well, Miss Voles?' the sheriff asked her grimly, as she came through the office and joined him outside the cell door. 'What do y'want here?'

'A word with Dave Norton, if you've no objections? I was passing on my way for my usual morning ride and I thought I'd drop in.'

Dave stared at her through the bars. He could not quite understand her attitude.

'Nothin' to stop you talkin' to him, I reckon,' Carson responded. 'That is, providin' I hears what it's about. He's not in here on any ordinary charge, remember. It's murder!'

'I know. I heard all about it.'

'Nice of you to drop in, anyway,' Dave commented, still puzzling over the girl's expression.

'I didn't even know that you knew Norton,' the sheriff remarked, his eyes narrowing. 'I'll bet Jeff Kelvin wouldn't like it either if he knew.'

The girl smiled faintly, put her hands in the side-pockets of her riding-skirt and leaned idly against the bars of the cell.

'It's because of what I told Jeff Kelvin that you've got your man behind bars, Sheriff,' she said calmly. 'I got to know from Norton here,' she flashed him an unfriendly glance, 'that he is an unconvicted murderer and so, calling to mind the number of people who have been shot and robbed in this territory, I thought I ought to do my bit to bring this footloose killer to justice.'

Dave stared at her blankly, his face hardening.

Sheriff Carson smiled and relaxed his formal attitude. The girl's surprising remarks had taken a good deal of suspicion from his mind as to the reason for her calling. In fact it had taken far too much suspicion from his mind for her right hand suddenly came out of her riding-skirt pocket and pointed an automatic.

'Never be fooled by a soft story if a woman tell
it to you, Sheriff,' she said drily. 'And now, I'll tak
your keys.'

'Why, you ornery little hellcat, I'll —'

'Oh no, you won't!'

Carson found his forward movement checke
by the automatic pressing into his stomach.

'I'm warning you, Carson. I'll let you have it
you don't do as I tell you! *Get the keys!*'

His face glowing with pleasure at the realiza
tion that he hadn't been mistaken in the girl afte
all, Dave watched anxiously as she forced the she
iff to go into his office for the key to the cell door.

With a sullen face Carson unlocked it and the
Dave whirled him inside. One terrific blow to th
jaw knocked the sheriff senseless on to the bunk

'Nice work,' Dave breathed, slamming the ce
door, locking it, and then pocketing the key. H
glanced at the girl. 'But what happens now?'

'I've got your sorrel waiting for you outside:
got it from your rooming-house stable. Also got m
own pinto. Both horses are loaded up wit
bedrolls and provisions. I've got everythin
worked out, Dave, don't you worry. Tell you as w
go, and we'll have to go fast. Come on.'

'A moment,' Dave said, as they came into th
lean-to office, and he wrenched open the drawer
the sheriff's desk.

As he had hoped his twin guns and gun belt
were lying there. He buckled them on, whirled hi
hat from the peg where it had been thrown, an
then took the girl's arm.

Cautiously they peered outside on the street, which was now livening into morning activity. The two horses were waiting sleepily beside the hitch rail.

'Okay, we can risk it,' Dave breathed. 'Not many people about yet.'

They hurried quickly to their horses, untethered them, and swung into the saddles. Spurs did the rest and sent the animals speeding out of town to the trail which led to Sunny Point. Then the girl took a sharp leftward turn which led them out on to pastureland.

Here, as she and Dave rode hard in the expanse, she began to speak.

'The gloves are off now, Dave! Last night, around midnight, Jeff Kelvin came to my hotel and told me that you'd been arrested for the murder of Ezra Munro. He just couldn't resist gloating over it and I realized he'd cashed in on my telling him earlier in the day that Munro was a good friend of yours . . .'

'He sure did,' Dave said grimly. 'And I suppose you realize that the similarity of the crimes proves conclusively that he *did* murder your fiancé back in your home town?'

'Yes. I suppose I have always known it, but I tried to push it to the back of my mind . . .' the girl tightened her lips.

'Anyway, it served to help me make up my mind to get you out of jail – and I think I've laid what is a pretty good plan. Up in the mountains, in a canyon called Long Shadow, there's an empty cabin. A prospector had it once and gave it up when he found his panning was no more use, because the creek had dried up. We can shake down there at least until we think out what to do next. Later we can either ride on to Tucson or try and get Jeff Kelvin where we want him.'

'Now you're talking my language,' Dave grinned; then as he looked ahead he began to frown. They were skirting the edge of the desert with its sage and cacti. To the west loomed the mountain range.

'This is the same course Kelvin took the other night when I followed him!' Dave exclaimed sharply.

'It is?' The girl gave him a surprised look. 'That might make it awkward for us.'

'Or useful,' Dave answered, thinking. 'We'll decide that when we see where we end up.'

They stopped talking for a while and gave themselves solely to their riding. Sure enough they presently arrived at the stony ground around the mountain foothills and, of necessity, riding became less easy as the horses picked their way.

'No doubt of it – this is the route Kelvin took,' Dave said, glancing about him. 'I particularly remember the view of the canyon ahead shaped like a gigantic V. How did you ever come to find a spot like this?'

'By accident,' the girl answered. 'One morning when I was out riding.'

'Any idea where it leads to?'

She shook her flaxen head. 'Not the slightest.

I've never followed it right through the mountains. All I know is that about two miles further on there's that prospector's cabin.'

They rode on into the deep shadows cast by the mountain heights, the horses picking their way amidst rocks, dry stretches of earth, patches of anemone, primroses, and whispering bells. The canyon had a sombre yet colourful beauty all its own, different from the glaring, torrid endlessness of the desert.

'You certainly came prepared,' Dave grinned presently, looking at the bedrolls on the back of each saddle.

She nodded. 'For everything! You've got to be that way when you throw the works overboard. Once I'd made up my mind I packed two bedrolls with necessities and came to get you. There are canned foods among other things, and cooking-utensils. I did quite a bit of buying in the general store. The cabin has a fireplace if I remember rightly.'

'In other words you've thrown in your lot with me?'

'Entirely.' The girl gave a grave smile. 'I know that you may be thinking it's hardly ethical, but you just can't *be* ethical when a murder charge is hanging over your head. And I owe it to Art Cranley's memory to bring his killer to justice. I think,' she finished, quietly, 'we can trust each other.'

'I reckon so,' Dave agreed, and again they were silent as their mounts picked their way onwards.

For nearly half an hour they continued along the

canyon, the mountains growing in on them from each side, until at length, well to one side of the canyon's centre, they came within sight of the abandoned cabin. Dave, having never seen it before, contemplated it interestedly as they approached.

Since it had a chimney of sorts the girl had evidently been right in her belief that there was a fireplace. As for the cabin itself, it stood near a freshwater stream and was made of rough, weather-stained boarding. The porch had become overrun with vines and around the place a garden had sprouted weeds and canyon anemone.

A little distance away from the cabin stood a barn made of sahuaro-poles and mud, surrounded by a small corral fenced in by ocotillo, through the prickles of which no horse would be able to penetrate. The gate to it, hanging on old mesquite-posts, was unlatched and swinging.

'Good enough!' Dave commented, nodding. 'The very spot – at least for the time being.'

They dismounted at the porch, tethered the horses, and Dave took the two heavily loaded bedrolls from the saddles. With the girl following behind him he mounted the two steps to the porch, pushed open the swinging door and entered the small, completely empty log-walled room that had once been living-quarters. Beyond it, through an open doorway, was another room which had presumably been a bedroom. Such was the entire layout of the place.

'Home from home,' the girl commented, and, evidently thinking of conventions she added with a faint smile, 'And a room each.'

Dave dumped the bedrolls on the floor and opened them. Inside them there seemed to be everything. A small lamp, a sealed tin of kerosene, tinned foods, cooking-utensils, food for the horses, matches – in fact practically everything that could be needed. Dave glanced up and grinned as he saw the girl watching him.

'Everything the doctor ordered,' he commented. 'And the fireplace right in front of us. We'll have to watch, though, that the smoke doesn't betray us. The same goes for the horses. We'd better put them in that barn.'

'But you don't think anybody will follow us this far, surely? My belief is that Kelvin and the sheriff and the rest of them will think we've headed for the next town – either Farnworth Bend or Tucson.'

'In that I agree,' Dave responded, 'but since Kelvin rode this way the other night there's nothing to stop him doing it *any* night – and that might be when we'd betray ourselves. I don't think he'll ride this way by day if his mission is supposed to be secret.'

'Yes, I suppose that's right.' Diana reflected for a moment. 'Look, Dave, what do you think we ought to do? I only thought of this place as a sort of base of operations. What plans have you?'

'To stay right here,' he answered promptly. 'It couldn't be better. Running away to another town won't solve anything for either us. There are three things to be done. One is to clear both our names from the murder frame-ups fixing us: the second is to find out who's behind the rustling, and wipe it out, and the third is to bring Kelvin to justice for murdering Ezra Munro.

'We're helped in that since he's admitted he did it, but unfortunately I had no witnesses. Lastly, the thing in our favour is that he rides this way sometimes. We'll stay around until the next time he comes along, and then follow him. Nothing but a very vital, secretive reason could bring him to this deserted canyon.'

'And if he notices that this cabin is occupied?'

'If he comes by day he *will* notice – no denying that. But if he comes by night and we blot out the window he's not likely to notice anything. Either way we'll take precautions. When we have to cook we'll kill the fire the moment we've finished. At night we'll take it in turns to sleep. You in the other room – me in here. Be tough going with no proper furniture or beds.'

'Better than a cell, though,' the girl commented drily. 'We've got the chance to act and that's the main thing.' She turned briskly. 'It's time we had a meal after that trip. Give me your knife, Dave, and I'll open one of these cans. You'd better get in some wood.'

He nodded and handed her his knife. 'I'll fix up the horses, too,' he added, filling two of the flat cooking-tins with meal.

With one pan in each hand he went out on to the porches and looked both ways along the cool, shadowed length of the canyon. Nothing was in sight – only the lonely, grey, deserted distances.

Once the horses were attended to and turned loose in the small corral he collected what wood he could find, all of it dry and brittle from the rainless months, and returned with it to the cabin.

To his surprise he found Diana looking woeful and holding up her right hand ominously. Down it ran a trickle of red.

'What on earth . . .?' Dave enquired blankly, tossing the wood in the fireplace and going over to her. 'What happened?'

'My hand slipped,' she sighed. 'The tin edge cut it.'

Dave inspected the injury and frowned. It was a deep flesh-cut across the top of her first finger, not bleeding very much but with a dull, purplish tint at the base which bespoke depth.

'Keep your hand up,' he instructed. 'I'll get some water.'

He hurried outside with a tin and filled it at the stream. Returning to the cabin he made the girl wash the cut thoroughly, then at her instructions found amidst her bedding a soft feminine trifle that he tore into a strip and used as a bandage.

'That's better,' Diana smiled, as he tied it in place. 'Just about like me to be a confounded nuisance . . . That's fine! All right, let's have the fire.'

Dave got it going in a few minutes, filled the can for coffee, and half an hour later, squatting on the boarding of the porch where they could instantly see anybody approaching, they had their meal. It was rough and ready but appetizing enough in its way.

'I just wonder where this canyon *does* go to finally?' Dave murmured, gazing into the distance.

'As far as I know,' the girl answered, 'it must end in the mesa. Certainly the nearest town is Tucson – in that direction, anyway.'

'To which Kelvin certainly wouldn't try and ride by night,' Dave commented thoughtfully. 'So there must be something much nearer than Tucson that interests him. Tonight, whether he comes or not, I'm going to try and find out what it is. One thing I do know: there are a lot of ranches between this canyon and Tucson. I'm wondering if a lot of the rustled cattle may not have been transported through this canyon to those other ranches, to be sent from there to wherever necessary.'

'It's possible,' the girl admitted, 'though of course Jeff Kelvin couldn't drive a herd of cattle single-handed. He must have a lot of helpers tucked away somewhere, and I don't think they're in Valley Shadow, either. Be too risky. One of them might talk and I can't see Kelvin taking that chance.'

They were quiet for a while, then the girl said: 'Naturally I shall come with you tonight.'

Dave gave her a quick look. 'Do you think you should? There is no telling what we'll run into.'

'I'll risk it. In fact it's probably safer than being alone in the cabin watching out for Jeff Kelvin. If he *did* happen to spot me I wouldn't be able to do a thing except shoot him, and I don't want to do that because then I'd *really* be a murderess.'

Dave nodded. 'Okay. We'll go together – after sundown.'

9

RUSTLER'S CANYON

As darkness was falling they both started off along the canyon, leaving it to the horses to pick their way as best they could amidst the loose stones. In the growing dark there was a forbidding sombreness about this huge natural cleft. Only a section of the starry heavens was visible, and mist cloaked the canyon floor. Every sound made by the horses echoed back from the towering walls.

It was after twenty minutes' riding that they came suddenly upon another smaller canyon bearing due left, its presence marked by a V-shaped wedge of stars. Dave drew rein, leaned on the saddle horn and looked about him.

'Now what?' he questioned. 'Do we go straight on or turn left?'

'We might do both,' the girl said finally. 'This one to the left can only go into the heart of the mountains. The one ahead goes out to the mesa – or should. Let's try the left first.'

'Okay,' Dave agreed, and turning the heads
their horses they followed the canyon floor for
distance of nearly two miles. Here they found
suddenly shelved deeply and went down in a lon
gentle slope to what seemed to be a huge natur
basin in the midst of the mountain range.

'Look!' the girl breathed.

Dave saw what she meant. Perhaps half a mi
away, to one side of them and apparently on th
mountain face, was a flickering yellow glow, blo
ted out now and again as somebody crossed i
front of it.

'Camp-fire,' he murmured. 'Somebody in a cav
– and there's also something down there in tha
basin,' he added, staring into the starlight.

'Something huge, and moving.'

He and the girl were both intently watchful fo
a space, forcing their eyes to penetrate the gloon
then Diana caught her breath a little.

'Cattle!' she exclaimed, turning to look a
Dave's dim form mounted on his horse beside he
'That's what's down there – hundreds of head o
cattle. A natural mountain corral!'

'Yeah.' Dave's voice was grim. 'Now I get it! An
I didn't guess far wrong, either. The cattle that ar
stolen are driven to this natural corral wher
they'll probably be rebranded. Then, by night
they can be taken from here to the main canyo
and driven out on to the mesa and the ranche
which must act as receivers for stolen herds.' H
gave the girl a sideways glance.

'After that they'll be disposed of in the way tha

suits the rustlers best. That means there must be a lot of ranchers out on the mesa working for Kelvin – if he's the boss of the rustlers, and I presume he is. Very profitable – and safe too! Until we found out about it!'

'Even now that we do know,' Diana said, her eyes on the flickering camp-fire, 'I don't see what we can do about it.'

'Rustling on this scale is a matter for a marshal to look into,' Dave answered. 'For obvious reasons I can't return to Valley Shadow and tell Sheriff Carson, but I can ride to Tucson and bring a marshal back with me to see for himself. That way it's possible Kelvin can be caught red-handed.'

'That would settle the rustling,' the girl agreed, 'but it wouldn't clear you of that murder charge, nor would it save me. Kelvin would never confess to either of those things.'

'Once arrested for rustling his entire affairs would be looked into, Diana, and that would start things moving. The truth would come out somehow. Once we get Kelvin behind bars and a marshal satisfied as to his dirty work we need have no fear. The proper authorities will sift everything to the bottom.'

Dave was silent for a moment and then added, 'We might do worse than see who's in that cave. It might even be Kelvin himself, though I doubt it. You willing?'

For answer the girl slid from the saddle. She and Dave pulled their horses into the shelter of the rocks, on the off-chance that Kelvin might yet appear, then in single file they followed the rocky pathway which went round the face of the mountain towards the yellow flame of the camp-fire.

It was further away than they had imagined and it took them a good fifteen minutes to get near to it. With the lessening of distance the real size of the cave-mouth became visible.

It was quite huge, though the fire itself was small. Moving slowly now, Dave with his guns ready and the girl with her automatic, they crept nearer and nearer, taking care that no stones tripped them or gave away their presence. So eventually they gained a vantage point from which they could see into the cave itself.

In all there appeared to be about a dozen men grouped round a fire in various lounging attitudes, some of them smoking and others talking in voices not loud enough to carry. The cave was obviously being used as a camp for it was provided with all manner of necessities – oil-drums, stacks of logs for the fire, cooking apparatus, camp-beds, and a dozen-and-one other necessities.

From the look of the men's faces they were chiefly saddle tramps and outlaws, every man-jack of them. Swarthy, unshaven, grim-faced men, probably fugitives and willing to take on any desperate game just as long as it gave them reasonable cover from the law and the elements and some money in their pockets.

'Nice-looking bunch,' Dave breathed in the girl's ear.

'Yes,' she whispered back. 'What do we do now?'

'Nothing we can do at the moment, and obviously we can't take on a dozen trigger-men and live to survive. We know where they hide out anyway and once we can get a marshal here —'

'Somebody coming!' the girl interrupted. 'Back along the pathway . . . .'

Dave gave one desperate glance about him and then caught the girl by the arm and pulled her over the edge of the pathway and into the dust and rocks which formed the steeply shelving side of the basin, at the bottom of which lowed and moved the rustled cattle.

They were not a moment too soon. Riding a horse with difficulty along the narrow way came a single figure. At the cave-mouth he dismounted and for a while the camp-fire threw his tall silhouette into relief. There was no mistaking it.

'Kelvin!' Dave breathed, peering with the girl over the edge of the pathway.

'OK, OK, it's only me,' came Kelvin's voice. 'You can put the hardware away . . .'

There was a murmur of voices, then Kelvin's clear tones came again: '. . . things aren't entirely ready yet. We can't move until the early morning, otherwise we might ruin everything.'

'But what's the boss a-waitin' for?' one man demanded. 'One time's as good as another, ain't it?'

'That's for the boss to decide,' Kelvin answered calmly.

Dave glanced at the girl in the starlight. He

could not see her expression even though he cou
imagine it. Her next words confirmed his belief

'Then he *isn't* the boss! Who on earth *can* k
then?'

'I dunno,' Dave murmured. 'This is something
never expected. Just the same he's close
connected with this racket, and that's wor
knowing. If we can get a marshal on his track h
can probably be made to tell us who's back of a
this. It's the only way we can work, not knowin
who's behind things.'

'Uh-huh,' the girl acknowledged, her voice lo
'Not much point in staying here any longer, is ther
I can't hear a word now he's gone inside the cave.

Dave looked about him. 'We'll start movir
right now, keeping below the pathway edge unt
we're clear of the cave. Come on.'

The girl followed him as he edged his way car
fully along, taking care not to make a single soun

It took them all of twenty minutes to mov
silently away from the cave's area, then the
climbed up to the pathway and went along it at
faster pace, reaching their hidden horses a fe
minutes later.

'I'm wondering if I ought not to go back to th
cabin for provisions and then set off for Tucso
tonight,' Dave said reflectively, climbing into th
saddle. 'And bring a marshal back with me.'

'It's a good idea, and I'd like to come with yo
only –' Diana hesitated. 'Only I don't feel up to i
she finished.

Dave could not help being astonished, and hi

voice showed it. 'You don't? Why, what's wrong?'

'I don't quite know. I feel sort of – queer. I felt it when we started off. A chill, a bit feverish. Excitement perhaps . . .'

'That settles it,' Dave said briefly. 'I'm not going any place until you can either come with me or stand up for yourself if you're attacked in the cabin. We're going back there right now and find out what's the matter with you.'

The girl said nothing. She jogged her horse along behind him and he kept glancing back, seized with the fear that she might collapse or something. She did not do so however, but when they reached the cabin he had to lift her bodily from the saddle.

Wearily she went into the cabin while he hurried the horses round to the barn, fed and watered them, then came back into the cabin's main room. The girl had fastened a blanket over the window to blot out the light of the oil-lamp and now she squatted on the floor, back against the wall, her flaxen head lolling lazily.

Dave knelt beside her. As she glanced up he saw her cheeks were flushed and her breathing short and husky. At intervals she shuddered convulsively.

'Must be a chill,' he said worriedly. 'I'll fix up a bed for you here on the floor. You'd better wrap up warm in these blankets.'

She opened leaden eyes after she'd closed them for a while.

'It's something – worse than a chill, Dave,' she

muttered. 'I'm not the sort to feel like this from a cold: never had a bad one in my life . . .' she gave a little sigh.

'My – my right arm's so stiff I can hardly move it. Been getting worse all day. I didn't say anything sooner because I wanted to come with you tonight. I'm thinking – maybe it's that cut I got from that meat-can this morning.'

Dave started. He had forgotten all about the incident. Now it was recalled to his mind he took the girl's hand and untied the rough bandage swiftly.

One look at the cut across her finger satisfied him. The tin edge had either had impurities on it or else her hand had been dirty from the ride to the cabin.

'Blood-poisoning!' he exclaimed. 'I'd know it any place.'

She nodded wearily. 'I thought so. What's the remedy?'

'Get a doctor, of course! I can't pretend to cope with a thing like this. I haven't the knowledge.'

He turned aside and began arranging a rough bed as the girl rebandaged her finger. Then he lifted the girl up and laid her gently amidst the blankets, drawing them close about her as she shivered at intervals.

'Dave, you *can't* go for a doctor,' she insisted weakly. 'It will mean going back to Valley Shadow and straight into a hangman's rope!'

'I've got to risk that,' he answered quietly. 'You're not fit to make the trip and you need medical aid. I'll be all right: leave it to me.'

He laid her automatic on the floor beside her. 'If by any chance anybody should come shoot first and ask questions afterwards. I'll be back as fast as I can. I'll put the lamp out, just in case. Unless he's already gone Kelvin has still to come back past here.'

The girl did not argue. She was too listless. Dave gave her a final troubled glance and then blew out the lamp-flame. Silently he stepped out on to the porch and latched the door.

As he went round to the barn for his horse he paused, instinctively drawing his gun and standing motionless.

The sound of a horse's hurrying hoofs had reached him and in a moment or two a lone rider came sweeping past within quarter of a mile of the cabin. Evidently he was not concerned with it for he continued on his way down the canyon, the noise of the horse becoming fainter and fainter.

'That's one relief anyway,' Dave murmured, slipping his gun back in the holster. 'Kelvin on his way home again. That makes Diana hundred per cent safer.'

He resaddled his horse, vaulting into it, and began the journey through the night to Valley Shadow.

Though he travelled fast he was alert all the time for some signs of Kelvin – with whom he feared he might catch up – but there was no evidence of him anywhere, either in the canyon or in the vast expanses of desert beyond it.

10
LYNCH LAW

It was towards midnight when Dave reached Valley Shadow. He approached it cautiously from the backs of the ramshackle buildings, though at this hour he was pretty sure that there was not much chance he would be observed. Eventually he was compelled to enter the main street in order to reach Doc Walters' home.

It was the doctor's son Pete who finally opened the door. He was hastily dressed in pants and shirt. Thin-faced, a man Dave had never liked on the few times he had encountered him, he poked his face out into the night.

'Well, who in tarnation is it?' he demanded unpleasantly, holding up an oil-lamp so the rays fell on Dave's face. Then he gave a little gasp.

'Sufferin' cats, it's Norton!'

'All right, you don't have to advertise it!' Dave retorted. 'Let me in, can't you? I've got to see your father right away.'

'Yeah? For why?' Pete's voice was bitter. 'What'd an escaped murderer be a-wantin' to see him for, eh? There's a price on your head, Norton, an' I —'

'This,' Dave snapped, whipping out his gun, 'is urgent! Get inside and stop bleating. And call your father!'

'Yeah . . .' Pete glanced at the gun. 'Just as yuh say.'

Dave kept his gun steady as the thin-faced young puncher had to back into the hallway, still holding the lamp. He put it on a table against the wall and then called up the staircase.

'Pop! Hey, Pop! Come down here, will yuh? There's that guy Dave Norton a-wantin' to see yuh.'

'*Who?*' came an astonished gasp from the top of the dark stairs.

'Dave Norton – him as the sheriff is a-lookin' for.'

There were sounds of hurried movements above and the thud of a door closing. Pete Walters lounged back against the hall table and considered Dave and his gun with sour interest.

'I reckon you do everythin' at the point of a rod, don't you?' he asked cynically. 'Without your hardware you'd make pretty small fry. There's a lot of folks around this territory as is a-waitin' to get their mitts on yuh, Norton. The sheriff told us how you got outa jail with that woman Nina Voles to help you. What we didn't know was that you're the rustler that's bin a-thievin' from us all, an' that you shot Ezra Munro – a harmless old feller who couldn't protect himself.'

'Get your facts straight before you start shooting off your mouth!' Dave retorted.

'They're straight as they is, I reckon. An' there's five hundred dollars for anybody who can tell the sheriff where you are.'

That the position was getting tough Dave well knew. A sneaking rat like Pete Walters would not think twice about giving the facts and collecting the $500 reward. His name had never ranked very high in the list of square shooters in Valley Shadow.

Then Dave gave up thinking the problem out as the middle-aged, grey-haired Dr Walters came hurrying down the stairs.

He looked at Dave in grim wonderment, as though his professional interest and personal antipathy were fighting for the mastery. Dave was not entirely a stranger to him. He had seen him on occasions when trifling injuries had needed his ministrations.

'Well?' he asked briefly. 'What do you want? Stickin' your neck out like this?'

'I want your help, Doc, and quickly.' Dave reholstered his gun.

'Not for myself: for Nina Voles,' he added, using the name by which the girl was known in the town.

'He's lyin!' Pete declared flatly. 'I'd sooner trust a rattler than this guy, Pop!' Walters glanced impatiently at his son.

'Get back to bed, Pete, and leave me to handle this.'

Pete hesitated, a malignant gleam in his dark eyes, then with a shrug he turned and went up the stairs.

'I've got the idea he'll sneak out to the sheriff,' Dave said uneasily.

'Can't blame him if he does, can you?' Walters asked quietly. 'The whole town's lookin' for you, Norton, and that woman Nina Voles who got you out of jail. What was it you were telling me about her, anyway?'

'She's ill – got blood-poisoning. She's up in a cabin in Long Shadow Canyon. If she doesn't have medical help there's no telling what may happen to her. I reckon blood-poisoning can be pretty dangerous if it isn't checked.'

The doctor set his mouth. 'How'd I know you're tellin' me the truth? Since you murdered a lawyer in cold blood how'd I know you ain't aimin' to do the same thing to a harmless doctor?'

'You really believe that of me?' Dave asked bitterly.

'Not much else I can believe, is there? Everybody in the town can't be wrong, I reckon.'

'They can in this case. I'm speaking the truth, Doc. I never murdered anybody, and I never rustled cattle. Nina Voles knows I didn't and that's why she helped me to escape. Do you really think I'd come riding into town like this if it wasn't deadly serious? You've got to come, Doc – you've *got* to!'

The doctor reached to the stand and took his hat from it. From underneath the stand he lifted his ever-ready medical bag. Then, from a holster that had been hidden by his jacket, he removed his gun and pointed it.

'All right, I'll come,' he agreed, 'because I'm a doctor first and a man second. But I'm makin' one condition: you ride ahead of me all the time. One thing you do wrong, Norton, an' I'll shoot to kill. I aim to take no chances.'

'Suits me,' Dave shrugged. 'Let's be going.'

He stepped out of the house ahead of the doctor and swung up into the saddle of his horse. He had to wait a moment or two while the doctor got his own mount from somewhere at the back of the house, then – Dave in front as ordered – the ride began.

As they left town Dave kept his eyes open anxiously for signs of anybody watching. He could not rid himself of the feeling that Pete Walters would not let $500 slip by so easily – but for all his worry he beheld nobody and he and the doctor presently gained the trail, and then the edge of the desert, without untoward incident. When finally they reached the darkened cabin the doctor eyed it as they walked together up to the porch.

'Picked yourself a nice quiet spot, didn't you?' Walters asked. 'If you're not guilty how come you're hidin' out like this?'

'So I can lie low and find out who *is* responsible,' Dave answered. 'But never mind me for the moment, Doc; it's the girl who counts.'

'Okay. Lead on. I'm right behind you.'

Dave entered the living-room of the cabin and murmured a word of greeting to the girl as he did so. Her tired voice responded with obvious thank-

fulness; then the oil-lamp came into being as
Dave lighted it. Doc Walters stood gazing down on
the girl for a moment and a change of expression
came to his face.

Snapping open his bag he put his gun inside it
and took out a thermometer. Dave remained
standing beside the closed door, watching as the
diagnosis was made. Presently Walters glanced
up.

'I'll want some boiling water, Norton. Get the
fire lit.'

Dave nodded and did as he was told, going out
to the stream to get water in one of the cooking-
tins. Once he had the water boiled he watched
again.

He did not understand one half of what the
medico did, but at the end of the time the girl had
her finger professionally rebandaged, and smoth-
ered in antiseptic, while some kind of medicine
had removed the unhealthy flush from her
cheeks. She lay back in the roughly made bed,
breathing heavily.

'Nice mess for a strapping girl to get into, eh?'
she asked, smiling faintly.

Walters contemplated her. 'If you hadn't got a
man beside you with the courage of Dave Norton
here you'd have been dead in a few days,' he
answered gravely. 'As it is you'll be all right
because you're constitutionally strong. You need a
few more days taking it easy. I've got the poison
out of the wound, and the rest is up to nature.
How come you got that cut?'

'Canned-meat tin.'

'Uh-huh. Nasty things sometimes, I reckon. Just bad luck.' Walters patted the girl's shoulder, smiled a little, and got to his feet.

Dave looked at him wonderingly.

'*What* was that you said about me?' he asked.

For answer Walters held out his hand frankly. 'I'm satisfied,' he said. 'I'm at an age to form my own judgement, an' to blue tarnation with what other people think. Any man who'd risk his neck comin' back to town so this girl could have help is a square-shooter from where I'm standin'.'

'Thanks!' Dave gave a smile as he grasped the hand. 'Nice to know you believe in me. And she'll be all right, you say?'

'Sure she will. I'll leave you fresh dressing and some medicine.' Walters put them on the floor beside the lamp.

'Change the dressing morning and evening. If I can get over by night I'll do so, but if it seems to me it'll make it dangerous for you I'll hold off. In any case, Miss Voles, you'll mend from now on. Soon as you're up to it get out into the fresh air.' Walters paused, and shut his medical bag.

'About payment . . .' Dave began. But Walters silenced him with a gesture. 'Forget it. We'll talk about it after you've gotten your affairs straightened out. Meanwhile, I've got to be goin',' he said, and with a final nod to both of them he went to the door.

Dave saw him on his way and then put his own horse in the barn. It was just beginning to dawn on him that he was feeling tired after all that happened. Re-entering the cabin he squatted on the floor at the girl's side and smiled.

'Well, it was worth it,' he murmured. 'That puts you straight. I'll wager you're feeling better already?'

'Uh-huh,' her blue eyes studied him. 'And you can open the next can of meat we have . . .' She broke off with a gasp and Dave swung round as with a crash the cabin door suddenly slammed open.

Dave's hands flew to his guns but he wasn't quick enough.

'Keep 'em up, Norton!' ordered the man in the doorway, and the lamplight gleamed on the twin barrels of .38s. Then as the man came further into the range of the light the vulpine features of Pete Walters became visible.

'I might have known it!' Dave breathed.

'Get up!' Pete ordered. 'And put your guns on the floor where the gal can't reach 'em.'

Dave obeyed slowly. If the girl had not been lying directly in the line of fire he would have taken a chance on a flying tackle, but with dice loaded so heavily against him he did not dare risk it.

His guns tossed to one side he got up, then watched in some surprise as Pete was elbowed on one side by a group of men behind him. One of them came forward, likewise armed.

The man was middle-aged, round-faced, and in normal circumstances probably genial enough. At the moment his face was grim.

'Don't know me, do you?' he asked shortly, and Dave shook his head. 'For that matter you probably don't know any of us – save Pete Walters. Not including him there's six of us here – each one of us men whose cattle you've stolen. My name's Vincent – Gary Vincent.'

'Never heard of you,' Dave said.

'I run the Grey L ranch, north of Valley Shadow, and thanks to you and your rustlers I'm three hundred head o' cattle short. When Pete knew you'd come back to town he didn't go to the sheriff: he came to us – the men who've lost most. The sheriff's let you slip through his fingers twice, so we're goin' to act for him. It was plumb easy for us to catch up on you and the doc and follow, then wait until the doc left. We're goin' to show you what justice is, Norton, since you're so good at escapin' it!'

'What are you going to do?' Diana demanded hoarsely, sitting up.

'Nothing you can alter,' Vincent told her. 'Don't worry – you'll be looked after.' He jerked his head to one of the other men.

'Keep her here, Bill,' he said, and to Dave he added, '*Outside!*'

Faced with a revolver and feeling appallingly giddy there was nothing Diana could do but relax again, her ears straining for every sound and her pulses racing.

Outside, Dave found himself forced to cross the weed-choked garden to the barn. The horses within moved uneasily. Unable to help himself he found his hands fastened tightly behind his back.

The dim figures of the men in the dawning moonrise were all he could see. Vincent's voice reached him.

'This is a necktie party, Norton,' he explained. 'Lynch law! We consider ourselves as judge and jury and unhampered by legal technicalities, as the sheriff is. You'll not steal our cattle and murder our townsmen an' get away with it!'

'But you're wrong!' Dave insisted hoarsely. 'For God's sake give me —'

'Shut up!'

Dave breathed hard, becoming silent only because he realized the uselessness of argument.

In a moment a lariat had been thrown over the centre-beam of the barn and the noose adjusted about his neck.

Dave was quite convinced this was the finish. When five strong men pulled on the other end of the rope . . .

'What's that?' Vincent asked abruptly.

Dave felt the tautness of the noose about his neck slacken as the men listened. Then he heard it too – the dull, distant thunder of a herd of cattle coming nearer through the night.

'Sounds like a herd headed this way,' one man said.

Dave made frantic gurgling sounds as the noose tightened a little – then it was suddenly pulled free by Vincent.

'You know what's going on, Norton?' he snapped.

'Yes – sure I do.' Dave gasped for breath. 'It's a herd of cattle that's being stolen tonight. The rustlers are driving them up this canyon to a hidden natural corral in the mountains. Miss Voles and I heard them making arrangements earlier on. There's a whole gang of owl-hooters hidden in these mountains.' Even as he spoke, the thunder of the herd came nearer.

'Say,' one of the men remarked, turning to Vincent, 'I guess we could've been wrong at that. Norton here's been runnin' after the doc most of the night. He couldn't direct a rustlin' at the same time, could he?'

'Don't I keep telling you I've nothing to do with it?' Dave demanded.

'He's lyin',' Pete Walters snapped. 'It's one o' his tricks!'

Gary Vincent made up his mind and whipped away the lariat. 'I believe what I see,' he said, unfastening Dave's hands. 'What about the rest of you men?'

Their acquiescence was grudging, but it was there. Pete was the only dissenter and Vincent snapped him into silence.

'I reckon we had you all wrong, Norton,' Vincent said, turning to him. 'What *do* you know about these rustlings?'

'Enough to bring it to a stop – if I can play a lone hand.'

Vincent listened to the approaching cattle.

'Lone hand? I reckon not! We're goin' to get the men directin' this.'

'An' how much good will it do you?' Dave demanded. 'You may be shot – and you can be sure the brains behind this won't put himself in your line of fire.'

Vincent reflected. 'Yeah, that sort of makes sense,' he admitted.

"Here they come!' Dave said abruptly. 'Lie low – and watch.'

The group obeyed the order, even Pete – who certainly had not the nerve to try anything single handed – and well hidden by the barn the party watched the herd go stumbling by, driven by the crack of whips and hoarse orders. In time the cattle had passed and the normal silence of the canyon returned. 'Seemed to be about six men in charge,' Vincent said.

'All told there are around a dozen,' Dave told him. 'Miss Voles and I saw a dozen, leastways. Mebbe more.'

'You don't know where those cattle came from?' Vincent asked.

'No – but we'll know soon enough. These aren't just ordinary rustlings: they're highly planned thievery with murder thrown in if anybody gets in the way. You can blunder in and do as you like, if you want. But if you'll let me handle it I'll have a marshal take care of things. You can be sure nothing'll go wrong. I've my own innocence to prove, remember.'

Vincent thought for a while and finally nodded

in the dim light. 'OK, do it your own way. Too many cooks spoil the broth, I reckon. If you're in need of help send for us.'

Dave heaved a sigh of relief. 'Thanks! You can rely on me.'

The men said no more. The solitary guard was recalled from inside the cabin and then the party rode off into the night.

Mopping his face Dave went back to the cabin porch. To his amazement Diana had got as far as the doorway. He caught her in his arms as she swayed.

'Dave! Oh, Dave, thank God you're safe! I thought they'd —'

'They didn't. They're on my side now. Come back inside and I'll tell you all about it.'

11
RETRIBUTION

The rest of the night and the following day passed uneventfully for Dave and Diana, and the girl at least was glad of it.

She spent all the daylight hours on the porch wrapped up in a blanket, her every want attended to by Dave. Only when the evening chill returned did Dave see that she retired comfortably to bed again.

'I'll not light the lamp,' he told her, 'because I want to watch at the window in case Kelvin makes a trip. If he does I'm going right after him. I've got the horses saddled ready – and this is in case I've no time for a goodbye.'

He put the automatic beside the girl and added, 'Since there doesn't seem to be the chance to ride for a marshal I'll take the only course, and next time I see Kelvin I'll beat the truth out of him.'

He turned, went across to the window and took up his stand. In half an hour darkness had come and the girl had dropped asleep. Dave glanced at her dim form, smiled to himself, and tiptoed out to the porch.

There were only the sounds of normal nightlife and the cool wind blowing down the mountain slopes and setting the cedars and juniper trees of the upper reaches stirring.

Then, after perhaps twenty minutes, there was a different sound – the hoofbeats of a speeding horse. Instantly Dave was alert.

He sped across the weed-ridden garden to his horse, untied the reins from the barn rail and leapt into the saddle. Quietly he jogged the animal forward to the side of the cabin – and waited.

Once the speeding rider had gone past, half-cloaked in the mist rising from the canyon floor, Dave started off in his wake. As they went higher the mists thinned unexpectedly and Dave found himself able to view the horseman ahead in the bright starlight.

The distance was too great to enable him to distinguish who it was, so he kept on riding, only dismounting as he saw his quarry take a sharp left turn which could only mean he was making for the natural corral in the mountains.

Still Dave followed, but as the distant horseman prepared to take the narrow trail which led round the mountain face above the depression he must have heard the sounds of pursuit. He jumped off his horse and Dave too slid from his saddle.

Silently Dave drew his horse behind a rock,

tethered the animal to it, and then crept forward like a ghost. The last thing he wanted was for Kelvin – if it was he – to use his gun and attract the attention of the other men.

Evidently Kelvin, as at close quarters he became revealed to Dave, was not sure whether he was being followed or not. Dave gave a grim smile to himself and sprang out of the shadows. In one wrench he tore Kelvin's levelled gun out of his hand and sent it flying.

'Time we met up, again, Kelvin,' Dave breathed. 'You and me have got some talking to do!'

He snatched away Kelvin's other gun and then stood facing him.

'Talking?' Kelvin panted. '*What* talking?'

'About lots of things – your murdering Ezra Munro, the evidence you've got against Diana Travers, alias Nina – and the name of the man behind the rustling. I'm going to get the answers, Kelvin, even if I have to beat the hide off you!'

Kelvin twisted, swung, and dodged out of the grip Dave had upon him. His advantage only lasted a second. A pile-driver blow on the jaw swung him round on his heels and he staggered over the edge of the narrow pathway and on to the sloping valley-side.

Instantly Dave flung himself after him, taking and giving blow after blow. Unable to stop themselves they rolled over and over, lower into the depression where the black mass of cattle stood.

A stretch of ground a little more level than the rest gave Dave his chance at last. He scrambled up, jerked his head away just in time to miss an uppercut and landed a blow on Kelvin's face that sent him staggering. A left in the stomach followed it and he doubled up. Another under the chin straightened him, then with an anguished groan he fell on his knees – to find his arms wrenched up behind him.

'For God's sake, Norton!' he gasped in anguish. 'You're breaking my arms —!'

'That's just what I'm aiming to do unless you get sensible! Here – see these? There's enough starlight.' Dave flung down a small notebook and a copying pencil. 'I'm going to release your right arm and you'll start writing. First the truth about Diana Travers—'

'I won't! Blast you, Norton, I'll . . .' Kelvin broke off with a gasp, sweat starting out on his face at the fiendish twist Dave gave his left arm.

'Write!' Dave ordered, and released Kelvin's right hand. 'Put: *Diana Travers is not in any way connected with the murder of Arthur Cranley.*'

Kelvin wrote as ordered and twisted a vicious face upwards in the starlight.

'Well, there it is! What more d'you want?'

'The name of Cranley's real murderer – yourself!'

'Why, you – I'd nothing to do with it!'

'Don't waste time lying to me, Kelvin. You did it, just the same as you fixed Ezra Munro. Write: *I hereby admit that I murdered Arthur Cranley and Ezra Munro.*'

Kelvin hesitated, then, goaded by the continuing creeping torture up his arm he obeyed the command.

'Good!' Dave snapped, watching intently. 'Now sign it!'

Kelvin did so. Dave snatched up the notepad and put it in his pocket. Still retaining his grip on Kelvin he forced him to his feet.

'There's just two more things. Who's back of this rustling and who killed Will Pilkington?'

Kelvin did not answer. Dave's fist lashed suddenly and Kelvin staggered a pace. Another punch knocked him on his face and then blows seemed to descend on his head from all directions.

'This'll go on until you speak!' Dave panted. 'Who's back of everything?'

'All right, all right, I'll tell you,' Kelvin gasped through bruised lips. 'It's —'

The explosion of a revolver close at hand split the night. Dave jumped with the unexpectedness of it and uneasiness surged over the cattle below. Kelvin gave one last gasp and then lay flat. Dave glanced at him, his hands flying to his guns.

There was a dim figure a yard or two behind him, hardly visible in the starlight.

Back at the cabin Diana Travers awakened suddenly as the door banged open, but before she could collect her wits and reach for her automatic a voice stopped her.

'Better not, Miss Voles – I've got you covered!'

She relaxed, staring at the two silhouettes against the grey of night. The foremost she recognized from the voice as Sheriff Carson, and the other she remembered the moment he spoke.

'Looks like that ornery cuss has gone after all, Sheriff. There ain't a sign o' him around.' Plainly it was Pete Walters.

'Where's Dave Norton?' the sheriff snapped.

'I should tell you!' the girl retorted. 'How'd you get here, anyway?'

'Pete here had the sense to behave like a decent citizen and put me wise – an' I want Norton! *Where's he gone?*'

'I've not the least idea,' Diana answered calmly, though her heart was thumping.

'Let me get to work on her, Sheriff,' Pete suggested. 'I can make her talk plenty quick.'

'You'll do nothin' of the sort,' Carson retorted. 'What you will do is stay here and keep guard over her while I go and look for Norton. He can't have gone a great distance.'

'Wait a minute!' Diana exclaimed, sitting up again. 'You're not going to leave me with this rattlesnake, are you? Take me with you! I'm fit enough now.'

'Yeah? So's you'd have a chance to give Norton the tip-off eh?' Carson asked drily. 'I reckon not!'

He went out and slammed the door. He vaulted into the saddle of his horse and he rode up the canyon, flogging the animal with a grim urgency.

When he came to the leftward-branching canyon he followed it quickly, dismounting as he came to two horses grazing – one belonging to Dave and the other to Kelvin. He glanced about him, frowning, moved to the edge of the narrow pathway and looked along it. A voice came to him clearly in the still night air.

'This'll go on until you speak! Who's back of everything?'

'All right, all right, I'll tell you,' gasped the voice of Kelvin.

The sheriff snatched out his gun and fired, point blank. Then he walked forward slowly and found himself looking at Dave's startled face in the starlight.

'You!' Dave gasped. '*You* are the brains behind everything!'

'Right,' Carson agreed, coldly. 'An' I've no more use for guys like Kelvin who shoot off their mouths, or guys like you who make 'em!'

Dave thought swiftly. 'Now I get it! No wonder the law never caught up on those rustlers! Now I know why you came on the scene so quickly the night I shot those two rustlers. You didn't see the ranch fire, like you said. You were *on the spot* some place, directing operations!'

'And I brought the cattle back because it was safer just then,' Carson sneered. 'So what?'

'Then you fixed that frame-up with Ezra Munro.'

'I sure did. I owed him that for the way he sprang you out of jail, and I had to figure a way to get you back in, too. I discussed it with Kelvin and he made the arrangements. It was that girl who upset things. She and you have meddled in my affairs too long, Norton. Fortunately I've got a good man in Pete Walters. He tipped me off that you knew of this hideout, so I came along.'

Premonition warned Dave in that instant that Carson's trigger finger was tightening. Another second and he would be dead. He took a desperate chance and whirled up his left arm.

It jolted the revolver upwards at exactly the moment Carson fired it – then before either man could make another move they were both aware of rolling thunder coming towards them.

'The herd!' Carson gasped. 'It's stampeded! The revolver shots must have scared 'em—' he glanced wildly about him. Terror made him garrulous.

'There's only one way out – along the canyon. The other way's barred with rock . . .'

Neither he nor Dave had time to think of settling personal scores, no time to think of anything except escaping the raging, maddened beasts sweeping up the slope towards them.

Dave swung and ran, stumbling up to the path. He heard shots from somewhere, presumably from the men drawn out of the cave, but he took no notice. The animals were close upon him, the starshine reflecting from their horns, the air heavy with the rumble of their hoofs.

'For God's sake . . .!' Carson gave one mighty yell for help and Dave glanced back. The sheriff had slipped and rolled backwards – and vanished under the raging, maddened feet. He gave one brief agonized scream – then he died beneath the pounding hoofs.

With only yards to spare Dave plunged for his

horse, at the same time slapping the other two horses across the withers to set them going down the canyon. It was their only chance of survival – then he swung into the saddle and dug his spurs into the sorrel's sides.

Even as the startled beast darted forward a numbing thought descended on Dave. Carson had said the canyon was the only way out, that the other way – presumably to the mesa – was barred with rock. Two miles or so further on, in the main canyon, and this battering herd would sweep down on the flimsy prospector's cabin where Diana was. Once that happened . . .

Sweat dewed Dave's face at the thought and he rode as never before, the horse stumbling and faltering over loose stones and shrubs, pursued by the crazed cattle. How quickly he covered the distance Dave did not know. As he came to the cabin he swung out of the saddle, raced up to the porch and through the doorway. For a moment the scene astounded him. The oil-lamp was burning. Diana, risen from the bed, was struggling frantically with a lean cowpuncher, raining blows into his face as he sought to embrace her. Further up the canyon came the roar of the coming cattle.

'You dirty, stinkin' polecat . . .!'

Dave seized the puncher by the shoulder and whirled him round. He just had time to see that it was Pete Walters, then he delivered a blow that hurled the man clean through the doorway, across the porch, and into the dust outside.

'He – he —' Diana made a choking gulp as she

tried to speak.

'No time now,' Dave panted, whirling her up over his shoulder. 'Stampede coming – from up the canyon. Got to move!'

He plunged outside and lifted the girl to his saddle, but before he jumped up in front of her he caught hold of one of Pete's feet and held on to it.

'What do you want him for?' the girl demanded.

'Can't leave him to be killed in cold blood, I reckon. 'Sides, he may be useful. The ride he'll get will take the sting out of him!'

Leaning down from his horse so he could drag Pete along the rough earth Dave spurred the beast forward as fast as it could go. Laden down though he was the sorrel responded, instinctively aware of danger. He kept up a frantic pace amidst the loose stones and rubble.

Once, as they glanced behind them, Dave and the girl saw the cabin go down before the living flood, splintered to matchwood.

But they were steadily winning the race. They came to the end of the canyon at last and here, on the open desert, the danger was over. The cattle had the chance to fan out and disperse, running on until their fright had abated, and they could be sorted out by their rightful owners and returned to the home corrals.

'Done it!' Dave breathed thankfully, drawing his horse to a halt and dismounting. He released his hold of Pete Walters and then helped the girl down. For a moment or two they stood still as the cattle overtook and ran thinly past them; then when the main rush had finished the girl turned.

'He's trying to get up,' she muttered, glancing at Pete.

Dave reached out a hand and yanked the bleeding, glowering puncher to his feet.

'Lay off me!' he snarled. 'I ain't done nothin' —'

'I think differently!' Dave retorted. 'You were a good man for Sheriff Carson because he told me as much. How much do you know about Carson?'

'I don't know —'

Dave raised his right fist. 'So help me, Pete, I'll kill you if you don't tell me the truth!'

'All right – all right, he's a rustler,' Pete muttered, cringing at the threat of further punishment. 'I found it out by accident, even though I takes my orders from Kelvin.'

'Just as I thought,' Dave murmured. 'You're going to tell all you know to a marshal to back up my story.'

The puncher mumbled something but Dave's next words silenced him.

'I see now what your little game was. First you tried to get me in a necktie party by telling Gary Vincent and his friends – then when that didn't come off by which time you realized I knew of the mountain corral – you went to the sheriff. You didn't do it to protect him, as boss, but to get rid of *me*, because you knew that if I exposed everything you would lose a nice, profitable little sideline. As for that five hundred dollar reward, I reckon you hoped to get that too.'

Diana had been listening in bewilderment. 'You

mean it was *Sheriff Carson?*' she asked, amazed.

'Yeah – and he's dead. And Kelvin too.' Dave turned to the girl. 'I guess Cranley and Munro have been avenged.' He was silent for a moment, as Diana looked at him soberly.

'I'll explain it to the authorities – but first we're going to tell Doc Walters, Gary Vincent, and the rest of 'em. They can start recalling the cattle.'

He glanced again at the cowed and bruised figure, who had now slumped on the ground beside him.

'Tomorrow, Pete,' Dave went on, 'you're going to Tucson with Miss Voles and me, after you've spent a night in jail in Valley Shadow.' He turned to the girl with a smile, shaking his head.

'What am I saying – Miss Voles? We can drop that pretence right now, and you can use your own name again! There's nothing to worry about any more. I got a signed confession out of Kelvin before Carson shot him. It'll be sufficient, I'm sure of it.'

The girl smiled as Dave's hand tightened on her arm.

'I'm glad. That was Kelvin's idea, and I was beginning to hate the name . . . and the first thing I'll do when I'm in Tucson is to send a telegram to Sycamore Halt, to let my father know what happened to me. He'll have been sick with the worry since I disappeared, and probably thinking I was guilty . . .'

Dave took the girl gently in his arms and looked at her frankly.

'Your own father? I don't think so, Diana. He

knows what kind of a girl you are, and won't have doubted your innocence for a second . . .'

The girl made no effort to remove herself from Dave's grip. Instead she put her own arms around his neck, and asked:

'And what kind of a girl am I, Dave Norton?'

'That's something I aim to find out,' Dave smiled, 'and while we're in Tucson. there's something else we should do,' he added. 'To make it sort of ethical for us to live together in future . . . .'

—

The Effective Dance Program in Physical Education

The Effective Dance Program in Physical Education

Clara Furst
and
Mildred Rockefeller

Parker Publishing Company
West Nyack, New York

Library of Congress Cataloging in Publication Data

Furst, Clara,
   The effective dance program in physical
education.

   Includes index.
   1. Dancing—Study and teaching—Curricula.
I. Rockefeller, Mildred,   . II. Title.
GV1753.5.F87   375'.7933'0712   81-9494
                    AACR2

ISBN 0-13-241505-4

Printed in the United States of America

Dedication

To Larry, Crystal, and Linda Furst
To Peter, Lisa, and Amy Rockefeller

who often waited for their dinners

Acknowledgments

The authors wish to express their gratitude to Nancy Schuman, Angelina Carbone, Elaine Haber and the staff of the Physical Education Department at Walton High School for their encouragement, suggestions and moral support in bringing this book to fruition.

Special thanks to Ray Beiner for his photography and to Michelle Russell who posed with skill and enthusiasm.

How to Organize and Develop
A Successful Dance Program

The Effective Dance Program in Physical Education is a practical guide to teaching dance for both the physical educator and the dance specialist. This book offers a variety of dance techniques and creative activities, with methods for adapting ideas to different ability levels. We offer a graded curriculum. Creative and movement ideas have been carefully selected to provide a developmental flow from one sequence to another. Although specifically geared to modern dance, our methods are applicable to a wide variety of dance styles including ballet, jazz and ethnic dance.

Each chapter provides a multitude of dance experiences that are easy to read, providing a ready reference for the teacher. Each dance experience includes suggestions for class formations, sound accompaniments and appropriate testing procedures.

The Mirror Image format, described in Chapter 1, offers an exciting and creative change-of-pace dance lesson. Through movement experiences in Mirror Image, beginning pupils become more at ease with dance and develop an awareness of body parts and how they move. Problem solving abilities are sharpened through our much enjoyed dance games, described in Chapter 2. We offer a series of graded game activities, which help spark the imagination of pupils and encourage their understanding of important movement principles. For example, "counting games" have helped many a pupil to learn the art of meter, while the "memory game" has helped to develop the discipline for remembering and accurately performing movement patterns.

In the four chapters (3,4,5,6) on the language of dance, we provide you with a collection of successful dance exercises, as well as explorations of movement and lead-up activities. Since this is a graded curriculum, it enables you to adapt the material to the needs of your pupils.

Chapter 7 gives you musical experiences to stimulate movement technique and creativity, including suggestions for creating unique sound accompaniments for dance class and performance.

In Chapters 8 and 9, we present the many aspects of teaching choreography to the student. Pupils learn the art of designing short, simple dances through group interaction and through appropriately graded movement problems. Pupils experience the joys of free improvisation as well as formal choreography for the dance performance.

Our teaching approaches have been developed from working with pupils on a daily basis. Our program, therefore, encompasses the natural growth patterns, along with the educational and psychological needs of the student. Our dance pupils are challenged to explore and discover their movement potential in an atmosphere that is conducive to growth. Emphasis is on the achievement of a satisfying and successful dance experience for all.

Clara Furst
Mildred Rockefeller

Contents

How Mirror Image Works, 15. Music and Mirror Image,
16. Suggested Activities, 17. Sample Presentation in Mirror Image—Mass Formation: Teacher as Leader, 20. Suggestions for Effectively Using Mirror Image in the Dance
Unit, 21. Mirror Image Activities with Partners, 23. Variations on Mirror Image—the Shadow Technique, 24. Advanced Mirror Image Ideas and Formats, 24. Suggested
Creative Activities: Advanced Mirror Image, 24.

Dance Games, 27. Game Formats, 26. How to Create
Original Games, 39. How Do You Know If Your Game Has
Succeeded? 40.

Locomotor Studies Walking, 55. Culminating Activity, 59.
Skipping, 60. Running, 61. Sliding, 62. Galloping, 63.
Hopping, 64. Jumping, 64.

General Reminders for Disciplining the Body Through Exercises, 69. A Summary Outline of the Series with Lead-
Ups, 70. Glossary of Positions, 72. A Useful Combination
Using Simple Abdominal, Foot and Body Bounce Exercises, 79.

1

Developing Body Awareness Through Mirror Image

One of our most successful dance techniques is Mirror Image. It is used throughout the graded curriculum, and it has particular value as an icebreaker for beginning dance students.

Through Mirror Image, students develop an awareness of body parts and an appreciation for movement exploration. For dancers on the beginning level, teachers can use Mirror Image as a natural and easy motivational device, helping pupils to lose inhibitions while encouraging them to focus on movement concepts. These students suddenly find themselves vigorously warming up or gracefully dancing on their floor spots.

When your beginning dance students seem bored by the daily routine of technique, or lapse into the common refrain "Let's stop exercising and start dancing!" ... try Mirror Image. It's a change of pace activity that sparks enthusiasm and love for dance.

HOW MIRROR IMAGE WORKS

Imitation is the key to Mirror Image. You, the teacher, perform various movements that are imitated, in unison, by the students.

TEACHER HINT:

1) Make sure your pupils fully understand the format by giving a preliminary test such as:
   a) lift both arms to side (slowly) and down
   b) lift right arm (pupils should lift arm directly opposite or parallel to teacher)
   c) lift left arm
2) Perform your movements slowly, with many repetitions to encourage a successful Mirror Image experience.

3) Explore different body parts in simple, deliberate patterns.

4) Instruct pupils to move exactly as you move; if you do this, they must do the same. Make sure pupils concentrate on every motion.

MUSIC AND MIRROR IMAGE

1) For beginning experiences in Mirror Image, use lively music to get the attention of your class. It's important to motivate new pupils!

2) Later, when Mirror Image activity is expanded, use different types of accompaniment such as: silence, strange effects, popular and classical music, rhythm machine, etc.

3) Enhance the dance theme through your musical choice. If you're working on sustained, smooth movement, pick music that is lyrical and sustained.

4) Use music as a contrasting element. Create unusual combinations of dance and music. For example, combine rock and roll with ballet movements, or explore jazz ideas with an electronic background.

5) Emphasize the humorous elements of dance, with music that is comical. Many pieces for the Moog synthesizer provide a humorous effect. Also, various popular pieces composed for novelty dances can be used, such as the Alley Cat, the Hokey Pokey, etc.

6) Bring variety into sound accompaniment. Instead of sticking to your personal favorites, be daring in your choices. Ask pupils for their own musical contributions. (Remember to take records home and listen to them before using them in class.) Musical areas to choose from include: rock and roll, jazz, popular, electronic, Moog, classical, chamber, symphony, and vocal.

7) Interpret the words of a song through movement and gesture. This is fun for beginning pupils because it provides a sense of security. For teachers who need some creative inspiration, there are hundreds of excellent songs on the market, ranging from popular tunes to opera!

8) Try creating your own sound accompaniments with original tape collages. Investigate the kinds of sounds to include on

the tape. Record the sounds of everyday activities such as street noises, voices of students talking about their interests, radio broadcasts, etc. Make unusual tape combinations of music and voice, of classical and rock music, etc. Be creative! Don't become a slave to your music. Remember, you are in command as the creative force. Later, pupils will bring their own interpretations to the music.

SUGGESTED ACTIVITIES

TEACHER AS LEADER—CLASS IN MASS FORMATION

Class Formation—mass grouping; use floor spots with the teacher at the head of the class, use a platform if one is available. Make sure you can be seen by all the pupils.

xxxxxxxxxx
xxxxxxxxxx
xxxxxxxxxx
T.

MIRROR IMAGE ACTIVITIES IN MASS FORMATION

1) Explore simple axial movements around a central axis, and locomotor movements that travel in space. Axial skills might include flexion, extension and rotation of body parts. Locomotor skills include walks, runs, hops, etc. Develop movements in time, space and energy, to provide a variety of dance experiences.

   a) Explore the element of *TIME,* by varying the speed of your movement. Perform it in different accents and rhythms; explore different rhythms by clapping out patterns or using other sounds (clicking, vocalizing, etc.)

   b) Explore *SPACE* elements by varying a particular movement in different ranges (small to big). Try performing the same movement in different spatial levels; move body parts in different directions.

   c) Create different *SHAPES* in space; explore symmetry and asymmetry; use letter shapes; use imagery from many sources (animals, insects, geometric forms, objects in nature, art objects, etc).

d) Explore *ENERGIES* using different body parts; help pupils to understand the difference between moving smoothly, sharply, and in a vibratory and swinging manner.

2) Isolate body parts to provide an easy movement for beginners.

a) Keep your movements simple and direct. Repeat patterns often to determine pupil understanding.

b) Investigate various ways of moving body parts, think of moving in a particular sequence, such as from head to toes or vice versa.

c) Challenge pupils by suddenly changing from one body part to another.

d) Keep your pupils' interest by sudden changes in tempo, energy, level, range, etc.

e) Move from a balletic pattern, to a rock and roll idea, back to a modern dance movement, to an everyday gesture.

3) Experiment with various dance positions to be used as a springboard for creating movement patterns.

a) Explore ideas in a variety of floor positions such as, cross-legged, kneeling, stride sitting, long sitting, etc.

b) Change the level of various movements, such as from the floor to standing.

c) Explore ballet and jazz dance positions.

d) Ask for pupil suggestions to create original dance positions. Develop the latter ideas in time, space and energy.

4) Begin to combine body parts into longer, more challenging phrases.

a) Move arm and head together.

b) Create movements using three body parts. For example, use head-arm-leg combination or four parts, head-chest-arm-leg, etc.

c) Try out problems in coordination, such as: touching your head while rubbing your stomach, or hopping on one foot while clapping and shaking your head. Be creative! Let yourself go and make up unusual combinations.

5) Perform different dance styles such as modern, jazz, ballet, Afro-Caribbean, etc., to expose beginning pupils to the distinctive qualities of these styles.

   a) Introduce the simple arm movements of a balletic port de bras.

   b) Use the contraction-release movements of the Martha Graham School and the fall-recovery movements of the Humphrey-Weidman School.

   c) Present simple jazz isolations with exciting rhythms.

6) Change the pace from totally original movement themes to recognizable patterns that are used in the daily technique lesson. Try to present these patterns in a new design. As students learn more exercises, teachers accumulate more material to explore in this format.

   a) Review a simple floor warm-up, such as the chest arch. Vary it in time; add a new arm movement; try a sharp head movement, etc.

   b) Perform a swing on different floor levels, such as: on one or two knees, sitting, standing, etc. Swing different body parts such as arms, head, chest, legs, etc.

7) Look to everyday life for movement ideas:

   a) Examine actions we use everyday to communicate our thoughts and feelings. Explore gestures such as a hand-shake, waving good-bye with your head, shoulder or hip; introduce yourself through a movement of the toes, elbows, etc.

   b) Analyze and explore the kinds of motions we use to get things done, such as work activities, like hammering a nail, sawing a piece of wood, making a bed, etc. Perform these activities using different body parts, at different speeds and rhythms, in different ranges, levels and directions, and in different energies.

   c) Explore school actions such as: reading a book, solving problems, writing on the board, combing your hair, running to class, cheerleading, talking to your friends, and eating in the cafeteria.

8) Utilize physical education as a movement source for Mirror Image explorations.

a) Utilize sports motions such as a lay-up shot, a tennis swing, and a throw and a catch. Remember to keep it simple for your beginning pupils.

b) Make unusual combinations of steps, using different sports actions in a single pattern such as: a tennis swing, into a basket ball jump, into a swim stroke.

TEACHER HINT

Always make sure you are prepared to lead your class in Mirror Image. Have a basic movement theme in mind, and focus on it for your lesson. However, try to remain flexible and open to pupil responses. Perhaps one of the most important aspects of a successful Mirror Image experience is the teacher's sense of humor. Try to keep your ideas interesting and unique, and stay away from daily technical exercises.

SAMPLE PRESENTATION IN MIRROR IMAGE— MASS FORMATION: TEACHER AS LEADER

SUGGESTED MUSICAL ACCOMPANIMENT— "Nairobi Trio"
Album: (or any Moog, electronic or comic piece).

1) On floor, in cross-legged positions:

2) Lift right arm up (sharply); lift left arm up (sharply). Drop right arm, drop left arm.

3) Tilt head right side-center-left side-center.

4) Lift shoulder and drop; repeat on left side.

5) Clap hands twice; click fingers twice.

6) Tap head with right hand, then left hand. Tap shoulders with right hand; tap left shoulder with left hand; tap tummy with right hand then left hand. Repeat motions faster and faster, from head to shoulders to tummy, creating a comic, speeded-up, movie-effect.

7) Stretch to parallel legs and reach over to touch head to knees. Bounce over eight times. Open to stride leg position and again bounce over with head between legs eight times. Move to frog-sit position and bounce with head to feet eight times.

8) Stand. Use a sneaky method of raising and lowering your body until you finally reach a standing position.

9. Do plies and releves in first and second position.

10) Stretch the arms overhead, then roll down and bounce over.

11) Isolate the head, right shoulder, left hand, hip, etc., in order, using one count per movement.

12) Isolate hips slowly and deliberately, using the following directions: circular, side to side, front to back. Pick up speed as you repeat the hip motions, then develop them further to include all body parts moving in jazz style.

13) Perform a locomotor study, maintaining face to face contact such as in: a slow tip-toe walk to the side. Move slowly, then make a sudden change in direction and speed up your walk to a run. Constantly change speed and direction and keep your class moving.

14) Perform some jumps in place (keep them simple).

15) Finish your dance with a slow, reeling collapse to the floor.

SUGGESTIONS FOR EFECTIVELY USING MIRROR IMAGE IN THE DANCE UNIT

Mirror Image is such a totally motivating activity that it can be used at the beginning, the middle or the end of a lesson. When used as a warm-up activity at the beginning of a class, Mirror Image leads nicely into any other planned activity, such as locomotor patterns or axial combinations. After a sufficient amount of technical warm-up, Mirror Image provides a zesty change of pace at the conclusion of the lesson.

The length of time devoted to Mirror Image exploration depends on your goals for the class. If you are attempting to solve a particular movement problem, then by all means, continue until you are satisfied with the pupil response. If you are merely sparking the atmosphere of the dance lesson with a needed change, keep going until you achieve your goal. If you are using Mirror Image to introduce a specific movement concept, then limit exploration and balance with other activities.

At various times throughout the dance unit, find out how much pupils really understand. Ask questions after Mirror Image activities to reinforce their learning. For example, after a lesson in isolation, find out if pupils can remember how the body part moved, and suggest other ways of moving that particular body part.

After pupils have developed a sense of body awareness through movement created by the teacher, they are ready for the partnership approach, in which they will develop original movement patterns and experience the stimulation provided by social interaction.

As pupils alternate the roles of leader and follower, they must be able to take the initiative and create original patterns, while at the same time being able to respond enthusiastically to the creations of others. This kind of activity provides the daily dance lesson, with just the right amounts of surprise, challenge and fun!

MIRROR IMAGE ACTIVITIES WITH PARTNERS

Class Formation—retain mass grouping (floor spots), but have pupils face each other in a partner formation. With uneven numbers of pupils, create a three-some, alternating roles of leader and follower among the three pupils.

xx xx xxx

xx xx xx

xx xx xx

There are many different types of problems to be explored through a partnership formation in Mirror Image. Students can create interesting movements based on changes in time, space, and energy, or develop totally original dance ideas. Many of the ideas described in mass formation can be utilized with partners. An outstanding aspect of working in groups is the possibility for creating a finished dance.

In this section, we will show you how one movement idea can be developed into a complete dance. We've selected *variations in energy as our main theme*. To prevent pupil distractions, it's a good idea to not use music for the initial exploration. The following are examples of the kind of directions you can give to your students:

1) Positions. Partners face each other and sit cross-legged. Those facing one wall are leader #1; those facing the opposite wall are leader #2. Partners imitate each other as they assume the role of leader.

2) *Instructions to leader.* Alternate the following movements between leader #1 and leader #2:

   a) Move arm slowly in different directions.

   b) Explore movement using the head and arms in a sustained fashion.

   c) Move to a new level and explore sharp movements of the head, arms and legs.

   d) Vibrate arms, head, legs, and torso.

   e) Combine smooth and sharp motions of all body parts on different levels.

   f) Combine smooth, sharp and vibratory qualities of all body parts on all levels.

The class is now ready to incorporate its explorations into a finished dance. Maintain partners, but have pupils move to separate places in the gym. Make sure that the partners can still see each other. Electronic music can be used as background. Actually, any music without a definite, overwhelming beat can be used. Pupils can move toward or away from each other, but they cannot turn their backs because this would destroy the Mirror Image format.

SAMPLE DANCE FORMAT FOR FINISHED DANCE WITH PARTNERS

1) Instruct leader #1 to start the dance with an interesting body shape on any spatial level. Some may choose a position on the floor, while others will remain standing in a pose.

2) Instruct leader #1 to explore all energies in all levels, using all body parts in any combination, to the sound of music.

3) Give pupils sufficient time to explore their themes.

4) End the dance at the sound of the drum.

5) Instruct your pupils in the many ways to end a dance creatively.

   a) Take seven slow steps to the center of the gym, form a group cluster; and on count eight, make a sharp pose.

   b) Stretch bodies upward, with eyes looking up to the ceiling to create a serious ending.

c) Descend to the floor with legs high in the air for a comic effect.

d) Create an unusual pose touching different body parts, such as elbows, hips and shoulders.

e) Unify the group with a tableau pose ending, or create variety with individual poses.

VARIATIONS ON MIRROR IMAGE—THE SHADOW TECHNIQUE

The Shadow technique involves imitation without the restriction of having to *face* a partner. Pupils can imitate each other by following from behind. Many possibilities can develop with this technique, either with partners or small groups.

ADVANCED MIRROR IMAGE IDEAS AND FORMATS

Select outstanding pupils to lead the entire class or small groups in Mirror Image. Provide leaders with specific problems to be solved, or give complete freedom. Give potential leaders a homework assignment focusing on a particular Mirror Image problem.

Challenge the student partner by allowing leadership to flow spontaneously from one partner to the other. For example, as one partner leads with various movements, the other partner might take over and begin a new movement idea. Students must really concentrate and be willing to give and take.

SUGGESTED CREATIVE ACTIVITIES: ADVANCED MIRROR IMAGE

1) Have pupils create their own musical accompaniments for Mirror Image activity. For example, they can create nonsense sounds, recite original poetry, read magazine and newspaper articles aloud, and play percussion instruments.

2) Help students develop movement patterns based on emotional ideas. Pupils explore patterns based on joy, sorrow, jealousy, or guilt. Ask pupils to suggest emotions and list them on the chalkboard. Explore the differences in expressing an emotion through words, gestures, facial expressions, and finally through movement.

a) Have partners select emotions from a given list, then explore these in static poses.

b) Allow poses to come alive in movement.

c) Select outstanding couples to perform for the class, and ask pupils to guess which emotions are being expressed.

d) Develop these ideas further by asking various couples to combine their ideas into a group dance based on the selected emotions.

e) Utilize musical accompaniments that can reflect the emotion being expressed or that can be used for contrast.

3) Present a wide range of ideas for pupil exploration. Ask them what they are thinking about or what is important to them, and use these ideas as movement sources. For example, their interests might include school activities, dating, careers, etc. Help them focus on certain problems in our society, such as crime, poverty, old age, drugs, and war. Explore these ideas in the Mirror Image format.

4) Make students aware of the senses of sight, sound, touch, and smell as sources for movement exploration.

a) Bring in an object; have pupils close their eyes and touch it. Have the students describe the object in words, then respond with body movements.

b) Explore colors and the various emotions they stimulate in your pupils. For example, divide your dancing area into three sections. Assign a different color to each section, such as yellow, blue or purple. Assign different numbers of dancers to proceed through these areas, to interpret each color in their own way. Structure their response, if necessary, to include changes in level, energy and direction. Have students finish their dance by remaining in a pose for a certain number of beats.

5) Create movements based on contrast. Explore the ideas of frenzied activity vs. stillness, ballet vs. rock and roll, slow vs. fast movements, arm vs. leg movements, etc.

6) Use exercises practiced in the technique portion of the lesson and perform them with a partner in Mirror Image. Combine known exercises with original movement pat-

terns. Students or teacher may vary and modify the exercises.

7) Use the idea of action-reaction. For example, using a sports motion theme, have one partner throw a make-believe ball, while the other partner catches or misses it.

The Mirror Image format provides an opportunity for pupils to observe and perform for each other. Help them realize the unique solutions possible in a creative setting. There is no *one* right or wrong answer. For many pupils, the chance to perform is an excellent opportunity to sharpen technical skills and develop confidence in a job well done.

2

Discovering Movement Potential Through Dance Games

Dance games have an important place in the dance curriculum because they provide an enjoyable, yet educational, form of movement exploration. Games challenge the imagination and help to motivate a love for dance. In addition to the recreational values, games also provide learning experiences in movement theories and concepts.

Like mirror image, it is best to use games sparingly and discriminately to provide a balance with the technique lesson. Overuse can sometimes lead to boredom and careless dance performances.

In this chapter, each game activity includes information on class formations, sound accompaniments and problems to be solved. In addition to our collection of games, we also provide hints for creating your own original activities. Games are chronologically organized to provide a graded skill progression. Dance games can be coordinated with learning activities discussed in other chapters. For example, when pupils are ready to structure their movement explorations, "Counting Games" can be used as an excellent lead-up activity.

DANCE GAMES

1. The Counting Game

2. The Memory Game

3. Statues

4. Relay Races

5. I Challenge You

6. Pass It On

7. The Magic Envelope

8. Follow My Orders

GAME FORMATS

GAME 1: THE COUNTING GAME

This game helps students become acquainted with the organization of movement into count sequences. They experience how it feels to move in a slow, 16-count phrase, and in a quick, 4-count phrase. Students practice moving various body parts in different count sequences. They move through different spatial levels, and learn how to move across the floor on cue. This game is an excellent lead-up activity to performing technical skills, because it provides a basic experience in listening and responding to the drum beat.

Class Formation

It is best to begin the game on the floor, using pupil floor spots, in mass formation. The floor not only provides a foundation for movement, but also a psychological security for new dance students. In addition to moving in unison, allow the class to practice in two or three groups. The latter provides opportunities for observation and rest.

Sound Accompaniment

You can aid pupils by counting aloud; later use a drum beat.

Problems to Solve

You can devise various problems for class exploration. The following counting games have been successfully presented to our pupils. Emphasize that pupils should move through all given beats.

1) *Using arm movements.* (cross-legged-Floor Level) Raise the arm in different count sequences:
   a) Can you raise your right arm to your side (shoulder level) in 8 beats?
   b) Lower it to your side in 16 beats; see how slowly you must move and how much control you must have.
   c) Raise your left arm to the front (eye level) in 4 beats.
   d) Lower your left arm in 2 beats.
   e) Can you feel the difference moving in 16, and then in 4 beats?

2) *Using total body movements* to move from one position to another. Lying prone on the floor, try moving into and out of a tiny ball position in a set sequence of counts.

a) Move into a ball, flexing all body parts in 8 counts.

b) Now stretch your body outward in 8 counts. Release all body parts: neck, chest, waist, arms, legs, etc.

c) Move into a closed-in position (ball) in slow, 16 counts; stretch out in 16 counts.

d) Close up in 8 counts; stretch out in 8 counts.

e) Close up in 4 counts; stretch out in 4 counts.

f) Close up in 2 counts; stretch out in 2 counts.

g) Close up in 1 count; stretch out in 1 count, and repeat.

Note—pupils really enjoy this sequence, because it builds up to an exciting climax! You can use this form of count accumulation and reduction with other dance activities. You may surprise your students by performing the above activity in different count sequences, for example, open in 16 beats; close in 2 beats.

3) Using body parts to move from one position to another. Beginning position: cross-legged, floor level.

a) Lie flat on your back with arms overhead in 8 counts.

b) Roll to your stomach and raise your head in 16 counts.

c) Rise to both knees in 4 counts.

d) Lie on your right side in 6 counts.

Teacher Hint:

Many variations are possible with this activity. Be creative and show your sense of humor with some of the following:

a) Touch your nose to your knee in 4 counts.

b) Touch your right elbow to your right hip in 8 counts.

4) Using two different levels—sitting and standing.
Try moving from one level to another in different count sequences: Beginning position—hook sitting-floor level

a) Get off the floor any way you like, in 8 counts: you can move in a spiral, focus on your arms to lift you, or make different designs with your legs.

b) Lower your body to the floor in 8 counts (Pupils must touch backside to floor each time they lower their bodies.)

c) Move away from the floor in 16 slow counts; lower to the floor in 8 counts.

d) Rise from the floor in 4 counts; return to the floor in 4 counts.

e) Rise in 2 counts; lower in 2 counts. (Make sure pupils don't land carelessly; this could be hazardous!)

Pupils will enjoy the challenge of these count changes. Let them be creative and think of unusual ways to raise and lower their bodies. Some form of demonstration, either by the teacher or an outstanding pupil, might help to stimulate interesting modes of movement.

5) Using bending and stretching.

Bend and stretch your body in different count sequences:

a) Beginning position—tall standing. Touch the floor with your fingers without bending your knees in 8 counts.

b) Stretch upwards, reaching for the ceiling, in 4 counts.

c) Bend forward in 16 counts.

d) Stretch upward in 2 counts.

Teacher Hint:

In this activity, you can provide a variety of sudden count changes to keep students literally on their toes. This is also an excellent sequence for warming up the spine and developing the muscles.

6) Using Locomotion movements in different count sequences.

In this activity, pupils get an opportunity to explore different ways of moving across the floor (running, skipping, hopping, walking) in different count sequences. In addition, they learn the importance of moving on a particular cue or beat, along with the "etiquette" of moving across the floor in definite lines and sequences.

Class Formation

Have the class line up in rows of 4 across, and use the drum to establish the count sequence and tempo.

a) Have pupils practice responding to the drum beat by clapping their hands to beat out the number of counts. For example, the teacher plays 8 beats, the pupils clap 8 beats; the teacher plays 4 beats, the pupils clap 4 beats, etc. The class is now ready to move across the floor in lines (Also refer to Chapter 3, "Exploring the Language of Dance," for more details on moving across the floor.):

b) Play 8 moderate beats: each line responds by walking in 8's across the floor. They must be able to walk 8 as well as wait the 8 counts before their line begins the movements. Vary beats and tempos; try slow 8, fast 8, slow 4, fast 4.

c) Use different locomotor steps and add a challenge with changes in direction. For example, skip forward 4 and backward 2; walk backward 8 and forward 4, etc.

The emphasis in this game sequence is not on the perfection of locomotor skills, but, more importantly, on the exploration of movement across the floor in different tempos and meters. Don't get the class bogged down in technical corrections.

Effective Use of Counting Games

This game should be used at the beginning of the dance unit. It incorporates many significant movement concepts that beginners need for success in future class experiences. In addition to the use of mirror image as a dance icebreaker, counting games can also be employed in the first week of the dance unit as a lead-up to performing technical sequences and movement combinations. Response to the drum beat is a precursor to learning and counting out exercise patterns.

GAME 2: THE MEMORY GAME

This is an excellent game for developing pupil concentration and dance memory. We've used this game often as a lead-up activity to developing and memorizing dance phrases. At the beginners level, dance sequences should be kept short and simple, with problems becoming more complex as pupils advance.

Class Formation

Divide your class into small circles of 5 or 6 pupils. It is important to keep the circles small because of the challenge to remembering long sequences. With some classes, you can let pupils organize themselves into circles, while with others, it is necessary to direct who goes into which circle. Let your particular situation be your guide!

It is best to begin with pupils sitting on the floor, since it provides a secure base, both psychologically and physically.

Sound Accompaniment

Supply a drum beat to help pupils maintain their count sequence.

Problems to Solve

Perform a single movement idea, using a definite body part. Move an arm or leg, or your head; you must remain on the floor. Each pupil in the circle should move in chronological order. Number 1 starts off, then # 2 must repeat the movement of #1, adding her own movements. The last student has the hardest job of remembering all the movements, plus adding one of her own. After the last student completes her movement, all members of the circle perform their pattern in unison.

We have found that pupils perform beautifully in this game. They seem to enjoy the cooperative development of movement patterns. Some patterns are so effective you can use them for class work. As pupils become more advanced, more movements can be added to the problem. For example, pupils can create two movements, rather than just one. For greater challenge, more pupils can be added to the circle.

After performing only on the floor level, challenge pupils with longer movement phrases on the standing level. The latter provides additional sources for movement creation. Expand this game by letting pupils travel through space.

GAME 3: STATUES

This is a device for teaching body control and balance. Pupils get a chance to experiment with locomotor movements they have learned and are challenged to use them in different patterns. Teachers can also provide variations in tempo, direction and level changes.

Class Formation

Organize the class in line formation to work across the floor. Determine the number of pupils in each line on the basis of your class size.

Sound Accompaniment

Drum and mallet

Problems to be Solved

1) Begin with a simple locomotor step, such as a run or walk. Ask pupils to balance on the sound of the drum for a certain number of counts; for example, run, freeze for 8; run, freeze for slow 16.

2) Add to the run a more complicated balance such as: balance on one leg for 8 counts, 4 counts, balance in a letter shape; balance in a shape on the floor for 8 counts, etc.

3) Vary the locomotor step, such as:
   a) Walk backwards 8 counts—collapse to the floor for 16 counts and balance on one body part for 4 counts or,
   b) Skip 4 counts forward and 4 counts backward and balance on 3 body parts
   c) Jump 4 times and balance off-center on one leg for 8 counts.
   d) Use turns to get across the floor then balance in a shape.

4) Problems to be Solved: Partner Formation
   a) Hop 6 times, create an interlocking design in 8 counts and balance for 4 counts.
   b) Create an interesting shape as partners travel across the floor, then separate to different positions and balance.

Teacher Hint

Expand the partner formation by organizing small groups of different numbers of pupils.

GAME 4: RELAY RACES

In this game, pupils explore different locomotor movements in a challenging, yet fun situation. You create movement problems or tasks to be solved by the students. Test knowledge of movements already learned, along with introducing new movement ideas. This game provides an opportunity to review and to introduce new ideas in an enjoyable way.

Class Formation

It is best to use a mass formation for this game, with pupils seated in their floor spots. The class can be organized into teams, with each line representing a team (line 1 = team 1; line 2 = team 2, etc.) Make sure all empty floor spots are filled, and test out pupil memory of floor spots by calling out numbers. Relay races work best in the gymnasium because of the large space provided, but the game can also be adapted to smaller studio spaces.

Sound Accompaniment

Usually only a drum or whistle is used to begin and end a relay race. However, any form of percussion instruments can be used to accompany activities. Student leaders can experiment with instruments such as: claves, bells, triangle, gong, bongo drums, etc. (The music department is usually helpful in suggesting and lending this kind of equipment—give it a try!)

Problems to Solve

The game procedure that has worked well is for the teacher to determine the problem, then call out the floor spot of various pupils. For example, "Hopping on your right leg, number 3, ready—go!" Pupils move to the front or back of their line, and then back to their floor spot. The first pupil to get back to place first is the winner. Get your class leaders to help observe and keep score. Of course, the primary goal of relay races is not just to win, but to enjoy the exploration of movement through time and space.

1) Use different locomotor steps to challenge pupils, such as: walking, running, skipping, leaping, sliding, galloping, jumping, hopping, etc.

2) Vary steps in time, space and energy, for example:

a) walk as slowly as you can;

b) run as fast as the wind;

c) take 4 slow walks, then a rapid run;

d) walk 8 steps then collapse 16 counts to the floor and crawl to place;

e) triplet, freeze, then jump 4 times and hop back to place. Endless possibilities exist!!

3) Vary problems further by adding body motions to the locomotor steps; for example:

a) Walk, contract your body into a little ball, then stretch out on the floor and run back to place

b) Run and move your right arm in circles

c) Skip and rotate your shoulders

4) Add different body parts to take the lead, for example:

a) Walk with your hips leading,

b) Make a walk with shoulders circling,

c) Walk with your chest bone leading you.

5) Vary steps further by adding vocal accompaniment supplied by the pupils themselves. For example:

a) Create movements to sounds such as "oohhh, yukky, bang, bang," etc.

b) Use nursery rhythms.

c) Use recorded musical accompaniment. Instruct students to: Move as slowly as the music; move sharply against the music; etc.

Use this game for a full period or more because it takes time to set up the class and explain the rules of the game. Sometimes we extend the game for several lessons, to give all team members a chance to participate. Select talented pupils to develop additional problems for the class.

GAME 5: I CHALLENGE YOU

The goals of this game are to explore and experiment with different movement skills. The act of challenging is an excellent motivation.

Class Formation

Use a mass formation with pupils in their floor spots. This is the most practical organization for your class.

Sound Accompaniment

A drum and mallet get pupil attention, and are sufficient for this game format.

Problems to be Solved

As in relay races, you can make this game a success by creating interesting movement problems that involve the craft of dance. Provide an opportunity for outstanding pupils to help create problems for the class. Inherent in this game is the possibility for pupil performance and an informal mode for testing class knowledge and understanding.

1. *Problems involving touch—to develop body awareness and flexibility—*
   a) Can you touch your fingertips to the floor from a standing position? Can you touch your palms to the floor?
   b) In a sitting position, can you touch your head to your knees? Touch your right elbow to your left ankle? Touch your left ear to your right knee?
2. *Problems involving movement—to explore motion through time and space—*
   a) Can you move your head in circles,
   b) Balance on one leg,
   c) Balance on two body parts, three parts?
   d) Can you jump up and down six times,
   e) Move your arm in circles,
   f) Rotate your torso right and left,
   g) Curve and straighten your spine in all directions?
3. *Problems involving body shapes—to develop awareness of design and line in space—*
   a) Can you create straight lines with your body? Curves? Angles?

    b) Can you make a letter shape using your entire body? Try it lying on the floor; standing up.

    c) Can you make a number with your body?

    d) Take an object in the room and copy its shape with your body.

    e) Choose an object in nature, bring it to class, and copy its shape with your body.

4. *Problems involving coordination—to develop an ability to move different parts at the same time—*

    a) Can you move a part of your body forward while another part moves backward?

    b) Can you move two parts back and two parts forward?

    c) Can you move one part right and another part left?

    d) Two parts right, three parts left, and one part forward?

    e) Can you move one part up and another part down?

    f) With a partner, can you attach body parts and move through space, for example: attach hip-to-hip or shoulder-to-shoulder.

    g) Can you create an interesting body design by attaching different body parts with two or three pupils? Vary these problems with changes in level, time and energy.

The following game experiences can be used with more advanced pupils:

GAME 6: PASS IT ON

In this game, pupils learn to move and create patterns in a successional manner. In successional movement, one body part starts the action with other parts naturally flowing from that point. For example, if the shoulder leads, then elbow, wrist, and hand movements follow after in a fluid or lyrical motion.

Class Formation

Divide the class into small groups of 5 or 6, and organize pupils into circles. Appoint a leader and have pupils count off numbers to the right of the leader. Begin the game in a seated position, but allow your pupils to use all levels.

Sound Accompaniment

Silence is best for this game, because it is the least distracting.

How to Play the Game—Pass It On

Pupils pass or transmit ideas around a circle. However, unlike the memory game, movements do not accumulate. The leader of the circle begins with a successional movement, using any body part (hip, shoulder, head, elbow etc.), then taps the person to his right in the circle. The body part touched initiates the next movement to be performed in succession. Each pupil in the circle gets a chance to explore successional movement using a different body part.

Help motivate pupils with a preliminary warm-up. Practice the following successional movements in the Mirror Image format, to show students the movement possibilities that exist. For example: ear, top of head, chin, finger tips, wrist, elbow, hip, knee, etc.

Teacher Hints

1) Present this game to pupils after they have had sufficient technical and creative experiences.

2) Provide additional rules for the game to stimulate creativity. Some pupils feel inhibited and limit their creative output. In this case, you can ask all pupils to move from the floor to a standing level somewhere in their dance, then return to their starting floor position. This forces pupils to create a longer pattern.

3) Movements developed can be linked together into a dance phrase and performed by groups for class observation.

GAME 7: THE MAGIC ENVELOPE

In this more advanced game, pupils learn to solve problems on the spur of the moment. Creative problems can be developed by both teacher and students. Ideas are collected on paper and contained in an envelope. Pupils pick problems randomly from the envelope.

Class Formations

1) Organize students in their floor spots, in mass formation. Select a student to pick a movement problem from the Magic Envelope and read it aloud to the class. Pupils respond to the problem in their own way and perform their solutions en masse.

2) Organize the class into small groups. Each group devises movement problems for their own Magic Envelope and performs their solution for class observation.

Sound Accompaniment

It is preferable not to use any sound accompaniment when you first introduce this game. At a later point, use music that is appropriate to the problem being solved. Have an assortment of sound accompaniments available (percussion instruments, records, tapes) as a background for student performance.

Problems to be Solved

A wide assortment of problems is possible, ranging anywhere from technical challenges to dramatic themes. For example:

1) Hop five times in place, collapse to the floor, turn, and rise.

2) Choose an animal and imitate its style of movement or create a static animal shape.

3) Select objects found in the home for movement creation.

Students respond in the way that the object moves. They can select a dishwasher, toaster, egg beater, etc. Expand further with entire groups representing parts of the appliance.

More Advanced Magic Envelope Problems

1) Pick a geometric object and adopt the qualities of that object. For example, the angles of the square can be represented in sharp, angular movements, while the curve of a circle can be reflected in flowing, lyrical motions.

2) Use dramatic themes and contemporary problems. For example, nuclear warfare, pollution, drugs, inflation, etc. After sufficient analysis and discussion, pupils can develop

movement phrases and finished dances to reflect their ideas.

Use this game only after pupils have achieved technical expertise. Vary the types of problems presented, try to link problems with ideas from daily technique lessons, or provide a definite contrast to the everyday lesson.

GAME 8: FOLLOW MY ORDERS

In this game, pupils explore a variety of themes and problems in an improvisational setting.

Class Formation

In floor spots—mass formation.

Sound Accompaniment

Use a drum to signal the beginning and end of a problem.

Problems to Be Solved

Ask pupils to travel to any spot in the gym, and on the sound of the drum, to freeze their position and listen for the problem. Given the problem, they must solve it as they return to their original floor place.

1) Using *characterizations:*
   a) Make believe you are a man from Mars; how would you move?
   b) Move as if you are a strange, ugly insect with 500 legs and 200 heads;
   c) Dance as if you are a famous ballerina.
2) Using *objects in nature:*
   a) You are sleet falling to the ground, how do you move through space?
   b) You are a flower blossoming;
   c) A cloud floating in the breeze, etc.
3) Using *non-living objects personified:*
   a) Make believe you are a cigarette being crushed out,
   b) A mirror shattering into tiny pieces,

      c) A toy doll, etc.

  4. Using *movement problems in time and space:*
      a) Move as slowly as you can. How quickly can you move back into place without bumping into anyone?
      b) Walk backwards to place; crawl on the floor.

This game can be used at the end of a dance lesson to reinforce learning. For example, if a class has just practiced a simple run and walk, use this game to vary the movement with changes in tempo or body shape. How slowly can pupils walk? How quickly can they run? Can they walk and swing their arms?

HOW TO CREATE ORIGINAL GAMES

Determine the *types of goals* you wish to achieve, for example: development of coordination, flexibility, awareness of body shape and spatial design, awareness of body parts and how they move, practice of axial and locomotor skills learned, variations of movements in time, space and energy, response to varied imagery, development of movement memory, balance, and body control.

Determine the *type of class formation* you wish to use, for example: circle, square, mass formation, floor spots, teams, partners, or small groups. Choose the level you wish to begin the game on.

Determine the *type of sound accompaniment* to use, for example: drums, percussive instruments; musical recordings, tapes, or human sounds.

Summary of Movement Resources for Games

a) *motional:* Use various movement concepts, such as: contraction/release, fall/recovery, bend/stretch, lift/collapse; problems using sports, work, play, and everyday motions; Use of different dance styles, such as jazz, ballet and ethnic.

b) *emotional:* Interpreting emotions through movement, such as: fear, love, hate, jealousy, conceit.

c) *sensory:* Use the elements of sight, sound, touch and smell to elicit movement; for *sound,* use different sources such as music, poetry, strange sounds, animal sounds, or sounds that objects make. For *sight,* use such sources as paintings (classical and modern), sculpture, collages, or colors. For *touch,* use sources such as velvet, sandpaper, glass, or stretch fabrics.

d) *ideational:* Use ideas drawn from different sources: war, competition, computers, poetry, movie themes, holidays, seasons, robots, toys, or appliances.

e) *relating to others:* Moving in small groups, or with partners. For example, partners make contact using different body parts. Groups represent parts of a machine.

HOW DO YOU KNOW IF YOUR GAME HAS SUCCEEDED?

If your pupils are applying skills learned in the dance technique lesson to the game situation, you've created a good game. If your pupils are not only having fun, but are also widening their dance vocabulary, it's a terrific game.

3

Exploring the Language of Dance

The exploratory techniques that follow, and those that are contained in the chapters on Mirror Image and Games, can be used as preliminary activities to any basic modern dance technique. Exploring the language of dance provides students with a heightened sense of body parts and how they move. Exploratory techniques can be used as a warm-up or a lead-up to movement exercises.

GETTING READY TO WORK

Generally, we divide class time into floor, standing and loco-motor exercises. Not only does this afford experiences in the use of different muscle groups, but it also provides students with a lesson that is varied in rhythms and dynamics.

We have found it best to start the class on the floor level, because it is physically more comfortable and psychologically more secure for the student.

EXPLORATORY EXPERIENCES

Exploratory exercises do not require count structures because this is an inhibiting factor. Students should be able to freely sense and internalize the movement. Later counts should be used to provide a structured activity that can be repeated for practice purposes and uniform performance.

TENSION AND RELAXATION—PART 1

Position—Tailor sitting

(sitting with body erect, legs crossed, knees flexed, feet under thighs, arms extended, fingertips touching floor)

Action Cues

1. Raise arm to shoulder level.
2. Make your arm very stiff, fingers extended, or make a fist.
3. Relax arm and hand.
4. Let your arm float to the floor.

Note:—May be repeated as often as necessary. Change arms frequently.

Teacher Hints

1. Walk among students and try to move stiff arms.
2. If needed, ask pupil to exert pressure against your hand.

TENSION AND RELAXATION—PART 2

Position—Long Lying

(on back, legs together, knees extended, arms at sides, palms down)

Action Cues

1. Close your eyes. Keep them closed throughout.
2. Feel relaxed. Teacher should take several minutes and walk around, noticing whether fingers are limp and feet are rotated outwards.
3. Tighten up toes, ankles, knees, thighs, abdomen, chest, fingers, wrists, elbows, shoulders, neck and head. Teacher should pause between body parts.
4. Hold position.
   a. Teacher should observe outstretched fingers or clenched hand, flexed toes and feet, or pointed feet, and
   b. Observe strained neck muscles.
   c. Teacher should: Tell pupils to pretend they are encased in ice.

Note—It is almost hypnotic, telling them how stiff they feel. Repetition is important. Use as many images as you can possibly think of (e.g., You are a zombie.) The same holds true in relaxing the muscles. Use terms such as sleepy, floating, limp, soft, jelly, etc.

5. Relax only those parts of the body that I mention, one at a time. (Start as above, then reverse on repetition.)

6. Ice is now melting your toes, ankles, etc. (with pauses)

Note—This tension and relaxation experience may be repeated as needed.

Culmination—End with the relaxed state and have them stay with eyes closed for a minute or so.

Action Cues

1. When I say the number one, open your eyes. (Pause), ONE.

2. Rest on the floor with your eyes open.

3. On the signal two, sit up. (Pause) TWO.

Note—A discussion usually follows describing the body reactions and feelings during this exercise.

BREATHING—PART 1

Position—Tailor sitting

(legs crossed, knees flexed, spine rounded, neck flexed forward, eyes focused downward, arms relaxed at sides)

Action Cues

1. Breathe in slowly.

2. Lift your body.

3. Start the movement in the hips, let it travel upwards through the waist, chest, shoulders, neck and head last.

4. Breathe out slowly.

5. Bend your body.

6. Let your hips pull you down, and continue the movement to the waist, chest, shoulders, neck and head last.

Teacher Hints

1. Demonstrate actions.

2. Repeat them a minimum of four times.
3. Use a slow tempo.
4. Suggested counts—four or eight for each movement.

BREATHING—PART 2

Position—Same as above

Action Cues

1. Inhale (same as above).
2. Lift your head and focus on the ceiling.
3. Exhale (as above).

BREATHING—CULMINATION

Position—Same as Part 1

Action Cues

1. Inhale.
2. Lift your spine.
3. Face the ceiling.
4. Lift arms-shoulder level and balance them.

The above techniques lead into Breathing and Bouncing series in Chapter 4.

RUBBERBAND STRETCH—PART 1

Position—Long lying

(lying on back, legs together, knees extended, both arms overhead on floor)

Action Cues

1. Stretch toes and fingers in opposite directions.
2. Relax, letting your lower back sink into the floor (body may flex).

Teacher hints

1. Repeat a minimum of four times.
2. Suggested counts—eight or four for each action.

RUBBERBAND STRETCH—PART 2

Position—Same as above

Action Cues

1. Concentrate!
2. Slowly stretch your right side, (arm and leg) while you relax your left side, (arm and leg).
3. Repeat on the opposite side.
4. Now this time, *flex* your right ankle as you stretch your right side, then your left side as you flex your left ankle.

FLEX AND POINT—PART 1

Position—Long Sitting

(legs together, arms extended, hands on floor, close to hips and behind to support a straight back)

Action Cues

1. Flex feet.
   a) Push heel forward.
   b) Bring toes toward you, extend them or fan them out.
2. Point toes.
   a) Flatten or smooth out your ankle.
   b) Make a fist with your toes.

Teacher Hints

1. Demonstrate.
2. It may be necessary to walk around and touch toes back or forward as the case may be.

EXPLORING A SIT-UP WITH ISOLATED BODY PARTS

Position—Long lying

(lying on back, legs together, knees extended, arms overhead)

Action Cues

1. Lift parts of your body in succession: arms, head, shoulders, chest, waist and hips.
2. Bounce forward from the waist—four times.
3. Return to the floor, moving hips, waist, chest, shoulders, head and arms in succession.

Suggested Counts

Four slow beats for each action

EXPLORING LEG MOVEMENT POTENTIAL—PART 1

Position—Long lying

(lying on back, legs together, knees extended, arms at sides)

Action Cues

1. Bring your right knee to your chest, flex your ankle. Use your right arm to hold the back of your thigh.
2. Extend your leg to the ceiling, point your toe.
3. Bring your knee to your chest.
4. Extend your leg to the floor (original position).

Teacher Hints

1. Repeat movement on the left leg.
2. Perform actions using both legs together.
3. Suggested counts—four for each action.

EXPLORING LEG MOVEMENT POTENTIAL—PART 2

Position—Same as above

Action Cues

1. Bring your knee to your chest.
2. Extend your leg to the ceiling.
3. Bring your leg down to the floor. Keep the leg straight; do not flex.

LEG ROTATION AND ALIGNMENT—PART 1

Position—Tall standing

(standing erect, feet parallel under hips, arms at sides)

Action Cues

1. Turn out your legs and feet.
   a) Make a "V" with your feet.
   b) Keep the weight on the outside of your feet.

Teacher Hint

1. Repeat parallel and first positions as needed.
2. Repeat the exercises with a view to proper alignment.

Action Cues

1. Take the wrinkles out of your leotard.
   a) Press your shoulders down.
   b) Try to touch the ceiling with your head.
   c) Make your waistline smaller, or thin out your waist.
   d) Turn sideways to the mirror to check your position.

Teacher Hints

Check for proper body alignment, including contraction of abdominals and a perpendicular pelvis.

LEG ROTATION—PART 2

Position—Long sitting

(legs together, arms extended, hands on floor behind hips, to help support a straight back)

Action Cues

1. Check to see whether both knees are facing the ceiling.
2. Roll the legs sideways, so that your knees face each side of the room.
3. Keep your knees straight.

LEG ROTATION WITH FLEX AND POINT—PART 3

Position—long sitting, feet parallel

Action Cues

1. Knees to the ceiling.
2. Point your toes.
3. Try to get your pinky toes on the floor by rolling your legs outward.
4. Knees to the ceiling or roll in and relax.
5. Flex ankles.
6. Roll legs outward.
7. Roll legs in.
8. Relax feet.

A STANDING STRETCH—PART 1

Position—Tall standing

(body erect, feet parallel under hips, arms at sides)

Action Cues

1. Reach for the ceiling.
   a) Raise your arms, still pressing shoulders downward.
   b) Show me you are reaching with your finger tips.
2. Relax—arms down.

Teacher Hints

1. Urge the girls to go higher and higher.
2. Check to see fingers are outstretched.
3. Repeat as needed.

STANDING STRETCH—PART 2

Position—Stride standing

(body erect, legs extended, feet apart facing diagonally, ballet second, arms at sides)

Action Cues

1. Raise both arms to shoulder level.
2. Make believe you will be able to touch both sides of the room at one time.
   —Stretch, try harder, hold it.
3. Relax.
4. Try it again, this time with your eyes closed.
   —Concentrate—feel as if you could reach those walls.
5. Relax.

Teacher Hints

1. Do this slowly. Give students time to stretch outwards.
2. Repeat a maximum of three times.

USING THE LOWER BACK

Position—Hook lying

(lying on back, legs slightly apart, knees flexed, soles of feet on floor, arms at sides)

Action Cues

1. Press your lower back to the floor.
   —Use your hand to check whether any air can get between the lower back and the floor.
2. Slowly extend your right leg.
   —Repeat 1.
3. Bring it back.
4. Extend your left leg.
   —Repeat 1.
5. Bring it back.

6. Straighten both legs slowly, but keep pressing your back to the floor.

7. Hold it and keep breathing!

8. Relax.

Teacher Hints

1. Elicit from the class what is happening to their abdomens as their backs sink lower into the floor.

2. Repeat as needed.

3. May be used in combination with the "Rubberband Stretch."

4. Suggested counts—slow tempo, four counts per action.

Here is an example of a culmination of exploratory activities using counts and changes in tempo.

Note—Complete the following combinations with counts listed in column (1) before proceeding to column (2).

Position—On floor, Tailor Sitting

Action Cues	Counts (1)	Counts (2)
1. Circle head to the right,	8	4
2. Raise right arm,	4	2
3. Lower right arm,	4	2
4. Straighten legs (parallel),	8	4
5. Flex feet,	2	1
6. Point feet,	2	1
7. Flex feet,	2	1
8. Point feet,	2	1
9. Bring legs back (tailor sitting) (Repeat to the left).	8	4

The following is an example of a culminating activity based on creative imagery, using counts and dynamic change.

Note—Complete the following combinations with counts listed in column (1) before proceeding to column (2).

Action Cues	Counts (1)	Counts (2)
1. Float to the floor.	8	4
(a) By count 8, you should be flat on your back.		
2. Make yourself tiny.	4	2
3. "Become an insect and travel to another spot on the floor.	6	3
(a) You can roll, slither, crawl, etc.		
4. Get your head to touch your knee.	4	2
5. Stand up as slowly as you can, and reach for a star in the sky."	16	8

Teacher Hint:

An action cue should take the entire count given. (e.g., in an action cue of 4-four counts, the student must move through all four counts, and it is only at count four that the head touches the knee.

Locomotor movements, whether in a basic study, combination, or a pattern, should provide students with an enjoyable and exhilarating dance experience.

This section provides basic locomotor studies exploring change, of direction, dynamics, levels, tempo and rhythms.

It also answers the question "How many different ways can we walk?" (skip, run, etc.)

Before starting any of our locomotor exploratory studies, it is necessary to do the following:

I Train your students to listen to the drum.

II Teach the necessary discipline in moving across the floor.

III Designate the correct starting leg.

IV Explain the need for silence.

I. A PROCEDURE IN TRAINING STUDENTS TO LISTEN TO THE DRUM (USING WALKS ONLY)

Action

Step on every beat of the drum.

Position

Line up in rows to move across the floor.

Teacher Cue

Verbalize: Ready, Set, Go! for each line.

Teacher Actions

Part One:

1. Drums a steady beat in a Medium walking tempo.

Part Two:

1. Varies the tempo with each line.

    a) Funderal walk (very very slow).

    b) Marching tempo (snappy).

    c) very fast walk (walking race etc.).

Class

1. Move one line at a time across the floor.

2. Repeat a part if needed.

Teacher Hints

1. Encourage different students to be leaders.

2. Challenge each line to do better than the one before it.

3. Praise those lines that do well.

II. A METHOD WHEREBY STUDENTS LEARN THE NECESSARY DISCIPLINE IN MOVING ACROSS THE FLOOR.

Actions

1. Line up across and fill in lines—at one side of the room.

    a) Number across is determined by:

        1) Size of the room

        2) Locomotor movement (a skipping turn needs more space than a walk forward).

2. Straighten up lines.

    a) Guiding right (eyes right),

   b) Raising of hands as lines are called,
   c) Last line may be the only uneven line.
       If one girl is alone, she moves with the preceeding line.
3. Starting on the first beat of a measure:
   a) Teacher explains that each line will start on the first beat of the measure and continue across the floor.
   b) Teacher counts aloud (1234, 2234, 3234, 4234 etc.)
   c) Girls count aloud as they cross the floor.
   d) Teacher drums:
       1) Accenting the first beat.
       2) Girls count to themselves.
4. Practice
   a) Use eights, twos, etc.
   b) Use slow and fast tempos.

Teacher Hints:

1. Begin with a walk in 4/4 time.
2. Move out on first beat with a line.
3. Aim for perfection through drill and repetition may be necessary.

Teacher Cue:

"Keep awake!"

III. DESIGNATE THE CORRECT STARTING LEG

1. Terms used
   a) Right leg, left leg.
   b) Upstage leg, downstage leg.
   c) The teacher can use physical features of the room to point out which foot to start with (e.g. mirror leg, window leg).

Teacher Hints

1. Always practice a study, combination or pattern from both sides of studio, alternating from right to left sides.

2. Maintain the same starting leg for the same side of the room.

IV. EXPLAIN THE NEED FOR SILENCE

Hints for the class:

1. You need to concentrate and review the step in your mind.
2. You must hear the last beat of the measure so that you are ready for your entrance.
3. You can learn by watching others.
4. You should listen to constructive comments made by the teacher.
5. You should listen for any new instructions.
6. You can rest while waiting your turn.
7. A student moving across the floor may feel more insecure and self-conscious if she hears whispering.

GENERAL REMINDERS:

A method for teaching locomotor movements (using the triplet as an example):

1. En masse:

Demonstrate for the class, going in the line of direction (students imitate). Break down the step, and work slowly. You can say "Down, up, up; repeat if necessary.

Class moves without the teacher's lead. They practice the steps using a slow tempo, and they say the cues or counts aloud.

2. In lines:

You are able to drum, accenting first beat of the measure and/or use verbal cues; observe any problem areas (incorrect footing, posture), and decide whether more repetition or breakdown is needed. You may withdraw those students who successfully perform and appoint them as leaders.

3. Group practices:

Each leader is given a group or line and assigned to teach peers in a specific area. The leader uses her own cues, tempo and method.

Meanwhile, you can walk around to each group, help with problems and check their progress. Allot as much time as necessary for the majority of the class to attain success.

4. Return to line formation

Use a definite tempo. As students become more skilled, tempo is increased. Students still having problems are placed into a group with a leader, and work in another area, while the teacher continues the lesson.

5. Partner practices

Practice sessions are repeated, using partners instead of group formation. Stress staying together, by having them use their own tempo.

6. On the diagonal—partners and singly

A degree of success should be demonstrated before your students cross the floor with partners or alone. Now cue your students and strive for perfection. You can motivate students to go higher, keep the body erect or keep the tempo. Speed up the tempo of a movement to challenge their skill. This works well with triplets. You can also allow time, before attendance, for students to practice. Remember to praise and encourage the class to help one another.

LOCOMOTOR STUDIES
WALKING

A walk has an even rhythmic pattern, and is a series of steps with transfer of weight from one foot to the other.

PART 1—DIRECTIONAL CHANGE

Action

1. Walk forward across the floor.
2. Walk backwards across the floor.
3. Change on four (four steps forward, four steps backward, in line of direction.)
4. Change on two.

Action Cues

1. Walk tall. (Body erect etc.)
2. Eyes up. (Focus on opposite wall.)
3. Relax arms. (Swing naturally.)

Teacher Hints

1. Begin with a brisk 4/4 meter.
2. Stress definite response to drum beat.
3. Vary speeds to determine concentration.

PART 2-LEVEL CHANGE

The following walking study provides a lead-up for teaching the triplet.

Triplet-Phase 1

Action

1. Walk low, bend knees across (Groucho Marx walk).
2. Walk high on toes (straight knees).
3. Walk four high, four low.
    a) First students come in after eight counts.
    b) Students then come in after four counts.
4. Walk two low, two high.
    a) Students may come in after four counts.
    b) Students may come in after two counts.

Teacher Cues

1. Low, low, high, high.

2. Down, down, up, up.

Leads into phase 2-triplet

Triplet-Phase 2

A triplet is done in ¾ time. Three steps are taken consecutively with the level change.

For example:

1. Right leg, low bent knee.
2. Left leg, high on toes.
3. Right leg, high on toes.

and continuing with:

1. Left leg, low bent knee.
2. Right leg, high on toes.
3. Left leg, high on toes.

Teacher Cue
Down, up, up.

Teacher Hints:

1. Do not demonstrate; make this a challenge for pupils to solve for themselves (allow time).
2. Ask for volunteers to demonstrate.

Formation

See "General Reminder"—A method for teaching locomotor movements.

Teacher Cues

1. Down, up, up.
2. Low, high, high.
3. Bend, toe, toe.

Teacher Hints (2)

Emphasize the following:

1. bent leg and foot flat on the floor
2. erect body

3. starting with the bent leg on the down beat
4. using the correct starting leg
5. pressing shoulders down
6. keeping arms still at sides:
    a) if arms swing, have students place hands on waist.

EXTENDED STUDIES—WALKING

Extended studies should not be given all at once, but only as the student becomes more competent.

1. Experience a circular walk-across the floor.
    Example:
        Action
            Walk four steps forward.
            Circle eight steps around.
        Teacher Hint
        1. Emphasize making a circle large enough to accommo-date eight steps.
            a) Students should not walk around themselves.
            b) Draw a circle on the floor or board.
2. Experience a walk, moving sideways, describing a square.
    Example:
        Action
            1. Make a square (floor pattern) facing front.
3. Experience a walk with isolated body parts across the floor.
    Examples:
        Action
            1. Using hips (sexy, swaying walk)
                a) Right foot, right hip, right shoulder.
                b) Left foot, left hip, left shoulder.
            2. Using shoulder circling
                a) May step out with same shoulder as foot or,
                b) Use right shoulder circling as left leg steps out.
4. Experience a walk using creative stimuli.
Ask the question: How would you walk across if you are _____?

Examples:

> 1. a hundred pounds overweight
> 2. ninety years old
> 3. on a boat during a storm
> 4. first learning to walk
> 5. a robot
> 6. an animal (bird etc.)

5. Experience a walk using arm gestures across the floor.

Example:

Action

> 1. Walking forward-eight counts stepping on each count (4/4 meter).
> 2. Raising arms sideways to reach overhead as you walk (four counts).
> 3. Reverse by lowering arms sideways (four counts).
> 4. Repeat.

CULMINATING ACTIVITY

A sample dance pattern using the walk in 4/4 meter, with appropriate musical accompaniment in this dance.

"Steppin' In Style"

Position

Facing in line of direction going forward

Action

1. Walk forward four steps:
   a) right, left, right, left.
2. a. Step side, together, step side, touch (hold), snap fingers on touch).
   b) Repeat, beginning with left foot.
3. Step and snap, four times:
   a) step side with right foot, left foot touch, snap fingers on touch.
   b) step with left foot right foot touch, snap fingers on touch repeat a) and b).

4. Three steps turn to the right and clap.

   a) right, left, right, clap.

5. Three steps turn to the left and clap.

   a) left, right, left, clap.

6. Repeat actions one through five.

Teacher Suggestions

1. After the progression is learned, use any popular record in 4/4 time with a brisk tempo.

2. Do the dance en masse.

3. Do the dance in lines coming in after the first four counts.

Variation on the Jazz Dance

1. Do the dance using partners.

   a) both facing forward,

   b) starting on opposite feet, turning away, and towards each other.

2. Use a stylized walk.

   a) hips swaying,

   b) shoulder circling,

   c) small shuffling steps.

3. Vary the direction.

4. Vary the order in which it is given.

5. Be creative! Use your own ingenuity.

Skipping

A skip is rhythmically uneven and has a step and hop combination.

Formation

In lines

Position

Facing forward, going across the floor.

Action

1. Skip forward across the floor.
2. Skip backward in the line of direction across the floor.
3. Skip four forward, four backward.
4. Skip two forward, two backward.
5. Skip one forward and one backward (a skipping turn).

Teacher Hints

1. Be aware of spatial relationships between students as they cross the floor.
2. Check body facing:
    Step is either done facing forward or backward (arms swing naturally).
3. Be aware that dizziness may occur on the skipping turn. Use spotting techniques.

Extended study:

Example:

Experience the skip with variations in tempo:

1. very fast, short quick skips close to the floor.
2. slow; high skips covering distance, challenge students— "Can you cross the floor in five skips?"

Running

A run has an even, rhythmic pattern similar to a walk, but with a faster tempo, and a greater spring from the floor.

Formation:

In lines

Position:

Facing line of direction

Teacher Cues

Cue each line with one drum beat.

Action

1. Run forward across the floor.
2. Run backwards in line of direction.
3. Run with knees behind,
    a) body slanted forward.
    b) feet touching backside.
4. Run with knees in front (May be used as a lead up to the prance.)
5. Run covering distance:
    a) Present it as a challenge—Can you run across this floor using only seven steps? (May be used as a lead-up to the leap.)

Extended Studies

Examples:

1. Use isolated body parts to lead you across the floor; elbow, chin, etc.
2. Have a race with each line.
3. Use imagery-make believe_____
    a) you are running to catch a bus,
    b) you are late for a date.
4. Play "Putting on the Brakes"
    a) on first drum beat-run,
    b) on second beat-freeze into a statue.

Safety factor for races:

The finish line should be placed at a safe distance from the wall.

Sliding

A slide is performed in a sideward direction. It has an uneven rhythmic pattern consisting of step, cut, step.

Formation:

in line

Position:

Side facing line of direction,
Body facing front,
Arms raised sideways, shoulder level.

Action

1. Slide with body facing front of room—across the floor.
2. Slide with body facing back of room.
3. Eight slides facing front, eight slides facing back.
4. Four slides front, four slides back.
5. Two slides front, two slides back.
6. Alternating slides front and back (one front, one back).

Teacher Hint:

Check whether feet touch each other in the air during actions one and two.

Teacher Suggestion:

The slide and half-turn on the hop are rarely broken down. Students learn by your demonstration and through imitation.

Galloping

A gallop has as uneven rhythmic pattern. It is the same as a slide but is done in a forward direction.

Formation:

In lines.

Position:

Facing in line of direction.

Action

1. Gallop across the room, repeat on opposite side.
2. Gallop
   a) with change of leg,
      right leg leading-four,
      left leg leading-four,

b) with arms—example:
arms rising parallel forward and over head on four gallops, and reverse down to sides on four gallops.

Teacher Suggestion

To maintain the body facing in a forward position, use the imagery of the hips being two headlights which must remain in a frontways position.

Hopping

A hop has an even rhythmic pattern. It is a take-off or spring from one foot to the same foot.

Note—The following sequence repeated is frequently used in the Gymnasium as a warm-up activity.

Formation:

On spots facing front.

Position:

Legs parallel.

Action

Eight hops on the right foot,
Eight hops on the left foot,
Four hops on right foot, four on left,
Two hops on right foot, two on left,
Alternate feet four times (right, left, right, left).

Jumping

A jump has an even rhythmic pattern. It is a take-off or spring from both feet to both feet.

Formation:

1. In spots,

2. Divided into two or more groups depending on size of class:

a) to avoid tiring, each action is repeated by the following group.

b) to be able to observe errors, such as pushing off, landing, etc.

Position:

Facing front
Legs parallel

Breakdown Cues

Breakdowns of the jump are necessary to avoid mishaps.

1. Press heels into the floor, flex knees; raise heels off and rise on toes; into the air—body vertical, stretch knees; on landing, touch toes, ball of foot, heel.
2. Plié, jump, plié: straighten your body and knees in the air and try to point your toes.

Action Studies—in 4/4 time

Experiencing elevation:

1. eight low jumps
2. four high jumps
3. four low jumps followed by four high jumps
4. three low jumps and one high jump—repeat
   a) tempo variation one, two, three and four
   b) preparation for jumping turns

2. Experiencing elevation and turns:

Three low jumps are executed facing the line of direction, and the fourth jump (a turn) is executed on the fourth beat (see number four above).

1. three jumps and 1/4 turns to the right, repeat to the left side
2. three jumps and 1/2 turns to the right, repeat to the left side
3. three jumps and one turn around, repeat to the left side

Note—Keep arms close to body on turns.

3. Experiencing a lead-up into elevation

    1. plié relevé four times (fast tempo) (bend knees, rise on toes).

    2. four low jumps

    3. four high jumps (slow tempo)

Teacher Cues

1. Bend your knees and imagine you are pushing off from a diving board into the air.
2. Touch the ceiling with the top of your head.
3. Imagine you are a straight line in the air (from head to toes).

Teacher Hints

1. Have the class perform a jump in slow motion. (See breakdown cues.)
2. Add the cue "Point your toes in the air" if your beginning students have the elasticity necessary for ankle and toe extension.
3. Drum a beat for the preparatory bending of the legs. (Plié.)
4. Use the drum to differentiate between the low jumps (softly) and the high or turning ones. (Very loud.)
5. Use verbal cues
   a) to motivate greater height
      And (plié) up (jump).
   b) to give directional cues
      Low, low, low, turn.
6. Have girls watch each other and comment on their posture in the air.
7. Have your students practice action studies in first (ballet) position.

Extended Studies

Examples:

1. Use the jump to cover distance in different directions: forward, backward, sideways right, sideways left

e.g. four jumps going forward
four backward
two sideways right
two sideways left

2. Present a challenge to each line:

a) How many different ways can you jump?

b) Can you jump with your:

1) legs out to the side?

2) knees in front of you?

3) knees behind you?

4) hands clapping above your head (behind you, in front of you)?

c) Use any combination of leg and arm positions.

To make *best* use of this section, you should use the following scheme:

1. Provide exploratory experiences for general movement.

2. Decide on series to be used; see Chapter 4.

3. Use the necessary lead-up techniques for that series.

·→❊ 4 ❊←·

Disciplining the Body
Through Exercise

After fully exploring the language of dance in Chapter 3, you are ready to present a selected series of exercises taught in a sequential manner in floor and standing positions. The series represents a progression of skills that flows from one idea to the other.

Because we feel that the success factor is of primary importance and is the best motivating device, we incorporate lead-up exercises whenever possible. Lead-ups represent the "breaking down" of a particular exercise in the series to its simplest components. (Please note that not all exercises in our series require a lead-up.)

ADVANTAGES OF THE SERIES

1. The series helps you to determine your goals for the lesson.

For example: a) to provide a change in dynamics, teach the swing.
           b) to develop abdominal strength, teach the roll down and chest arch series.

2. You can plan your lessons more easily. For example:
           a) You can conveniently and easily organize the series into your daily lesson plan because it is presented in chronological order with developmental flow.
           b) The exercises in the series are arranged so that they are easily adapted to the time limits of your lesson.

3. You can plan for the ability level of your class. For example:
           a) You have the option of using explorations of movement, lead-up exercises, or going directly to the exercises in the series.

b) Because the series is broken down for you, you are able to select the aspect that is consistent with the achievement level of your class.

4. You can view your class objectively.

a) You are able to step aside while your students move independently of your directions and cues.
b) You can easily determine the needs of the class.
c) You are able to test for technical learnings.
d) By memorizing the proper sequence and counts, a class obtains a sense of follow-through, completion and independence.

5. You can use the series format as a springboard to develop your own ideas.

a) Our technical format is adaptable to other styles of movement (jazz, ballet).
b) You may add your own variations to a series.

6. You can be assured of success within a set time period.

These series were chosen because skills are easily achieved on a beginner's level, within a particular time limit.

GENERAL REMINDERS FOR DISCIPLINING THE BODY THROUGH EXERCISES

1. Only our lead-up experiences have action cues. They are given so that students may focus on the correct working muscles.

2. Only our lead-up experiences contain challenges. As pupils progress, insert more difficult challenges to maintain interest and encourage practice.

3. Alternate rest with work periods, and be observant as to whether there is muscle strain. Though these exercises may be defined as lead-up, they are of a strenuous nature for the beginning dancer.

4. Exact counts and tempos are not always given in the lead-up section because each class begins with different needs and progresses at different rates.

5. Provide procedures for the evaluation and testing of pupil learning. Dance evaluation should include the testing of specific skills.

   a) Do not test lead-up exercises because they primarily involve movement exploration, where a unique, rather than uniform response is encouraged.

   b) Inform your pupils of the goals to be achieved through the series, and assign points to each of these goals. By having a point system (as in gymnastic scoring) students may take an active role in grading. By helping you test, students attain an awareness for correct performance, as well as respect for dance discipline and training.

A SUMMARY OUTLINE OF THE SERIES WITH LEAD-UPS

Floor

SERIES A

Bounce Series Based on Breathing

A 1   Body bounces—head to feet—Frog sitting
A 2   Body bounces—head to knees—Long sitting
A 3   Body bounces—chest to thigh—Stride sitting
A 4   Culminating position—Stride sitting

SERIES B

Flexion and Extension Bounce Series in Sitting Position

Lead-up activities to Stretch Series B—(Ldp.)
Series B:
B 1   Flex and point toes—Stride sitting
B 2   Body bounces with flexed feet—Long sitting
B 3   Body bounces with pointed toes—Long sitting
B 4   Culminating position—Erect sitting

SERIES C

Abdominal Strength Series

Lead-up activities to Strength Series C (Ldp.)
Series C: Hook sitting to long lying

C 1   a Roll down, midddle spine leading
       b Roll up, top of head leading

C 2   a Roll down, middle spine leading
       b Arch up, chest leading

C 3   a Side twist roll down—right side
       b Side twist roll up—left side
       c Side twist roll down—left side
       d Side twist roll up—right side

C 4   Culminating position—coccyx balance

Standing

SERIES D

Body Warm-up and Stretch Series

Lead-up activities to Series D
Series D: Stride standing

D 1   a Bounce, bending forward
       b Bounce, bending backward

D 2   a Bounce, side bend on right side
       b Bounce, side bend on left side

D 3   a Culminating combination—Bounce, forward, right, left, backward
       b Culminating position—Bend forward, roll up to erect standing

SERIES E

Heel Stretch and Weight Balance Series (Pliés and Relevés)

Lead-up activities to Series E
Series E:

E 1   Plié and relevé in a three-count phrase
E 2   Plié, relevé combination in a two-count phrase
E 3   Plié, relevé combination in a one-count phrase
E 4   Culminating position
E 5   Repetition of actions E 1 through E 4 in first position

SERIES F

Coordinating Weight Shift with Swings Series

Lead-up activities to Series F
Series F:

F 1   Swinging and circular movement of arms (in spots)

F 2   Coordinate arm movements with shift of weight (stepping sideways)

F 3   Coordinate arm movements with shift of weight using a leg lift

F 4   Coordinate arm movements, shift of weight, and leg lift with a step hop and slide

F 5   Culminating combinations

SERIES G

Toe, Ankle and Leg Extension Series (Point, Brush, Kick)

Lead-up activities to Series G
Series G:

G 1   a Points in parallel position
      b Points in first position

G 2   a Brushes in parallel position
      b Brushes in first position

G 3   Free kicks forward

G 4   Culminating action

GLOSSARY OF POSITIONS

FROG SITTING

Sitting, spine erect, legs flexed, soles of feet together, arms relaxed at sides.

TAILOR SITTING

Sitting cross legged, spine erect, arms relaxed at sides.

LONG SITTING

Sitting, spine erect, legs together, knees extended, toes pointed, arms at sides.

STRIDE SITTING

Sitting, spine erect, legs apart, knees extended toes pointed, arms extended sideways below shoulder level.

HOOK SITTING

Sitting, spine erect, legs together, knees flexed, soles of feet on floor, arms at sides.

LONG LYING

Lying, back on floor, legs together knees extended, toes pointed, arms at sides.

TALL STANDING

Standing, spine erect, feet parallel under hips, arms oval-shaped at sides.

STRIDE STANDING

Standing, spine erect, feet apart, facing diagonally, arms at sides.

LUNGE STANDING—FORWARD, PARALLEL OR SLIGHTLY TURNED OUT FEET

Standing, spine erect, front leg bent, foot flat on floor; back leg extended, heel off floor; weight of body is centered, arms extended sideways below shoulder level, palms down.

Floor Series—A

BOUNCE SERIES BASED ON BREATHING

Position—A 1

Consistent Features:
1. All bouncing actions in all positions are preceded by a breathing exercise that involves exhalation and inhalation in a smooth flowing manner, repeated two times.
   a) exhale—round spine in a successional manner (hips initiating movement, head is last to come down)—4 counts
   b)inhale—extend spine in a successional manner (hips initiating movement, head is last to come up)—4 counts

2. Counts:
   a) breathing—use a count sequence appropriate to the breathing action: 8 or 4
   b) bouncing—use 16 or 8
   c) transition—use 4 or 2

Frog sitting
> hands clasping ankles
> elbows out to side
> focus ahead

Action—A 1

Body bounces—head to feet, bounce from back of waist line
> Transitional steps:
>> Extend spine in successional manner to long sitting position

Action—A 2

Breathing—long sitting.
Body bounces—head to knee, arms reaching forward
> Transitional Steps
>> extend spine in successional manner to stride sitting position

Action—A 3

Breathing—stride sitting
Body bounces—chest to thigh
1. kneecaps face ceiling
   a) over right leg
   b) over left leg
   c) center, head to floor
2. arms reaching toward ankle
3. focus is down

Action—A 4

Culminating position—stride sitting, erect body, legs extended, toes pointed, focus forward

> Extend spine in successional manner 4 counts, hold with arms sideways, below shoulder level—4 counts

Leadup to Series B—Flexion and Extension Bounce Series in Sitting
Position
Ldp = Leadup

LDP B 1

Flex and point toes

Position—Long sitting

Actions

Rotate feet

> arms extended down at sides, hands placed near hips, on floor, to support a straight back

Action Cues

1. extend ankles, flex ankles
2. circle one foot at a time
3. circle both together
   > in opposition
   > in same direction

Challenge

Can you flex your feet so that your heels come off the floor?

LDP B 2

Actions

Point toes

Action Cues

1. flex ankle
2. curl toes
3. stretch ankle

Challenge

Can you hold your toes curled while they reach forward?

Floor Series B

FLEXION AND EXTENSION BOUNCE SERIES IN SITTING POSITION

Position—B 1

Stride sitting with hands on floor for support

Action—B 1

Flex and point toes with erect torso, and extended legs

Transitional Step

Change to long sitting in four counts

Action—B 2

Body bounces with flexed feet

1. arms reaching over toes
2. head up
3. focus straight ahead

Action—B 3

Body bounces with pointed toes

1. head down
2. hands resting on floor close to knees
3. focus down

Action—B 4

Culminating position: long sitting, erect body, legs extended, toes pointed, focus forward. Extend spine in successional manner for 4 counts, with arms raising sideways, shoulder level.

Lead-up to Series C—Abdominal Strength Series

Strengthening the abdominal muscle for the roll down, roll up series

LDP C

C 1 a

Roll down, middle spine leading

Position—Long lying

Action

Press middle back to floor

Action Cues

1. feel space between floor and waist with own hand
2. flex feet, raise knees slightly off the floor
3. press middle back down
4. keep breathing throughout

Challenge

1. Keep your back pressing against the floor as I count up to number _____.

Teaching Hints

1. Walk around. Check positions while alternating counts between abdominal tension and abdominal relaxation.
2. Have students check each other to see whether they can see "daylight" underneath

C 1 b

Roll up, with top of head leading

Position—Long lying

LDP C 2

Action Cues

1. head lift
2. head and shoulder lift
3. come up to sitting position

Challenges

1. How long can your head (shoulders) remain off the floor?
2. Do you have to use your arms to help you? Try placing your hands on top of your thighs.

Teaching Hints

1. Increase the number of counts during abdominal tension as strength develops.
2. Repeat this exercise with toes pointed and with toes flexed.

C 2 b—Arch up, chest leading

LDP C 3

Action

Neck and back arch

Position—Long lying

> arms extended sideward, shoulder level, palms down

Challenges

1. Can you arch your back so that the top of your head remains on the floor? You may use your hands to help you by pressing against floor to raise chest.

2. Can you see what is upside down behind you?

Teaching Hints

1. In some cases, it may be necessary for you to straddle the student and very gently lift the chest from underneath, telling the student to relax the head and shoulders, letting the head fall back naturally.
2. Check students' progress. If they are successful, have them come all the way up to a sitting position "let the chest lead you."

A Useful Combination Using Simple Abdominal, Foot and Body Bounce Exercises.

Position—Long sitting

Action 1
Roll down slowly, back of spine leading—four counts

Action cues

1. feet are flexed
2. small of the back sinks into floor
3. head is last to touch floor
4. arms move sideward shoulder level, palms down

Action 2
Arch up, chest leading—four counts

Action Cues

1. toes are pointed
2. head remains back as long as possible

Action 3
Body bounces forward—four counts

Action Cues

1. toes are pointed
2. arms reaching forward

Teaching Hints

1. Repeat maximum of three times continually.
2. Divide class into three groups and use this combination in a round.

C 4

Culminating position

Action

Coccyx balance with bent legs

Position—Hook sitting,

arms clasped around legs

Challenge

1. Can you balance with your feet off the floor?

Action Cues

1. rock back and forth until your best balance spot is found.
2. balance while holding on to legs.
3. balance as arms extend forward, parallel to floor, palms facing each other.
4. balance as lower legs move upward, parallel to the floor, point toes

Teaching Hint

Begin a counting game: "How long can you balance?"

Floor Series C

Abdominal Strength Series

CONSISTENT FEATURES

1. Starting and closing positions
   a) hook sitting
   b) elbows flexed parallel to floor, with fingertips on shoulders

    c) head close to knees

    d) focus downward

    e) heels off the floor

2. Counts

    a) roll-downs 6—3

    b) roll ups 6—3

3. Unfolding to a long lying or rolling down position

    a) legs extended, toes pointed

    b) arms extend to sides of body, palms up

    c) head is last to touch the floor

4. Roll-downs and roll-ups are done in a successional manner, unless otherwise mentioned

5. Class Arrangement

    Divide class into two groups. Group one rolls down in six counts and folds up in six counts. This is duplicated by group two. Group one repeats the same actions in three counts, again followed by group two. The culminating position is simultaneously done by both groups.

Actions—C 1

a) roll down, middle spine leading

b) roll up, top of head leading

Actions—C 2

a) roll down, middle spine leading

b) arch up, chest leading

    long lying

    arms extended sideward shoulder level

    palms flat on floor

    head drops back and is last to come forward

Actions—C 3

a) side twist—roll down right side, first count

    1) twist body from waistline

        elbows right

head turned to right side

focus back over right shoulder

2) unfold, lying on right side

3) long lying

roll head to left side

b) side twist—roll up, left side

1) twist body to left side

head lifts up on left side

focus back over left shoulder

elbows are on left side of body

2) hook sitting, closing position, last count

c) side twist—roll down, left side

1) repeat C 3a action on opposite side

d) side twist—roll up, right side

1) repeat action C 3b on opposite side

Action C 4

Culminating position—coccyx balance
knees flexed, lower legs parallel to floor, toes pointed, arms parallel, extended forward at shoulder level, on either side of legs palms facing, fingers together

Lead-ups to Series D
Body Warmup and Stretch Series (Standing) 19

A combination utilizing breathing, stretching, bending and bouncing

LDP D 1

Position

Tall standing, arms relaxed at sides

Action 1

Body stretch reaching upward

Action Cues

1. stretch arms overhead
2. focus eyes to ceiling
3. reach upward, alternating arms

Challenge

Can you extend your body, with arms alternately reaching overhead, while you inhale for eight counts?

LDP D 2

Action 2

Bend forward to the floor using a successional movement

Action Cues

1. bring arms down
2. exhale for eight counts
3. relax and hang down

Challenge

Can you roll down to the floor initiating the movement in your hips? Remember you head is the last body part to move!

LDP D 3

Action 3

Body bounces forward

Action Cues

1. fingertips are reaching for the floor.
2. knees are straight.
3. breathe naturally.

Challenge:

Can your back stay rounded and relaxed while bouncing eight times like a ball? Focus down.

LDP D 4

Action 4

Straighten body using a successional movement

Challenge:

1. Can you roll up to a standing position while inhaling for eight counts? Begin the movement in the hips. Slowly, let each spinal bone build up to an erect state. The head is last, focus straight ahead.

Teaching Hints:

This sequence is repeated four times.

Standing Series D

BODY WARMUP AND STRETCH SERIES

Consistent Features

1. Counts

   Unless otherwise specified, the sequence of bounces for each action is as follows:

   > eight bounces
   >
   > four bounces
   >
   > two bounces, repeated twice
   >
   > one bounce, repeated four times

   (Eg. bounce forward 8, bounce backward 8, forward 4, backward 4, etc.)

2. Position—Stride standing

Actions—D 1

a) Bounce bending forward, center spine rounded
   hips pushed back
   knees extended
   hands reaching for floor
   head down
   focus between legs

b) Bounce bending backward, spine arched
hips pushed forward
knees flexed
hands on back of thighs for support
head back
focus on ceiling or beyond

Note—Actions D1a and D1b bounce on one count four times, become full body swings forward and backward

Actions—D 2

a) Bounce, side bend on right side
knees extended
right hand on waist
left arm overhead (reaching towards right side of room)
neck and head flex to the right
focus under left arm
b) Bounce, side bend on left side
Same as above, using opposite body parts

Actions—D 3

a) Culminating combination

Note—Counts are similar but start with four bounces for each action

1. Bounce forward
2. Bounce, side bend right
3. Bounce, side bend left
4. Bounce, backward

b) Culminating position
After completing the last action, (D3a4) do the following in sixteen counts:
1. Round forward in one count
2. Slowly roll up to an erect standing position; use a successional movement of the spine (head is last).

3. Rise up on toes and balance;

   a) focus straight ahead,

   b) arms extended out to sides, below shoulder level

Lead-ups to Series E
Heel Stretch and Weight Balance
Series
(Pliés and Relevés)

LDP E 1

Position—Tall standing

Action—Plié
feet parallel under hips
arms at sides

Challenges

1. Can you bend your knees and still keep your back straight? Keep your heels on the floor.
2. As you bend, can the top of your head reach for the ceiling?
3. As you straighten up, can you press your shoulders down?

Teaching Hints

1. Have one of your students model the correct position.
2. Proper alignment is one of the most difficult techniques to master because of the need for concentrated effort and body awareness. With continued encouragement and correction, sensitivity can be attained.

LDP E 2

Position—Tall standing
feet parallel under hips, arms at sides

Action—Relevé (rising up on toes)

Challenges

1. Raise your heels off the floor and find a comfortable balance.

2. How long can you balance?
3. Can you move your arms sideways and stay balanced?
4. Can you move your arms overhead and maintain your balance?
5. Can you look at the ceiling and maintain your balance?

Teaching Hint

Start counting, "Let's see whether we can raise that number tomorrow."

Standing Series E

HEEL STRETCH AND WEIGHT BALANCE SERIES
  (Pliés and Relevés)

Consistent Features

1. Plié (demi)
    a) flex knees
    b) heels remain on floor
2. Relevé
    a) extend knees
    b) heels off floor
3. Position
    tall standing with arms oval shaped at sides, feet parallel

Actions—E 1

Plié and relevé in three-count phrases
    a) plié, three counts; straighten knees, three counts repeated four times
    b) relevé, three counts; heels down, three counts repeated four times

Action—E 2

Plié, relevé combination in a two-count phrase
    plié, two counts, straighten knees, two counts; relevé, two counts, heels down, two counts; repeated four times

Action—E 3

Plié, relevé combination, in a one-count phrase

plié, one count, relevé, one count, (down-up) repeated four times

Action—E 4

Culminating position

On the fourth relevé (action E 3), balance for eight counts, arms rising slowly to below shoulder level

Actions—E 5

Repeat actions E 1 through E 4 in first ballet position

Note—This series may lead directly into either standing series G (toe, ankle, leg extension series) or jumps (see Chapter 3 Exploring The Language of Dance, Locomotor studies, jumping.

**Lead-ups to Series F—
Coordinating Weight Shift with Swings Series**

LDP F 1

Action
Swinging different body parts

Challenges
1. Can you swing only using your head?
2. Can you swing your arms?
    one at a time
    forward and back
    side to side
3. Can you swing both arms together?
    moving concurrently
    moving in opposition
    using different directions
4. Can you swing from the elbow, wrist, ankle, knee?

5. Can you swing your body?

6. How would you swing your legs?

Teaching Hints

1. Show an object that has a swinging motion. For instance, using a necklace with a pendant, have the class analyze the motion by describing it and imitating it using different body parts.

2. Explore movement used in sports, such as pitching, batting and bowling.

3. Allow students to experiment with different body parts on different levels.

LDP F 2

Action1—Forward swing, 3 counts

Position

Parallel fourth position, right leg forward

Action Cues

1. bend knees

2. flex forward

3. swing arms forward and upward

4. extend entire body upward
   straighten knees
   focus eyes upward
   lift chest high
   extend arms overhead
   balance on the balls of the feet

LDP F 3

Action 2

Backward swing, 3 counts

Action Cues

1. pull body downward in succession,

   arms come down

   hips lead, head is last

   bend knees

2. straighten knees,

   body flexes forward

   arms drop to back position

   focus eyes downward

   balance on balls of feet or feet

   remain on floor

Challenges

1. Can you do a forward and backward swing in slow motion?
2. Can you swing forward and backward with your left foot in the forward position?
3. Can you inhale while swinging upwards and exhale on the downward swing?
4. When you reach the highest point on the forward swing, can you balance on your toes with your back arched and your head back? Take a breath.

Standing Series F

COORDINATING WEIGHT SHIFT WITH SWINGS SERIES

Note—This series may follow standing series D (bounces) or series E (pliés, relevés)

Consistent Features

1. Counts:

   24 measures in ¾ time, unless otherwise noted.

2. Swings and circular motion of both arms in the extended position.

   The swing finishes with both arms overhead together, in a diagonally upward position.

3. Body, head and focus follow the movement of the arm swing

4. A forward and backward swing may be added on to any action

   forward swing, 3 counts

   backward swing, 3 counts

Position

Stride standing

Action—F 1

Swinging and circular movements of the arms (in spots).

1. swing to the right, 3 counts
2. swing to the left, 3 counts
3. make a circle to the right ending on right side, 6 counts
4. swing to the left, 3 counts
5. swing to the right, 3 counts
6. make a circle to the left ending on the left side, 6 counts

Action—F 2

Coordinate arm movements with a shift of weight (stepping sideways).

1. weight on right foot, left toes on floor
2. weight on left foot, right toes on floor
3. step right, together with left, step with weight on right, left toes on floor
4. weight on left foot, right toes on floor
5. weight on right foot, left toes on floor
6. step left, together with right, step with weight on left, right toes on floor

Action—F 3

Coordinate arm movements with shift of weight, using a leg lift (slightly raised off the floor).

1. step right, lift left leg
2. step left, lift right leg
3. step right, together, step right, lift left leg
4. step left, lift right leg
5. step right, lift left leg
6. step left, together, step left, lift right leg

Action—F 4

Coordinate arm movements, shift of weight, and leg lift with a step hop and slide.

1) step hop on right foot
2) step hop on left foot
3) slide right, together, step hop on right foot
4) step hop on left foot
5) step hop on right foot
6) slide left, together, step hop on left foot

Action—F 5

Culminating combination, Combination of swings sidewards, step hops and slides with swing forward and backward. Connect Actions F 3 and F 4 with forward and backward swings.

Lead-ups to Series G:
Toe, Ankle, and Leg Extension Series (Point, Brush, Kick)

LDP G 1

Position

Tall standing, feet parallel under hips, or turned out in the ballet first position arms at sides

Action 1

Ball, toe, ball, heel

Action Cues

1. Ball of the foot—press all toes, ball of foot, against floor push ankle forward, heel off

2. Toe—

   bring foot into top of toe position on floor
3. Ball of the foot—

   return to action cue one
4. Heel—

   place heel down

Challenges

1. Can you do this exercise without moving the rest of your body?
2. Can you do this exercise while maintaining an erect posture?

Teaching Hint

You may use one count for each action cue (4 counts). Repeat four times on each foot

LDP G 2

Action 2

Ball, toe push off, ball, heel

Teaching Hints

1. This action is similar to action one, except the toes push *off* the floor in the pointed position.
2. Use four counts, repeat four times.
3. Repeat in first position, arms oval shaped.
4. Challenges remain the same.

LDP G 3

Action 3

Quick toe push off and ankle extension
(The same as above but done in one count)

Teaching Hints

To get proper dynamic quality challenge your students with the following ideas: have girls touch floor with one hand, and tell them the floor is hot to the touch; or have them move their hands away on a loud sound or clap.

Challenge

3. Now have your students react in the same way using their leg and foot.

Teaching Hints

1. Accent the push off
   Say "and up" clap on the "up"
2. Repeat in first position, and use the same challenge as in action one.

Note—Actions one, two and three may provide a lead-up to the prance (advanced study).

LDP G 4   Points in a Parallel Position

Position

Tall standing, arms at sides

Action 1

Slow extension of toes, ankle and leg forward (toe remains on floor)

Challenges

1. Can you move your foot and leg without tilting your body? Press your shoulders down while your head presses against the ceiling. Keep your legs straight.
2. Make believe you are pushing a peanut forward with your big toe. Push it as far as your leg allows without moving any other body parts (only used for points).

LDP G 5

Action 2

Return foot to place

Action Cues

1. Slide foot backwards along floor, keeping both knees straight.

   top of big toe

   five toes

   ball of foot

   sole of foot

   heel down back into place

Challenges

1. Can you lift yourself high as your foot returns to position? Keep your hips still and your abdomen pulled in.
2. Can you shift your weight without showing any body movement?

Teaching Hints

1. At the beginning, counts should be slow and even in tempo to allow for concentration and correct alignment. Later, however, dynamic changes are advised to prevent boredom.
2. Repeat in first position.

G 2 a—Brushes in parallel position

LDP G 6   Brushes in a Parallel Position

Position

Tall standing

Action

Slow extension of toes, ankle, and leg forward (toes rise off the floor)

Action Cues

Point your foot, touching floor.

Lift your foot slightly off the floor.

Return to place.

Teaching Hints

1. Arms may be lifted more away from the body to help balance.
2. Change standing leg frequently, to avoid tiring and strain.

LDP G 7   Free Kicks Forward

Position

Lunge standing, forward direction, left leg flexed forward, right leg stretched behind

Action

A leg swing upward and back to place

Action Cues

1. Swing right leg forward, straighten left leg, body remains erect.
2. Return to the lunge position.

Challenge

Lift your leg as high as you can without bending your body or legs. Keep your toes pointed.

Teaching Hint

Teach and practice the lunge position.

Notes

1. A kick may be broken down by the following two methods:

LDP G 8

Position

Tall standing, feet in parallel position or turned out, arms extended sideways, below shoulder level.

Action Cues

1. Point forward.
2. Kick high.
3. Point forward.
4. Return to place.

LDP G 9

Method # 2

Position—Tall standing, feet parallel or turned out, arms extended sideways below shoulder level.

Action Cue

Brush leg directly up high and return to place.

Standing Series G

TOE, ANKLE AND LEG EXTENSION SERIES (POINT, BRUSH, KICK)

Position

Tall standing, feet parallel, arms at sides, oval-shaped

Actions—G 1

a) Points in parallel position (forward) right leg, left leg; 4 counts each

Transitional Step

Open to first position, 2 counts

b) Points in first position (to the diagonal) right leg, left leg; 4 counts each

Transitional Step

Change to parallel position, 2 counts

Actions—G 2

a. Brushes in parallel position (forward) right leg, left leg; 4 counts each

Transitional step

Change to first position, 2 counts

b) Brushes in first position (to the diagonal) right leg, left leg; 4 counts each

Transitional step

Change to forward lunge position, 2 counts left leg steps forward, right leg behind is the working leg, arms raise sideways, below shoulder level

Action—G 3

Free kicks forward; returning to lunge position. Kick right leg high; 4 counts

Transitional step

Step forward with right leg and kick left leg high; 4 counts, slow down tempo.

Action—G 4

Culminating actions
1. Bring left leg into first position, arms go down to sides (oval shape) two counts
2. Plié, 2 counts
3. Straighten knees, 2 counts

5

Moving Through Space

Now you are ready to expand the fundamental locomotor movements of Chapter 3 to more challenging locomotor patterns in this chapter.

The structured exercises that you read about in Chapter 4 can now be used as linkage ideas to create new combinations and patterns.

This chapter is divided into two parts. Both parts are devoted to developing locomotor movements on the beginner's level.

Our code for locomotor movements, arranged in order of difficulty of execution, is as follows:

PART I

LXS Locomotor Exploratory Studies (see Chapter 3)

LX Moving an Exercise

LS Expanding an Exploratory Study

LCL Stretching a Study into a Combination by Joining a Locomotor Study with a Linkage Idea

PART II

LC Joining Two Locomotor Studies to Form a Combination

LP Extending a Combination into a Pattern

LPL Stretching a Pattern with a Linkage Idea

A combination is defined as two locomotor movements or one locomotor movement and one connecting step or linkage idea. A pattern is defined as three or more different locomotor movements, or two or more different locomotor movements with one or more connecting steps.

LX MOVING AN EXERCISE

First, we take several exercises from our series in Chapter 4 and move them across the floor. This is the time to have your students move in pairs on the diagonal. This formation is usually viewed as a welcome change in routine. Because they are on "show," you will find your students exerting great concentration. They also enjoy this opportunity to demonstrate their skills acquired on floor spots. Meanwhile, you can more easily observe that the students are correctly executing the exercise, body position, and proper weight transfer. After sufficient practice, add some appropriate music and you can have your class doing a "dance step" across the floor.

LX 1 Using the walk with points and brushes

LX 2 Using the walk with small leg swings, forward and back

LX 3 Using the walk with body bounces forward, roll-ups, and relevé

LX 4 Using a stylized walk with isolated body movements

LX 1 *USING THE WALK WITH POINTS AND BRUSHES*
     alternating sides
     four counts

(1) Step left
     Point right
     Step right
     Point left

(2) Step and point three times
     Step forward on count one

(3) Repeat a and b, using a brush forward

Arms: remain at sides or, move in opposition to working leg.

LX 2 *USING THE WALK WITH SMALL LEG SWINGS FORWARD AND BACK WITH EXTENDED KNEES, ALTERNATING SIDES, FOUR COUNTS*

(1) Step left
     Brush right leg forward, backward and forward
     Step right on count one

Arms: raised sideways

LX 3 *USING THE WALK WITH BODY BOUNCES FORWARD, ROLL-UP AND RELEVÉ*

> ⁴⁄₄ meter
> four measure
> sixteen counts

(1) Walk forward, left—right—left, three counts.
step right sideways (second position), on fourth count.

(2) Body bounces forward, rounded spine four times.

(3) Roll up, hip leading, four counts.

(4) Relevé, arms raising sideways, two counts
Return to flat position, arms lower to sides, two counts

Variations

(1) Insert a plié in second position; omit the relevé.

(2) Add a plié to the relevé, making it five measures of twenty counts.

LX 4 *USING A STYLIZED WALK, WITH ISOLATED BODY MOVEMENTS*

> may alternate
> ⁴⁄₄ meter
> four measures
> sixteen counts

(1) Jazz walk; swing the hips and circle the leg step left, right, left, right 4 counts.

(2) Bend and straighten knees in a parallel stride position four times, for 4 counts and snap fingers at the same time.

(3) Right shoulder roll, 2 counts left shoulder roll, 2 counts.

(4) Head roll, four counts.

LS EXPANDING AN EXPLORATORY STUDY

Next, we redefine and expand a study. It is from these expanded studies that we build our combinations and patterns.

LS 1 Expanding a skip into a step-hop in a high, flexed-knee position

LS 2 Expanding a step-hop into a straight leg back in arabesque

LS 3 Expanding the walk by toes touching first, followed by the heel

LS 4 Expanding a run by using the legs in a bent back-knee position, with toes barely touching backside

LS 5 Expanding the triplet

    A. using a triplet and one triplet turn with no alternation

    B. using a triplet and two triplet turns with alternating sides

    C. adding arm movements

    D. using a triplet with two pliés and a relevé

LS 1 *EXPANDING A SKIP INTO A STEP-HOP IN A HIGH FLEXED KNEE POSITION. (NOTE: WE DEFINE A ONE-SIDED SKIP AS A STEP-HOP)*

Warm Up

Have students practice low step-hops in place to experience the uneven rhythms of this movement

Action

step-hops with no alternation

Position

1. legs

   right leg straight

   left leg in high flexed knee position, toe pointed downward

   toes are pointed in the air

2. arms—in opposition

   right arm forward, shoulder level, palm down

   left arm sideward, shoulder level, palm down.

   swing arms from down to up as you hop to increase elevation

Action and Rhythm Cues

rhythm is uneven
step left (and)
step right and lift leg in high flexed position (one)
repeat with no alternation across the floor (and one, and one, etc.)

Teaching Sequence

1. Practice position and steps in spots
   a) on a flat foot
   b) rising on toe
   c) off the floor
2. Repeat a,b, and c, going across the floor

Challenges

Emphasizing form

   Can you see your ankle?

   Keep your body and working leg extended.

   Remember to use your arms!

Emphasizing distance

   Can you go across the floor in eight, (six, four) step-hops?

Emphasizing height

   How high can you step-hop into the air?

LS 2 *EXPANDING A STEP-HOP INTO A STRAIGHT LEG BACK IN ARABESQUE*

Action

A step-hop with leg extended behind in arabesque, no alternation, uneven rhythm.

Positions

1. Legs

   Legs are in the game position as in the step hop except the leg is in arabesque rather than in a flexed knee position

2. Arms

Both arms lift forward high

3. Body

remains upright throughout with eyes focused up on hop

Variation on step-hop-arabesque

Perform step-hop on each leg alternating sides. The rhythm is even. Emphasize the push off to achieve elevation.

Practice Sequence

Practice movements emphasizing plié and push off on flat and toe level before going off the floor.

LS 3 *EXPANDING THE WALK BY TOES TOUCHING FIRST FOLLOWED BY THE HEEL*

Converting a simple walk into the dancer's walk takes a great deal of practice and time. Introduce an uncomplicated walk to your beginners and they will easily perfect it as they become more advanced.

Action

Walk with toes touching first, followed by the heel

Teaching Cue

Reach forward with your toes

Teaching Hints

1. Emphasize
   a. smooth transfer of weight
   b. correct body alignment
   c. focus of eyes in line of direction
2. Suggested arm movements
   a. arms remain down at sides
   b. rounded arms lift forward as you walk four counts

   c. arms open wide sideways and down to sides as you
      walk

      upper back arch

      eyes to ceiling

      four counts

3. Use a creative assignment, by having students make up
   original arm movements that are continuous and flowing as
   they walk.

LS 4 *EXPANDING A RUN BY USING THE LEGS IN A BENT, BACK-KNEE POSITION WITH TOES BARELY TOUCHING BACKSIDE.*

Position

The run may be done in an upright position or at a slight angle, with head forward. The degree of success is high at the beginner's level

Action

Run with toes pointed, barely touching backside. Keep arms down at sides

Teaching Hint

Emphasize a light, bouncy run

Teaching Cue

Try to hit your backside with your feet.

LS 5A *EXPANDING THE TRIPLET BY USING A TRIPLET AND ONE TRIPLET TURN WITH NO ALTERNATION*

Before teaching the triplet turn, review the triplet in our exploratory locomotor section in Chapter 3. Remind your students to place their weight forward. An additional lead-up exercise for the triplet is having your students go across the floor in a lunge position.

Action

Triplet forward starting with right leg, triplet turn on left leg

Breakdown of triplet turn

1. Step-plié, on left leg
2. Step-pivot-relevé on right leg, ¼ turn to left
3. Step-pivot-relevé on left leg, ¾ turn continuing to the left, till you face the line of direction.

Teaching Cues

1. Turn in the direction of the plié leg
2. Down up, up. Down, turn, turn

LS 5B *EXPANDING THE TRIPLET STUDY BY USING A TRIPLET AND TWO TRIPLET TURNS WITH ALTERNATING SIDES*

Action

One triplet with two triplet turns alternating sides

Breakdown Cues
1. (triplet) down on right
   up on left
   up on right
      count: one, two, three
2. (turn) down on left
   turn on right leg
   turn on left leg
      count: two, two, three
3. (turn) down on right
   turn on left leg
   turn on right leg
      count: three, two, three
Repeat entire combination beginning on left leg.

Teaching Cue

Always step forward in the line of direction on the pivot turns.

Teaching Hint

1. Use "slow motion" teaching
2. Use any combination of triplets and triplet turns.

LS 5C *EXPANDING THE TRIPLET STUDY WITH ARM MOVEMENTS.*

1. Arms remaining in a static position for the beginner
   (a) hands on hips

      help maintain correct posture
   (b) arms in first position, oval-shaped, down at sides
2. Arms swinging simultaneously forward and back
   (a) first triplet

      both arms swing forward below shoulder level, palms down
   (b) second triplet

      both arms swing behind

LS 5D *EXPANDING THE TRIPLET STUDY WITh TWO PLIÉS AND A RELEVÉ*

Action

Step—plié, step—plié, step—relevé
   alternates
   ¾ meter
   arms at sides

Breakdown and Cues

Down on right, count one
down on left, count two
up on right, count three; raise left leg low in arabesque

Variations

1. Free leg lifts extended forward
2. Free leg lifts extended sideways

3. Combine forward, sideways and backward lifts with extended leg

4. Flex free leg in all directions

Teaching Hint and Variation

1. Emphasize the feeling of lift by starting the triplet with a low arabesque on toe

   cues: up, down, down

2. Arms may spread sideways during the low arabesque

Part I

LCL *STRETCHING A STUDY INTO A COMBINATION BY JOINING A LOCOMOTOR STUDY WITH A LINKAGE IDEA*

Linkage ideas for locomotor studies provide interesting variations in level dynamics, or body design. These linkage ideas are essentially stationary in nature to provide a breathing spell between locomotor movements. They have been successful because they can be easily attached, and require only beginner's technique.

LCL *JOINING A LOCOMOTOR STUDY WITH A LINKAGE IDEA*

LCL 1 *CHANGING LEVEL*

a. Relevé: see Chapter 4 "Lead-ups to Series E—Relevé" (LdpE2)

b. Standing crouch

c. Back fall and rise

LCL 2 *CHANGING DYNAMICS*

a. Percussive or sustained movements

b. Forward and backward swings; see Chapter 4, "Lead-ups to Series F—Swings Series" (LdpF2 and LpdF3)

LCL 3 *CHANGING BODY DESIGN*

a. Body shape—see Chapters 8 and 9.

b. Plié in second position

c. Straight back lean on knees

d. Arabesque

LCL 4 *UTILIZING AN EXERCISE AS A LINKAGE IDEA*

LCL 1 CHANGING LEVEL

LCL 1b *STANDING CROUCH*

Position

Standing, body erect, feet parallel, under hips, arms down at sides, eyes focus straight ahead

Actions

1. Knees flex, heels remain on floor
body flexes forward at waist, back is rounded,
arms flex, fingertips close to shoulders
head downward, eyes focus in toward body
2. Return to starting position

Teaching Hint

Use this movement in a sustained manner. It is simple to execute and effective in appearance.

LCL 1c *BACK FALL AND RISE*

Position

Standing, body erect, feet parallel under hips, arms at sides

Action 1

Step forward on right leg (parallel or turned out fourth position) extending the body upward.

Action Cues

Focus up
Swing arms overhead
Lift left leg in back attitude position

Action 2

Move downward in a successional manner
  flex spine
  focus down
  lower arms
  place left foot on floor for balance

Action 3

Move body onto floor level.

Action Cues

Place ball of foot on floor, keep legs in flexed position
Place hands on floor for balance
Place backside on floor
Unravel legs to hook sitting position

Action 4

Roll down on floor and arch up with chest leading (for action cues see Chapter 4, Floor Series C)

Rise to standing position using an accelerated tempo

Action Cues

Keep left leg in hook position
Flex right leg under left leg on floor
Place weight forward on left foot
Place both hands on floor to maintain upward momentum

Teaching Hints

1. Alternate backfall on different legs
2. Repeat in different tempos (eights, fours, sixes, threes)
3. Add a hop off the floor to emphasize the dynamic quality of the movement.
4. Use the momentum of the chest arch to rise off the floor

LCL 2 *CHANGING DYNAMICS*

LCL 2a *CHOOSE ANY BODY PART OR EXERCISE AND PERFORM SHARPLY OR SMOOTHLY*

LCL 2b *USE FORWARD AND BACKWARD SWINGS; CHAPTER 4*

LCL 3 *CHANGING BODY DESIGN*

LCL 3a *USE A BODY SHAPE: CHAPTERS 8 AND 9*

LCL 3b *PLIÉ IN SECOND POSITION*

Position

Stride standing, arms at sides

Actions

1. Bend knees

   arms raise sideways below shoulder level, palms down
2. Return to starting position

Challenge

Can you plié in second position keeping your body erect and your knees over your toes?

Teaching Cue

Keep heels on the floor

Teaching Hints

1. Use different arm movements
   a. raise arms sideways up to a rounded overhead position
   b. raise arms forward parallel to floor, palms facing each other

LCL 3c *STRAIGHT BACK LEAN ON KNEES*

Position

Double kneeling

   kneeling on both knees, spine erect, knees under hips, legs and feet slightly apart, toes uncurled, arms down at sides, focus ahead

Action

Lean back from the knee joints and return to original position

Challenge

Can your body keep a straight line from the top of your head through your shoulders, waist, pelvis and knees?

Teaching Hints

1. Practice this movement for thigh stretch using a slow tempo and repeat no more than four times.
2. Challenge students to lean farther back as their abdominal strength increases.
3. Give your students an opportunity to check each other's alignment.
4. Use different arm positions.

LCL 3d *ARABESQUE*

Variations to change shape of arabesque

a. Arch torso slightly backward, head up, focus up, arms sideways, shoulder level, standing leg extended.
b. Pitch torso forward, parallel to floor, head parallel to floor focus down

   arms parallel forward

   standing leg flexed

Teaching Hints

1. Stress oppositional pull between arms, and leg.
2. Use any mixture of arms, torso and standing leg positions

LCL 4 *UTILIZING AN EXERCISE AS A LINKAGE IDEA*

Use an exercise with a locomotor study to create a combination. This provides a practical application of skills learned.

Procedure

1. Use a basic exercise and review its proper execution.
2. Use a locomotor study that has been practiced successfully.

3. Pair off students of approximate height. Have them work together and travel across on the diagonal.

4. Use this procedure as a device for review, correction, or evaluation.

5. Use this format as the basis for a creative assignment to be practiced and demonstrated in one period.

Example of an Assignment

Connect two triplets with a standing movement based on an exercise in class, making a total count of four threes. Create your own arm movements to be performed with the triplets. Be sure you can repeat your sequence.

Example of a Combination

a. triplet (right, left, right)

b. triplet (left, right, left)

c. point forward (right leg)

d. point sideways (right leg)

Arms

a. right arm circling; triplet

b. left arm circling; triplet

c. both arms circle overhead; point toe forward

d. both arms out sideways; point toe to the side

Counts

a. one, two, three

b. two, two, three

c. three, two, three

d. four, two, three

Use this creative assignment as a valuable teaching aid. Your students will:

1. learn to incorporate counts into an exercise

2. determine the starting and working legs

3. create arm movements

4. learn how to determine the continuity of a combination

5. practice for synchronization

6. interact with one another through assistance and encouragement

7. demonstrate a performance awareness

Teaching Hints

1. Emphasize synchronization and dynamic performance

2. Allow outstanding pupils to perform for the class.

3. Add more counts to a sequence by using several different exercises to form a locomotor pattern.

Part II
Locomotor Combinations and Patterns

Remember, our definition for a locomotor combination consists of two different movements. For example, a combination may be two different locomotor movements, or one locomotor movement and one linkage idea.

A locomotor pattern can include three or more movement ideas. For example, three different locomotor movements, or two different locomotor movements and one linkage idea.

GROUP PROBLEM-SOLVING TECHNIQUES

As you begin working on combinations or patterns, it is advantageous to introduce group-solving techniques. The class is divided into small groups in order to create combinations or patterns within a framework of guidelines and general rules. General rules are as follows; uniformity of performance, definite counts or rhythms strictly adhered to, and transitions made so that repetition is possible. Each group performs, and comments by the class are encouraged.

GUIDELINE A—CREATING A MOVEMENT COMBINATION

1. Give one locomotor movement to the entire class.

2. Ask each group to add another locomotor movement or linkage idea, for example: 4 runs forward and four jumps in place, or 4 runs forward and an arabesque.

GUIDELINE B—CREATING A MOVEMENT PATTERN

1. Give one linkage idea to the entire class.
2. Ask each group to select two different locomotor movements and attach these to the linkage idea.

   Example—Plié in second position and 2 triplets and 2 step-hops; or 4 walks forward and standing crouch and 2 jumps in place.

GUIDELINE C—CREATING A NEW PATTERN BY VARYING THE COUNT SEQUENCE

1. Give a pattern to the entire class, for example: four walks, four jumps, 4 step-hops.
2. Ask each group to select the number of times a movement is repeated, for example: six walks, 2 jumps, 2 step-hops.

GUIDELINE D—

1. Give a pattern comprised of five or more different movements to the entire class moving in the line of direction, for example: 4 runs, back fall and rise, 2 triplets, standing crouch, 2 jumps.
2. Require each group to evolve a new pattern by rearranging the original sequence and direction of the movements, for example: 2 triplets forward, backfall and rise, 2 jumps, standing crouch, 4 runs backward.

CREATIVE VARIATIONS BASED ON GROUP SOLVING TECHNIQUE

Using each group's original pattern, or your own, other variations can be made.

1. Change the original position of the arms
2. Use different spatial formations
3. Imitate a musical round
4. Change direction of a movement
5. Require each group to make up their own variation

As you can see, locomotor combinations and patterns have been creatively applied for use in your lessons. To further explore the creative application of movements learned in the technique class, see Chapters 8 and 9.

YOUR GUIDE TO COMBINATIONS AND PATTERNS

(In Order of Difficulty)

LC 1—Walks and Runs

LPL 1—Walks, Crouch and Skips

LC 2—Slides and Gallops

LC 3—Slides and Jumps

LC 4—Gallops and Jumps

LP 1—Slides, Gallops and Jumps

LPL 2—Walks, Shape, Jumps and Slides

LC 5—Runs and Jumps

LC 6—Runs and Step-Hops

LC 7—One Triplet, One Triplet turn

LC 8—Two Triplets, One Triplet turn

LP 2—Triplet, Triplet turn, Leg swings

LC 9—Triplet, Two Alternating Triplet turns

LC 10—Two Triplets, Arabesque

LPL 3—Triplet, Triplet turn, Arabesque

LC 11—Two Triplets, Two Step-Hops

LC 12—Triplets and Walks

LP 3—Triplet, Triplet turn, Two one-sided Skips

LP 4—Triplet, Triplet turn, Swings, Backfall, Chest arch and Rise, Step-Hops

LC 1 *WALKS AND RUNS*

(Using Changes in Direction)

Description

walk forward, circle walk, walk backward, run forward

Example

four walks forward, lift arms forward and overhead

four walks in a circle, open arms sideways and down to sides four walks backward, lift arms forward shoulder level

eight runs forward, open arms to sideward position

Teaching Hints

Practice locomotor movements

Practice arm movements in place

Perform combination with arm movements

Creative variations using group solving techniques

1. Problem: Vary the sequence of movements

   Example:

   runs forward

   walk backward

   circle walk

   walk forward

Stretching a combination into a pattern using a linkage idea (LPL)

2. Problem—Add an eight-count axial motion to your own phrase, or to the original combination

   ### Extending a combination into a pattern by adding additional locomotor movements

3. Problem—Add two jumps somewhere in the combination

   ### Stretching a combination into a pattern by using a linkage idea with locomotor studies

LPL 1 *WALKS, CROUCH AND SKIPS*

Description

walks forward, crouch, skips forward

Example

four walks forward, arms at sides

four count crouch, (see crouch—linkage ideas)

four counts to original position.

four skips forward, alternating sides—normal skip, natural arm swing

LC 2 *SLIDES AND GALLOPS*

Description

slide right, slide left, gallop forward

Example

Moving in line of direction:
    two slides right, arms out sideways
    one-half turn, arms down at sides
    two slides left, arms out sideways
    one-quarter turn—to line of direction, arms down at sides
    four gallops forward, arms forward shoulder level

LC 3 *SLIDES AND JUMPS*

Description

slide right, slide left, jump

Example

Moving in line of direction:
    two slides right, arms out sideways
    one-half turn, arms at sides
    two slides left, arms out sideways
    one-quarter turn, arms at sides
    four jumps in place, arms at sides

Variation

Jumps may be done in one-quarter, one-half, or full turns

LC 4 *GALLOPS AND JUMPS*

Description

gallop forward, jump in place

Example

Moving in line of direction
    four gallops forward, arms forward shoulder level
    four jumps in place, arms down at sides

Extending combinations 2, 3, 4, into a pattern

LP 1 *SLIDES, GALLOPS AND JUMPS*

Description

slide right, slide left, gallop forward, jump in place

Example

two slides right
one-half turn
two slides left
one-quarter turn
two gallops forward
two jumps in place

Extending combinations 2, 3, 4, into a pattern with a linkage idea

LPL 2 *WALKS, SHAPE, JUMPS AND SLIDES*

Description

walk forward, assume a letter shape, jumps in one-quarter turns changing direction, slide right, slide left, walk forward

Example

Moving in line of direction
    four walks forward, arms at sides
    four counts to form a letter shape
    four counts to original position

four jumps with quarter-turns, (jumps complete a full turn) arms down at sides

two slides right, arms sideways

two slides left, arms sideways

four walks forward, arms down at sides.

Creative variations based on walks, shape, jumps slides (LPL 2)

Problems

1. Vary the sequence of movements
2. Vary the number of times you repeat a movement
3. Add a percussive movement which portrays a sense of reaching. Hold pose for four counts.

Example

Moving in line of direction

two walks forward

six counts to form a letter shape

percussive reaching movement in 2 counts, hold pose 4 counts

jump one full turn around

3 slides to the right sideward

two walks forward

LC 5 *RUNS AND JUMPS*

Description

run forward, jump in place

Example

two runs forward

two jumps in place

arms at sides, body extended

Variation of jumps

one-half turns or full turns

jump with knees to chest, hands slap thighs

jump with legs apart, hands clapping above head

jump with toes touching backside

Creative variation using group solving technique

Problem

Combine any number of runs with different types of jumps

LC 6 *RUNS AND STEP-HOPS*

Description

run, run, step-hop alternating sides

Example

run on right

run on left

step-hop on right

Repeat combination beginning on left leg

Teaching Hint

Stress the distance covered on runs and elevation on step-hops.

TRIPLET COMBINATIONS AND PATTERNS

Triplets are valuable to a beginner's course of study in dance. Students become highly motivated because they experience success early in its performance. Triplets provide a simple traveling step and a marvelous transitional step.

Triplets performed with turns or another locomotor movement or connecting step make a combination. These triplet combinations can be as varied as your imagination will allow. The following list may be used as a point of departure. (LC 10 is presented as an example)

LC 7 One Triplet, One Turn

LC 8 Two Triplets, One Turn

LC 9 One Triplet, Two Alternating Turns

LC 10 Two Triplets, Arabesque

LC 11 Two Triplets, Two Step-Hops

Teaching Hint

Always complete the triplet steps or the triplet turn before going onto the next movement.

Example LC 10: Alternating combination

Triplet: step on right, left, right

Triplet: step on left, right, left

Arabesque: step on *right* leg, and left leg extends upward behind

Repeat combination beginning with left.

LC 12 *Triplets and Walks*

Description—Triplets forward, 2 walks forward, in line of direction—no alternation.

       arms down at sides; triplets

       add original arm movements to the walk

       (Note: Each walk takes 3 counts)

Creative variations based on triplets and walks

Problems

1. Insert a standing exercise as a linkage idea anywhere in the combination.
2. Insert a twelve-count body shape as a linkage idea anywhere in the combination.

Stretching a triplet combination into a pattern:

    Using the linkage idea—

        LPL 3 Triplet, Triplet Turn, Arabesque

    Using a standing exercise—

        LP 2 Triplet, Triplet Turn, Leg Swings Forward and Back

Using a locomotor movement—

> LP 3 Triplet, Triplet Turn, Two Step-Hops

Using axial and locomotor skills in various directions, levels, and dynamics—

> LP 4 Triplet, Triplet Turn, Swings, Backfall, Chest arch and Rise, Step-Hops

LP 4 TRIPLET, TRIPLET TURN, SWINGS, BACKFALL, CHEST ARCH AND RISE, STEP-HOPS

Description

Facing line of direction:

> two triplets forward—begin on right leg
>
> two alternating triplet turns
>
> traveling swings to the right
>
> traveling swings to the left
>
> > (see standing series F 2)
>
> back fall, chest arch and rise
>
> > (see linkage idea LCL 1c)
>
> 4 step-hops in a circular pattern to the right and 2 step-hops to exit

The following list provides some of the essential ingredients for creating interesting movements, combinations, and patterns.

1. Variations in time:

   tempo, meter accent, rhythm

2. Variations in energy:

   sustained, percussive, vibratory, swinging

3. Variations in space:

   direction, range, focus, level, design

4. Incorporation of various movement styles:

   ballet, jazz, ethnic, folk

5. Isolation of body parts and contrasting body parts:

   movements of arms against legs

6. Creation of transitional ideas by using axial movements, turns, falls, rolls

7. Use of a specific dance theme:

   fall-recovery, flex-extend, contract-release

8. Use of various movement themes as the core of a dance pattern:

   suspension vs. collapse, control vs. out-of-control

9. Use of established exercises and modifying them

10. Creation of original movements may be derived from a distortion or exaggeration of a practiced dance step, or taken from everyday gestures, or motions used in sport and work activities.

A Sample Technique Plan For Beginners

Approximately forty minutes

CHAPTER 4

Starting position

A1   Body bounces, head to feet

A2   Body bounces, head to knees—long sitting

A4   Culminating position

B1   Flex and point toes, stride sitting

A3   Body bounces, chest to thigh, stride sitting

Transition to long sitting

B4   Culminating position, erect sitting

Transition to hook sitting

C1a   Roll down, middle spine leading

   b   Roll up, top of head leading

C2a   Roll down, middle spine leading

   b   Arch up, chest leading

Transition to double kneeling

On Spots

CHAPTER 4

Lead-up steps to Series D

Ldp   D1 Body stretch upwards

Ldp   D2 Body flexing downwards using a successional movement

Ldp   D4 Straighten body using a successional movement

**A Sample Lesson Plan For Advanced Beginners
(Approximately One Hour)**

Starting position: frog sitting

CHAPTER 4

    A1   Body bounces: head to feet

           Transition to stride sitting

    B1   Flex and point toes

    A3   Body bounce: chest to thigh, stride sitting

           Transition to long sitting

    B2   Body bounces with flexed feet, long sitting

    B3   Body bounces with pointed toes, long sitting

           Transition to frog sitting

CHAPTER 6

    A5   Knee bounce to floor stretch, frog sit

           Transition to hook sitting

CHAPTER 4

    C1a   Roll down, middle spine leading

     b   Roll up, top of head leading

    C2a   Roll down, middle spine leading

     b   Arch up chest leading

    C3a   Side twist, roll down, right side

     b   Side twist, roll up, left side

CHAPTER 5

    LC7 Triplet, triplet turn

CHAPTER 4

    F4 Traveling swings to the right and left with step-hops

Creative Variations Based On
Group Solving Technique

1. Create arm placements for the triplet and triplet turn.
2. Connect an arabesque for six counts anywhere within the pattern.
3. Add a change of direction in one of the following:

   a. triplet, triplet turn

   b. swinging movements

   c. arabesque

·→✤ 6 ✤←·

Refining the Language of Dance

This chapter assumes your class has experienced the activities as described in Chapters 3, 4, and 5, and is ready for further refinement and challenge.

We introduce this chapter with a challenging series titled Spanish Arch. The supplements continue the progression of skills in the series. They should be combined with or joined to the previous series for optimum results. We have added more transitional movements to expand our linkage ideas. Use them to connect one series to another, or include them in a combination and pattern for dynamic change.

The effective method of moving an exercise across the floor is also continued. Exploratory studies are expanded to include prances, leaps, and an advanced jumping sequence.

Additional locomotor combinations and patterns are presented on a more advanced level. They will facilitate preparation of lesson plans and provide your students with a progressive learning experience.

To facilitate your understanding of this chapter, we have divided the material into three sections; Section I, Series and Supplements; Section II, Transitional Ideas and Moving an Exercise; and Section III, Expanding an Exploratory Study, Combinations and Patterns.

YOUR GUIDE TO REFINING THE LANGUAGE OF DANCE

SECTION I

Series H Spanish Arch—Floor

Supplements to Series A—Floor

127

A5 Knee bounce to floor stretch—Frog sit

A6 Body bounce with straight and round spine—Frog sit

Supplements to Series B—Floor

B5 Side body bounces—ear to thigh—Stride sitting

B6 Knee foot flexion and extension—Stride sitting

B7 Extend B7 with a roll down and up with bounces forward—Stride sitting

Supplement to Series C—Floor

C5 A leg stretch using abdominal muscle control—Long lying

Supplements to Series D—Standing

D4 Alternate forward bounces with round and extended spine

D5 Bounce sideways with arms extended overhead

D6 Bounce bending downward to the floor close to the outside of leg with a round spine and arms reaching downward

D7 Bounce on the diagonal with an extended spine parallel to the floor and arms reaching outward

D8 Bounce forward with flexed knees, round spine

Two examples of a bouncing sequence

Supplements to Series E—Standing

E6 Use all ballet positions with appropriate arm movements

Example of a simple port de bras:

E7 Plié with a raising and lowering of heels (grand plié)

E8 Relevé with a flexion of knees and lowering of heels

E9 Plié with a raising of heels and extension of knees

Supplements to Series F—Standing

F7 Swing to the side using a three step turn

F8 Deep swing to the side with a plié

Supplements to Series G—Standing

G5 Include third and fifth positions and/or vary the rhythm

G6 Raise and lower the leg using a toe-knee touch position

G7 Combine a toe-knee touch position with a brush or kick

G8 Développé forward, sideward, backward

G9 Leg swings using a bent leg in a fixed position

SECTION II

Transitional Ideas

T1   Body curl into a knee scale—Floor

T2   Hip lift—Floor

T3   Roll over—Floor

T4   Standing spiral turn to a sitting position and rise

Addition—Standing spiral turn to the floor with body circling

T5   Side fall from a sitting position

T6   Side fall from a kneeling position

T7   Side fall from a standing position

LX Moving An Exercise

LX5 Stepping with a bent leg swing

LX6 Développé with balance and walk

SECTION III

LS Expanding an Exploratory Study

LS6   a Prances

             b Pedals

LS7   A run evolving into a leap

LS8   A walk evolving into a leap

LS9   A triplet turn with two pivot turns

LS10   A triplet with a balance on toe

LS11   A jumping sequence

LC Locomotor combinations

LC12   Runs and leap

LC13   Pedals and jumps

LC14   Walk and leap

LC15   Triplet, plié-hop-arabesque

LP Locomotor Patterns

LP5   Triplet, triplet turn, pivot turn, plié in second, plié hop arabesque

LP6   Triplet, triplet turn, triplet balance, two step-hops

LP7   Triplet, triplet turn, arabesque with a hop

LP8   Triplet, triplet turn, plié-hop-arabesque, fall and rise

LP9   Runs, jumps, arabesque, plié-hop-arabesque, crouch

SECTION I

SERIES H

Spanish Arch

Spanish arch is an extension of our series on the floor level. It is a sequence of movements divided between a stretch of the body in an extended back arched position and a curling up of the body into a ball

POSITION—(See Photo 1)

Sitting in fourth position:

right flexed knee in front

left leg flexed behind

right arm curved across—chest level

left arm extended sideways—shoulder level

Action 1a Circle body and left arm forward low ending in a high arched position; pelvis remains on floor (See Photo 2)

chest facing right side

left arm ends in curved position overhead

right forearm flexed on floor, palm up, aligned with left knee

Photo 1. Series H—Spanish Arch Position

Photo 2. Series H—Spanish Arch, Action 1A

weight on right forearm

focus upward on left palm

1b Reverse circle to original position

Action 2a Fold over forward in a tight ball on the right side (See Photo 3) pull left knee, left arm inward

Photo 3. Series H—Spanish Arch, Action 2A

tuck head in

right hand on floor

2b Return to original position

Action 3a Circle left arm around and push pelvis thru and upward off the floor (See Photo 4)

balance weight on knees and right hand

right arm extended

left arm curved

focus on left hand

3b Circle back to original position

Action 4 Repeat ball-like position

Action 5 Circle around, push pelvis thru off the floor and open left knee outwards (See Photo 5)

move toes of left foot closer to toes of right foot

open left knee outwards

lift both heels off ground

balance on right hand, right knee and toes of both feet

use arm movements as described in Action 3a

Photo 4. Series H—Spanish Arch, Action 3A

Photo 5. Series H—Spanish Arch, Action 5

Action 6a Assume ball-like position
Action 6b Return to original position

Suggested Cues

1. Circle body, hips on floor
   Return

2. Curl up
   Return

3. Circle body, hips off
   Return

4. Curl up

5. Circle with hips off, open knee

6. Curl up
   Return

Note—Counts vary with your objectives. Four-quarter time is used for each action if a smooth quality is desired. Vary the meter accordingly to produce dynamic changes at any point within the series. For example, Action 3a may be performed in a percussive manner.

SUPPLEMENTS TO SERIES A

A5 Action Knee bounce to floor stretch

Position

Frog sitting (A1)
   hands grasping ankles

Description

Bounce both knees to floor
   sixteen counts
Push right knee to floor
   allow rebound
   use right hand
   slow eight counts
Repeat on left side

Press both knees to floor allowing for rebound
 bend body forward
 place elbow pressure on knees
 slow four counts

Culmination

Press forward with extended spine
 low to floor
 two counts
Move to upright position
 two counts

A6 Action Body bounce with straight and round spine

Position

Frog sitting

Description

Bounce forward with a round spine
 focus inward
Bounce forward with a straight spine

 body is on a low diagonal plane from base of spine to top
 of head
 focus diagonally forward on floor

Teaching Hints

Use a mirror or buddy system to check placement
Use diminishing counts

SUPPLEMENTS TO SERIES B

B5 Action Side body bounces—ear to thigh

Position

Stride sitting
 arms sideways shoulder level

palms down
toes pointed

Description

Bounce to the side over right leg
    right ear to thigh
    right side, waist flexed
    left side, waist stretched
arms
    left arm curved overhead
    right arm curved underneath
Repeat on opposite side
Bounce forward with straight spine
    arms in original position
Move to upright position

Variation

Alternate with flexed feet

B6 Action Knee foot flexion and extension

Position

Sitting in wide second with legs extended
    arms extended sideways
    focus center

Description

Flex knee and ankle
    arm on working side curved overhead (See Photo 6)
Extend knee, ankle
    arm extends parallel above leg palm up
    focus toward working leg
Repeat on opposite side
Flex both legs at the same time
    arms curved overhead (See Photo 7)

Photo 6. Description—Flex Knee and Ankle

Photo 7. Flex both legs at the same time, with arms curved overhead.

Extend both legs
   lower arms sideways to shoulder level
Push hips forward to widen legs; use hands behind hips on

floor to assist stretch

Repeat sequence

B7 Action Extend Action B7 (leg flexion—extension) by adding a roll down and up with bounces forward Perform with appropriate arm and head movements

Cues and suggested counts

Position—Stride sitting

Flex right leg, extend four counts

Flex left leg, extend four counts

Roll down with a round spine and close legs simultaneously

    arms meet together in front of body

    two counts

Roll up

    round spine

    two counts

Bounce forward four times

    round spine with relaxed neck, arms relaxed on legs

Spread legs wide percussively on one count

    hold for three counts

    arms spread sideways, shoulder level

    focus forward

SUPPLEMENT TO SERIES C

C5 Action A leg stretch using abdominal muscle control

    Movements other than bounces are performed in a sustained manner.

Position

Long lying

Description

Bring one knee to chest

Bounce knee against chest

  arms hugging knee

Extend leg toward ceiling with a flexed foot; then lower leg in an extended position to floor

Repeat on other side

Bring both knees to chest

Bounce knees against chest

Extend legs toward ceiling with flexed feet; lower legs in an extended position to floor

  arms out at sides, palms on floor

Suggested counts

four counts for each step

Variation

Raise each extended leg toward ceiling using an extended foot and bring extended leg to floor with a flexed foot

Teaching Hint

Repeat sequence in a smooth manner by eliminating the bounces. Use two counts for each movement.

SUPPLEMENTS TO SERIES D STANDING

The following actions are performed standing in parallel second.

D4 Action Alternate forward bounces with a round and extended spine

Position (See Photo 8)

Torso flexed forward at hips; chest parallel to floor;

Arms extended alongside ears; palms facing;

Focus down

Photo 8. Position D4

Teaching Hint

Reach forward with arms.

D5 Action Bounce sideways with arms extended overhead
            (See Photo 9)

Position

Similar to D2 except for the placement of arms.

Arms extend overhead (D4) to one side.

Teaching Hints

Start movement at center and return to center before change
of side

Maintain a frontal posture throughout the movement.

Lift torso and arms to upright position with a deep breath.

D6 Action Bounce bending downward to the floor close to
            the outside of the leg (See Photo 10)

Photo 9. Action D5

Photo 10. Action D6

Position

Similar to D1a except for the direction of the bounce,
    spine rounded

arms reaching downward

focus down

D7 Action Bounce on the diagonal with an extended spine parallel to the floor and arms reaching outward (See Photo 11)

Position

Similar to D4, except for body direction

arms are parallel to the floor

Teaching Hints

Keep the extended parallel position when changing sides.

swing body forward (D4)

knees are extended

Alternate this action with D6.

Alternate this action with D5.

D8 Action Bounce forward (D1) with flexed knees, round spine

Position—loose body position

focus between legs

rounded spine

relaxed arms

Teaching Hints

Alternate this action with any other D action to relax back, arm and neck muscles.

Use when changing sides, (D7)

Variation

Drop forward in the flexed-knee position and remain still for the required number of counts.

Photo 11. Action D7

Series D provides you with numerous actions so that you have the opportunity to create your own bouncing sequence, and counts to challenge your more advanced students.

Two examples of a bouncing sequence:

1. Position—Stride standing, feet parallel or turned out, arms down at sides

D1   Bounce bending forward, arms downward

D4   Bounce forward with extended spine; arms parallel, swing to the side with extended spine

D6   Bounce bending downward to the floor close to the outside of the leg, arms downward

D7   Bounce on the diagonal with an extended spine, arms parallel

D5   Side bend with arms overhead lift upright to center, and repeat the sequence on the opposite side

2. Position—Stride standing, feet parallel or turned out, arms extended overhead

D4   Bounce forward with extended spine, arms parallel swing to the side with extended spine

D5   Bounce, side bend with arms extended overhead on right side

D7   Bounce on the right diagonal, extended spine, arms parallel, swing to left side with extended spine

D5   Side bend with arms extended overhead on left side

D7   Bounce on left diagonal, extended spine, arms parallel, swing to center with extended spine, arms parallel

D4   Bounce forward with extended spine, arms parallel

D8   Rest forward with flexed knees, round spine, arms and head relaxed, downward

D3b   Culminating position, slowly roll up to erect standing, arms at sides

SUPPLEMENTS TO SERIES E STANDING

E6 Action Extend series E by introducing the grand plié and using positions with appropriate arm movements

A demi-plié may be defined as a bending of the knees with heels remaining on the floor. A grand plié is a deeper bending of the knees so that the heels rise naturally from the floor. In both instances, pressing the heels to the floor is the first step in recovery.

All the actions within series E should be performed in all ballet positions, with arm movements. Practice with the use of a barre or its equivalent.

Introduce simple arm and head movements to encourage proper bearing and grace.

Example of a simple port de bras

In a sustained manner

Position

Standing in fifth position, arms rounded below, focus forward

Description

Raise rounded arms to forward position, chest level

Right arm moves sideward, shoulder level, focus follows right hand

Left arm moves sideward, focus follows left hand

Lower both arms simultaneously to original position, focus forward

Repeat with rounded arms raising above head, and each arm descending sideward to shoulder level.

Turn palms down when lowering to original position

A sequence using plié and relevé need not be monotonous if you experiment with changes in meter. Use the following actions to vary the plié and relevé.

Each step in the following actions is performed in one or two counts.

E7 Action Plié with a raising and lowering of heels

In a percussive manner

Cues

Demi-plié

Heels up

Heels down

Straighten knees

E8 Action Relevé with a flexion of knees and lowering of heels

Cues

Relevé

Flex knees

Heels down

Straighten knees

E9 Action Plié with a raising of the heels and extension of the knees

Cues

Demi-plié

Heels up

Straighten knees (relevé)

Heels down

SUPPLEMENTS TO SERIES F STANDING

F7 Action Swing to the side using a three step turn
Use the arms, on the third swing to propel the body into a three-step turn.
This action can be used as a variation to F2 and can be inserted anywhere within the series.

F8 Action Deep swing to the side with a bending of the knees (plié position)
Synchronize the descent of the arms with a bending of the knees in stride position. (See Photo 12)

Body drops forward

focus down

arms downward with hands brushing floor

The position on the lateral lift involves a moment of suspension.

Body, legs, arms, extended,

arms extend diagonally upward

focus toward hands

SUPPLEMENTS TO SERIES G STANDING

G5 Action Extend series G (Point, Brush, Kick) by including third and fifth positions and/or varying the rhythm
Practice series G in third and fifth positions. Use forward, sideward, and backward directions. Challenge your class by using variations in time. Do the movement on the beat in quarter-note time and alternate with eighth note rhythm.
The following actions (G6, G7 and G8) are based on the ballet position développé. In développé, the toes of the working leg glide up the side of the standing leg and stop at the knee; from this position, the leg extends toward the required direction.

G6 Action Raise and lower the leg using a toe-knee touch position
This action is practiced in a percussive manner; the foot goes directly to the knee.

Photo 12. Action F8—Synchronize the descent of the arms while bending the knees in stride position.

Position

Standing parallel feet under hips

arms at sides

Description

1. Lift flexed knee in forward direction to toe-knee touch position
2. Swing knee to side in turned out position
3. Swing knee forward

   Lower leg to place

G7 Action Combine a toe-knee touch position with a brush or kick

Use forward, sideward and backward directions. Practice in a percussive manner, with foot going directly to knee.

Position

Standing parallel or turned out first position

Description

1. Lift knee in toe-touch position
   Lower knee back to place (return)
2. Kick or brush leg forward in extended knee position
   return to place with extended leg
3. Lift knee in toe-knee touch position
   Développé the leg forward return to place with extended
   leg
4. Repeat on opposite side

G8 Action Développé forward, sideward, backward
   This action is practiced in a sustained manner using all
directions from a ballet first position.

Description

Développé and extend leg forward

Return to place with extended leg

Repeat to the side

Repeat to the back

Teaching Hint

Try to keep the knee in a fixed position during the extension of
the leg.

Variation

Bend the standing leg as the leg goes into développé.

G9 Action Leg swings, using a bent leg in a fixed position

Position

Standing in parallel or first

Arms extended sideways shoulder level

Description

Swing knee forward and back, going through first position as
you swing toes brushing floor

Teaching Hint

Flexed leg remains constant from hip to toes

Body is erect, toes are pointed

Swing leg through first position as leg moves forward and back

Variation

A combination of a flexed knee and extended leg swing.

Description

Swing flexed knee inward across the body

Swing an extended leg turned out to the side, moving through the first position as you swing the leg

SECTION II

TRANSITIONAL IDEAS

Linkage ideas were discussed in Chapter 5 "Moving Through Space." They were used to stretch a locomotor study into a combination. The following exercises are used as transitional ideas to connect floor, sitting or standing movements, as well as locomotor movements.

T1 Action Body curl into a knee scale

Position

Crawl position on all fours

Description

Touch right knee to forehead (See Photo 13)

    curl body inward, round spine

    flexed neck, focus inward

Arabesque on knee (See Photo 14)

    extend right leg backward high

    arch back

    raise head, focus forward or upward

Photo 13. Action T1 Description—Touch right knee to forehead.

Photo 14. Action T1—Arabesque on knee.

Teaching Hint

Repeat movement four times on a side before returning to the crawl position.

Use a transitional movement from a floor to a standing series. After arabesque, bring right leg through to a half-kneeling position and stand up.

T2 Action Hip lift

Position (See Photo 15)

Half-hook sitting
    legs
        left leg extended, toes pointed
        right leg flexed, foot flat on floor
    arms
        left hand flat on floor, behind left hip
        right arm flexed at elbow on inside of right knee
        fingers touch head or shoulder
    body
        rounded spine, between legs
    focus inward
        chin on chest

Photo 15. Position T2

Description (See Photo 16)

Perform the following two steps simultaneously, initiating the movement with the right arm extending upward.

Stretch right arm vertically upward

Raise hips high off the floor
  body extended backward with a slight arch
  legs maintain original placement:
      right leg, slightly flexed
      right foot, under hip
      right heel, lifted off floor, weight carried by toes
      left leg, extended to floor
      left foot, flat on floor
  arms
      right, extended toward ceiling, fingers stretched
      left, extended with hand flat on floor, hand supports weight
  focus
      upward to right hand

Note—There are three points of contact with the floor—left foot, left hand, and the toes of the right foot.

Lower body and flex right arm; return to original position

Teaching Hints

Raise and lower into position, using four counts each.

Change the count so that the movement becomes slow and sustained.

Raise the hips in a percussive manner, and lower slowly.

Be innovative and use all three hints in your sequence.

Addition Roll-Over

The following movement precedes the hip lift, and can be easily inserted within the culmination of series C in Chapter 4.

Photo 16. Description T2

T3 Action Roll-over with leg flexed behind into a hip-lift

Position

Prone, arms flexed, hands flat beneath shoulders
elbows close to sides of body

Description

1. Move into the hip-lift position (See Photo 17)

   Initiate movement with a raised right foot, followed by
   torso rotation toward the flexed leg:

   > flex right knee with toes leading,
   >
   > place leg in half-hook position, foot flat on floor
   >
   > rotate body forward into a sitting position
   >
   > place arms in hip-lift position, left hand slides closer to
   > hip

2. Perform a hip-lift and return to original position

3. Reverse the roll-over

   turn body toward extended left leg

   lower body into a prone position, straighten right leg, place
   hands in roll-over position

Photo 17. Description T3-1

4. Begin again with left foot moving to half-hook sitting position

Cues and Suggested Counts

Roll-over:		one, two, three
Position:	hip-lift sitting	four
Lift:	hips off floor	five
Hold:	extension	six
Position:	hip-lift sitting	seven, eight
Turn:	and lower to prone position	nine, ten

Teaching Hint

Decrease the number of counts as proficiency is acquired. Stress the dynamics of the movement.

T4 Action Standing spiral turn to a sitting position and rise

Position

Standing in stride
   arms out sidewards—shoulder level
   palms down

Description

1. Twist torso to the right with a one-half turn to a sitting position

Breakdown Cues

rise on toes, maintain foot placement throughout

rotate body towards right side

lower hips to floor and sit (See Photo 18)

Finished position:

right leg crossed over left knee; leg is flexed vertically; foot flat on floor close to left knee; left leg flexed; flexed leg and foot resting underneath

2. Unwind with a one-half turn to the left, returning to your original standing position

Breakdown Cues:

place weight on right foot

turn torso to left side and rise to standing position

3. Repeat spiral turn to opposite side

Photo 18. Action T4-1—Lower hips to floor and sit.

Teaching Hint

Beginners can use their hands pushing against the floor to facilitate the rise. As proficiency increases, arms remain at shoulder level throughout the entire movement.

Suggested Application

1. Spiral toward right side into a sitting position
2. Unwind legs to hook-sitting
3. Perform C2 (roll down—arch up) of Series C, Chapter 4
4. Cross right foot over left knee
5. Unwind to stride standing

Addition

Standing spiral turn to the floor with body circling

Description

Spiral turn to the sitting position,

    unwind legs to hook-sitting,

    place legs in fourth position, right flexed in front, left flexed behind

arms

    right curved forward chest level

    left extended sideways

    Circle arms on floor, starting from left toward right, torso duplicates arm circling

        body flexed low to floor

    Form a diagonal line from left knee to right hand on floor (See Photo 19)

Continue arm circling to the left. Torso follows circular pattern set by the arms.

    turn on back (See Photo 20)

Reverse the circle, to return to original position, sitting in fourth by initiating action in left hip:

    reverse circling of arms, with left arms leading

    thrust head forward and around; this gives momentum to body circling

**Photo 19. Form a diagonal line from left knee to right hand on
floor.**

**Photo 20. Continue arm circling to left. Torso follows circular
pattern set by arms. Turn on back.**

return to hook-sitting

cross right leg over left knee and rise, making a ½ turn to
original stride position, facing front.

Teaching Hint

Facilitate the rise from the floor to a standing position by pushing against the floor with the right hand. As proficiency is achieved, speed is increased. It becomes a complete, smooth rotation from the standing level to a low level in a curved position. It is performed with acceleration, without the aid of the right hand.

THE SIDE FALL

Before performing a side fall from a standing position, one should experience this movement from a sitting and kneeling position. These positions and actions are used as linkage ideas to create further innovative combinations.

T5 Action Side fall from a sitting position

Position

Side sitting:

    right knee flexed forward, right foot close to left thigh

    left leg extended sideways, toes pointed

    both arms sideways to left side

Description

Circle arms in a counter clockwise direction into a low level slide to the floor

    slide right lateral side of body onto floor:

        both legs in extension, torso extended with right side on floor—left arm flexed right arm extended

        head leaning on right arm

Recover to original position

    press left hand against floor, lifting torso to original side sitting position

    move arms to original placement

T6 Action Side fall from a kneeling position

Position

Kneeling

arms extended above head in parallel position

Description

Duplicate the movements of arms and body as described in T5;

lower body to the floor and slide to the right

Return to original position

press left hand against floor

raise torso off floor

bend both knees

rise to kneeling position

arms to original position

Teaching Hint

Emphasize the oppositional pull of the upper body to the arms.

T7 Action A side fall from a standing position

Position

Standing, arms at sides

Description

Step forward on left foot; arms swing upwards above head, right leg bent behind

swing arms in prescribed pattern

lean torso away from the direction of the fall

lower hips to floor, bend left leg, tuck right leg underneath, right knee touches floor

slide sideways to the right ending in an extended position

return to original standing position

follow directions to T6 (to a kneeling position)

move left foot forward: weight on left foot and right knee transfer weight forward and stand

Variation

Perform the standing side fall with a hop. Start the movement with a hop.

Suggested Use of the Side Fall

Precede the side fall with F4. Swing to the side with coordinated arm movements. Use the slide, and step-hop into a side fall and add the roll-over hip-lift, (T3, T2) on the floor. Rise to standing.

LX MOVING AN EXERCISE

Any of the standing exercises as described in the advanced series G may be converted to a moving exercise by stepping forward on the working leg.

Challenge your students by using quarter-turns, spatial variations and directional change, such as moving backwards.

Use any of our linkage or transitional ideas for a level change. This will provide you with a creative combination based on an exercise. Add another locomotor movement and a more complex pattern will emerge.

LX5 Action Stepping with a bent leg swing (based on G9) 5 Description

Alternation

Step forward lift

Swing high with right bent leg, forward, backward, forward

Step right

Continue across the floor

Variations

Any one or more exercises in series G can be added to this action.

Example— Alternate the action of large bent swings with that of small straight leg swings. (LX2 brushes)

LX6 Action Développé with balance and walk

This movement reinforces the développé as described in action G8.

Description

No alternation

Step forward on left

Développé and extend right leg forward

Step forward right

Step forward left

Développé and extend right leg to the side

Step forward right, step forward left

Développé and extend right leg backward

Repeat on opposite side

Arms:

Raise arms sideways, shoulder level on the développé.

Lower arms on the walk.

SECTION III

LS EXPANDING AN EXPLORATORY STUDY

Expanding a run by using the legs in a front flexed position.

This movement has an even, rhythmic pattern similar to the run. An exaggerated high lift of the flexed leg is a prance. A lower leg lift from the floor is a pedal.

LS6a Prances

Action

Run with knees high in front; tilt body slightly backward, point toes, arms sideways, shoulder level.

Variations

Try prancing backward

Alternate with LS4 (knees in bent back position)

Example:

Four runs with flexed knees back

Four runs with flexed knees forward

LS6b Pedals

Action

A spring from one foot to the other with toes pointed off the floor

Position

Standing in parallel position, arms at sides

Teaching Hints

Practice on spots with tips of toes remaining in place.

Emphasize pressing the ankle and lower leg forward, pushing off the standing leg, standing tall, feeling bouncy.

Variations

1. Pedal backward

2. Use first position

Move sideways in third or fifth ballet position, alternate leg in front and back. Move across the floor using four prances and four pedals.

LS7 Expanding the Run into the Leap

The leap is a spring from one leg to the other, characterized by a moment of suspension in the air. It involves a burst of force and energy. Its purpose can be one of achieving height or gaining distance. Leaps have an even, rhythmic pattern.

The leap may be approached through different methods, but all methods are interrelated in one way or another. As noted in the locomotor exploratory section, runs can be one of the lead-up movements to leaps. A slow run may evolve into a leap.

Using Runs

Factors in common:

The run is performed at an even tempo.

There is a transfer of weight forward, from one leg to the other.

The leg, on landing, is in plié position.

Action

Leap with legs extended forward and backward

Description

Arms raised sideways, shoulder level or in opposition

Step left,

Brush and swing extended right leg in an upward and forward arc; tilt body slightly back. Push off with left leg,

Thrust body upwards; raise arms higher to help upward thrust.

Mid-air

Extend right leg forward and left leg back simultaneously,

Keep torso erect

Landing

Arabesque with right leg in plié position

Leaps are usually preceded by quick running steps.

LC 12 Combination Runs and Leap

Example

Run, run, leap

Run, run, leap

Variations of the leap

scissors leap

forward leg flexed in mid-air

both legs flexed in mid-air

LS8 Expanding the Walk into the Leap

Continuous leaps for distance in a low plié position may evolve from fast walks.

Action

A fast walk with legs outstretched in a lunge position, with rear foot raised off the floor swing arms freely in opposition, turn head side to side in opposition to forward arm

Teaching Hint

The practice of lunges emphasizes an extended leg brushing forward onto a plié position, with the back leg extended to the floor. Arms are placed forward on an upward diagonal. Keep the back leg *off* the floor and you have a modified lunge. This can be a useful aid in reinforcing the movement.

LS9 Expanding the Triplet Turn with Two Pivot Turns (chaînée)

Description

No alternation

   Triplet on right
   Triplet turn on left
   Pivot on right
   Pivot on left

Suggested Cues

Down, up, up   one, two, three
Down, turn, turn   two, two, three
Turn, turn   four, five

Teaching Hint

   Step forward in line of direction with each pivotal turn, so that there is a continued rotation to the same direction.

LP 5 Pattern Triplet, Triplet Turn, Pivot turn, Plié in Second Position, Plié-Hop-Arabesques

Description

With alternation

    Triplet on right

    Triplet turn on left

    Pivot on right

    Pivot on left

    Step sideways on right

    Plié in second position (LCL-3b)

    Plié-hop-arabesque on left

    Plié-hop-arabesque on right

LS10 Expanding the Triplet with a Balance on Toe

Description

Alternation

    Triplet on left

    Step and balance on right leg

    Raise extended left leg forward, elevate body and arms higher with feeling of suspension; use six counts.

    Lunge forward with left leg to repeat study

Variations

1. Raise working leg in different directions sideways, backwards

2. Use a flexed leg with pointed toes

LP 6 Pattern Triplet, Triplet Turn, Step Balance, Two Step-Hops

Description

No alternation

    Triplet on right

    Triplet turn on left

    Step on right

    Balance on right leg, extend left leg backward

    Step-hop on left leg, step down on right

    Step-hop on left leg.

Variation

Extend left leg sideways and replace the step-hops with the body swing series. (Series F, Chapter 4) Another movement which can challenge your more advanced students is the arabesque with a hop on the standing leg. Balance is maintained on a flexed leg, foot flat on the floor. It is easily added to any triplet combination.

LP 7 Pattern Triplet, Triplet Turn, Arabesque with a Hop

Description

With alternation

   Triplet on right

   Triplet turn on left

   Step forward on right leg into an arabesque position, hold for three counts,

   Hop on right leg three counts

LS11 Expanding the jump by the use of different positions in a sequence

Jumps begin in a plié position, where both legs push off at the same time from the floor and end simultaneously in a soft landing. This is made possible by the consecutive actions of the toes, balls of the feet, heels, and the flexion of ankles and knees.

Review the exploratory section on jumping and LC 5—Runs and Jumps.

Expand jumps by using all ballet positions.

Create your own jumping sequence or use ours.

A JUMP SEQUENCE

Position

Stand in first position, arms at sides. Arms raise sideways, shoulder level, when legs are in mid-air and in second position.

Description

   1. Jump and land in first position
   2. Repeat

3. Jump with legs extended sideways, in air land in first position
4. Jump and land in first position
5. Jump to second position
6. Jump and land in second position
7. Jump to first position
8. Jump with legs extended sideways, in air land in first position

Teaching Hint and Cues

The position on take-off and landing is the first, unless otherwise noted. The action of the legs in the air is cued.

Cues:

1. Together
2. Together
3. Wide, in air
4. Together
5. Second
6. Second
7. Together
8. Wide, in air

The use of "Group Solving Techniques" (Chapter 5) becomes more significant when your students attain a degree of proficiency. It provides a challenge to their performing skills and to their creative ability. It provides you with additional combinations and patterns that are innovative and progressive. For illustrative purposes, a number of problems are presented.

LC 13 Combination Pedals and Jumps

Description

Four pedals forward

Four one-quarter turn jumps

Variation (using prances)

Four pedals forward

Two pedals backward

Two jumps in place

Four prances forward

Four one-quarter turn jumps

Teaching Hint

Perform to music with a steady yet vigorous beat.

Creative variations using group solving technique

Problems

Vary the sequence and/or direction of steps.

Create a locomotor pattern by including eight walks in a circle somewhere in the variation.

LC 14 Combination Walks and Leap

Another approach to the leap is using a slow motion technique.

Action

Slow walks and leap

Description

Alternation

Arms at sides;

Walk on right

Walk on left

Arms sideways at shoulder level;

Kick forward high with extended right leg

Land in a plié position; body tilted forward, left leg extended backwards, high off the floor.

PLIÉ-HOP-ARABESQUE (LS2)

A step hop with leg extended backward, as described in Chapter Five (LS2), is known as a plié-hop-arabesque to our advanced classes. This movement can also succeed the teaching of a modified lunge. (Teaching Hint—Leap LS8)

LC 15 Combination Triplets, Plié-Hop-Arabesque

Description

No alternation

Triplet on right

Triplet on left

Step forward on right, plié-hop-arabesque

Step forward on left, plié-hop-arabesque

LP 8 Pattern Triplet, Triplet Turn, Plié-Hop-Arabesque, Back Fall and Rise

Description

With alternation

Triplet on right

Triplet on left

Plié-hop-arabesque on right

Plié-hop-arabesque on left

Plié-hop-arabesque on right into a back fall and rise

To repeat pattern step forward on left

Creative variations using group solving technique

Problems

1. Vary the number of times you repeat a movement.
2. Intersperse a familiar floor movement and/or two jumps within the pattern.

LP 9 Pattern Runs, Jumps, Arabesque, Plié-Hop-Arabesque, Crouch

Description

Run on right

Run on left

Jump (preparation)

Jump a full turn around

Step forward onto right leg into a slow arabesque

Plié-hop-arabesque on left

Plié-hop-arabesque on right

Step forward onto left leg into a slow standing crouch (LCL-1b)

Teaching Hint

For alternation, repeat the pattern starting the run on the left leg.

Creative variations using group solving technique
Problems

1. Use your own counts.

2. Change the sequence of movements.

3. Add one percussive movement anywhere in the pattern and hold the pose for four counts.

A SAMPLE TECHNIQUE LESSON FOR INTERMEDIATE STUDENTS

(Approximately forty minutes)

Starting position—frog sitting

Chapter 4 A1	Body bounces with breathing; head to feet
Chapter 6 A6	Body bounces with straight and round spine
	Transition to stride sitting
Chapter 4 A3	Body bounces; chest to thigh with pointed feet; alternated with
Chapter 6 B5	Body bounces ear to thigh
	Transition to hook sitting
Chapter 4 C2 a	Roll down, middle spine leading
b	Arch up, chest leading
a	Roll down, middle spine leading
Chapter 6 T3	Roll over with leg flexed behind into
T2	Hip lift
	Transition to long lying
Chapter 6 C5	A leg stretch using abdominal muscle control

Chapter 4 C1b Transitional step; roll up, top of head leading

B3 Body bounces forward; head to knees, long sitting

Transition to double kneeling

Chapter 6 T6 Side fall from a kneeling position

Transition to tall standing pattern

Chapter 4 F4 Swings to the side using a leg lift, step-hop and slide into

Chapter 6 T7 Side fall from a standing position into

T2 Hip lift and

T3 Roll-over

Across the Floor

Combination

Chapter 5 LX2 Using the walk with brushes and

E2 Plié, relevé in a two count phrase

Combination

LX2 Variation—Using the walk with large leg swings forward and backward and

Chapter 4 E2 Plié, relevé in a two count phrase

Chapter 6 LS8 Expanding the walk into the leap

On Spots

Chapter 6 D8 Easy bounces forward with flexed knees, round spine

Roll up to erect position using successional movement of the spine

A SAMPLE LESSON PLAN FOR ADVANCED STUDENTS APPROXIMATELY ONE HOUR AND A HALF

Starting position—Standing in parallel position

Series D

Chapter 6 Example 1 A bounding sequence using an extended and round spine, in various directions

Chapter 4 E1   Plié and relevé in a three count phrase, using first, second and third positions interspersed with:

Chapter 6 E7   Plié with a raising and lowering of heels in a percussive manner and,

E8   Relevé with a flexion of knees and lowering of heels

LS11 A jumping sequence using first and second positions

Lead-up exercises—transitional step

Chapter 4 Ldp   F2 Forward and back swings into

Chapter 5 LCL—1c Back fall

Transition to long lying

Chapter 6 C5   A leg stretch using abdominal muscle control

Transition to wide sitting

B7   Leg flexion and extension with a roll down and up with bounces forward

Transition to sitting in fourth position

Series H—Spanish Arch

Transition to kneeling and standing in fifth position

Chapter 4   Series G

Points, brushes and kicks in fifth position using all directions

Chapter 6 G8   Développé forward, sideward, backward

Across the Floor

LX6   Développé with balance and walk

LS6b Pedals

Pattern

Chapter 5 LC8   Two triplets, one triplet turn combined with

LS2   Plié-hop-arabesques (four)

Combination—no alternation

LS1   Step-hop with a

Chapter 6 LS7   Step leap

CREATIVE VARIATIONS BASED ON GROUP SOLVING TECHNIQUE

1. Add any fall to the combination (LS1 and LS7) into an original twelve-count phrase on the floor. Rise to repeat the combination.

2. Given the following movements, rearrange into a pattern with a change of direction:

   four runs

   two leaps

   two step-hops

   your fall and original twelve-count phrase with a rise

   two triplets

   two triplet turns (your choice)

   four plié-hop-arabesques

·→❧ 7 ❧←·

Improving Dance Skills Through Musical Explorations

The arts of music and dance are closely related. Knowledge and sensitivity to the elements of rhythms, dynamics and timing affects the caliber of dance performance. In developing the dance curriculum, we include a variety of musical experiences.

There are many aspects to the use of music in the dance lesson. In addition to direct instruction in the mechanics of music, you can indirectly educate pupils through different types of dance accompaniment. Draw the student's attention to the musical elements of rhythm, tempo, dynamics and accent, while they are learning dance skills, and provide various kinds of sound accompaniment to develop creative explorations.

Select different kinds of accompaniment for the various parts of the dance lesson. For example, the music used for dance technique should be different from the music used for creative activities. In general, it is your responsibility to choose music discriminately. Even the amount of music used in the classroom must be carefully monitored, so that pupils are not overwhelmed by too much sound.

VALUES OF STUDYING MUSIC IN THE DANCE PROGRAM

1) Development of knowledge of the elements of music (rhythm, meter, tempo, accent, note value, dynamics, phrasing).

2) Development of a knowledge of musical styles, forms and composers.

3) Appreciation for the art of music and its interaction with dance.

4) Improved dance skills through musical exploration.

5) Increased motivation of beginning dance pupils through stimulating sound accompaniments.

6) Development of skills that can be used in choreography. For example, knowledge of musical forms (ABA, Theme and Variations, Rondo) and technical elements such as unison, canon, fugue, etc.

7) Development of musical skills, such as tapping techniques to help pupils compose their own musical scores for choreography and performance.

8) Development of a positive self-image through successful experience with music and dance.

LEARNING ABOUT MUSIC THROUGH DANCE

Suggested Activities
Provide instruction in the elements of music such as: rhythm, tempo, note values, meter and analysis of musical instruments.

1) *Building a Rhythmic Response in Pupils*

a) Have pupils listen to rhythms; use drum, rhythm machine and recorded selections. Create dance patterns illustrating various rhythms.

b) Select a leader to clap out rhythmic patterns with different accents. The class responds by clapping out what they hear and then responds through movement.

2) *Experiences with Tempo*

a) Develop an understanding of musical tempos through varied experiences in dance class. For example, provide pupils with movements in slow and quick tempos; challenge their understanding of tempos by using different accompaniments such as drum, rhythm machine and records.

b) Provide movements with potential for variation in speed. For example, teach a simple swing in moderate tempo; ask pupils to perform swing in slow, then fast motion. Develop a short combination using the swing in various speeds, and have pupils perform phrases for each other.

3) *Experimenting with Note Values*

a) Study of note values is important to expand dance knowledge. The ability to perform a dance phrase requires understanding of time and duration. Quality of motion is closely aligned with note values. For example, a series of sixteenth, eighth and quarter notes has a different quality when compared to a phrase made up of half and whole notes.

b) Compose exercises and movement patterns to illustrate different note values; provide experiences with whole notes, half, quarter, eighth, sixteenth, etc.

c) Provide opportunities for pupils to actively study notes and their durations through such illustrative materials as charts, chalkboards and musical scores.

d) Organize simple games to test pupil understanding of note values. For example, teams can be arranged with pupils choosing specific note values and creating patterns of movement illustrating these values. Teams attempt to evaluate patterns and identify the specific note values performed. Require teams to write up their patterns using musical notation.

4) *Experiences with Meter—Count Divisions*

a) Students should be able to concentrate on the number of counts comprising a dance phrase. The ability to memorize a dance pattern depends heavily on pupil understanding of count structures. Devise dance patterns with simple metrical outlines such as ²⁄₄ or ⁴⁄₄ or ³⁄₄. Later, opportunities can be provided to mix meters (combine movements in ²⁄₄ with movement in ³⁄₄ meter).

b) Use musical examples to test pupil understanding of meter. Select examples which reflect specific duple, triple and mixed meters. Pupils can try to identify these meters.

c) Write up note patterns in different meters. These "scores" can be danced out by pupils to determine understanding. For example:

Organize testing situations around these experiences. For example, create scores with pupils required to illustrate the patterns in dance movement.

In addition, games can be organized. For example, pupils can create short musical scores, exchange them with other pupils, and attempt to dance them out.

Another game would require teams to dance out scores created by the teacher. Correct responses could be rewarded with extra credit or prizes.

5) *Analyzing Musical Instruments*

a) Instruct pupils in the tonal qualities of various musical instruments. Call upon your colleagues in the music department to demonstrate different types of musical instruments. Use various musical recordings for the illustration of different instruments. Provide illustrative materials to encourage understanding. For example, use bulletin boards with pictures of instruments.

b) Take trips to concerts to help illuminate the musical experience.

c) Create interesting movement activities around the theme of instruments. For example, create dance actions that reflect the quality of various instruments. (Violin could be portrayed with lyrical movements using long lines of action; percussive instruments can be represented with sharp, dagger-like actions of all parts of the body; wind instruments can be portrayed with elevated movements). Many possibilities exist with this form of exploration.

Effective Ways to Use Music in the Dance Technique Lesson

There are many opportunities to use music effectively in the dance technique lesson. For example, various types of accompaniment can be used:

A progression of sounds can be developed and used at different times in the lesson, for example:

1) count aloud as movement is taught

2) have pupils count aloud as they imitate you

3) accompany the class with drum

4) have pupils count to themselves as they move

5) use a rhythm machine to accompany the lesson releasing the teacher to move more freely through the class; cue movements with the machine.

6) use the rhythm machine by itself (no teacher cues)

7) use silence while pupils keep the count

8) use music as an accompaniment

The *Drum* can be used. The most popular for modern dance is the Mary Wigman Drum. There are various ways to use the drum effectively: use the palm of your hand to create effects; use a mallet on the drum head and rim. Other percussive instruments include: bongo drums, claves, maracas, cymbals, triangle, piano.

If no drums are available use books, tin cans, etc.

The *rhythm machine*—can be used to provide a variety of beats. It frees you from playing the drum and allows you to move about the class and make corrections. Also, the rhythm machine is mechanically dependable and can maintain a steady, accurate beat. The speed on rhythm machines can also be varied. Thus, movements can be performed in all speeds. As various skills are practiced, you can challenge pupils' performances by slowly increasing speeds. Pupils enjoy trying to keep up with the beat!

Voice and Body Sounds can be used to accompany the class. Snap fingers, clap hands, slap hips, stamp feet. Vocal sounds can be used.

Tape Recorded Music can be used. This approach is inexpensive and more efficient than records. Many different sound accompaniments are possible with cassettes. For example, in addition to recordings, you can tape sounds from television, radio, and the environment.

Recorded musical selections can be used to help stimulate pupil performance. A listing of suggested composers can be found at the close of this chapter.

TEACHER HINTS

1) Accompany the class with contrasting devices to provide interest and excitement. Pupils may get bored if the same accompaniment is used for all portions of the lesson. Keep them motivated and eager to learn with variety and balance in the accompaniment.

2) Test pupil knowledge and understanding of movements learned, by using different types of accompaniment. Pupils can be

evaluated for musical response and sensitivity as well as dance performance.

3) Stress musical elements as the main theme for developing movement patterns. For example, if you want to teach syncopation, create a movement phrase with this element in mind. If you wish your class to explore different meters, then create phrases in 4/4 time, 5/4 time, etc.

Effective Ways to Use Music for Creative Activity

1) Make collage tapes, linking together various ideas (spoken word, music, etc); attach ideas with a splicing tape. Voice and music can be distorted in the following ways:

    a) record voice at 3¾; play back at 7½; effect = speeded up

    b) record voice at 7½; play back at 3¾; effect = slowed down

    c) play music with normal speed of 33 at 45 or 78; effect = speeded up. Record on tape at 3¾ or 7½.

    d) play music with normal speed of 45—at 33; effect = slowed down. Record on tape at 3¾ or 7½.

2) Create unusual music scores through imaginative use of various tape techniques. For example, pupils can select a piece of music and distort it by speeding it up, slowing it down, running it backwards. Tape loops can also be used. This technique involves recording a short selection of music or other sounds. The material is then distorted by cutting the tape to a length several inches long. Connect tape into a circular shape or tape loop. The results of this technique are interesting because sounds produced are original and unpredictable.

3) Use sound effects as accompaniment. Students can produce their own scores by taping sounds (city noise, cafeteria at school, sounds of nature, etc.). Records devoted to sound effects can also be used. It is important to establish definite dance themes before sound effects are selected. However, sometimes accompaniments help to motivate the choreographic idea.

4) Have pupils create their own sound scores with homemade instruments such as: pots, pans, spoons, sticks or glasses.

Effective Ways to Use Music for Dance Performance

Dance concerts can use recorded or live music for accompaniment. Accompaniments can be original ideas or traditional works. The following suggestions can be utilized in the dance program:

1) Recorded music should be taped carefully with leaders separating numbers. Record players should not be used for performances because they are too sensitive to stage vibrations. Records can break and needles get stuck in grooves, so avoid them.

Taping suggestions:
   a) Set the proper tempo—make sure class uses the performance tape for rehearsals.
   b) make sure the pupils can hear the opening bars of music.
   c) Make sure leader tape precedes music so that the dance can proceed smoothly. A delayed opening can be demoralizing to your pupils and throw off their timing.
   d) Check the volume level of tapes for any distortion. Most recorders have normal and distorted levels to check. In addition, evaluate the type of sound system available in your school auditorium.
   e) Decide who should operate the tape recorder. Ideally, a stage squad should be trained to handle sound equipment.

2) Live music can be provided by music departments:
   a) use talented pupils to provide small chamber accompaniments such as piano and violin; drum, cello and piano, etc.
   b) Use school bands or orchestras to accompany dance. Tremendous satisfaction can be achieved through this type of interaction.
   c) provide vocal music by soloists or groups. Talented dancers can accompany themselves vocally.

3) Dramatic readings provide interesting accompaniments. Have dancers speak lines to accompany the dance. Use nonsense

sounds as well as lines from poems and plays. Students can create original poems for accompaniment.

4) Commissioning a score from the music department. There are various approaches to use:

1) *create the dance first*
   a) invite musicians to see the finished dance
   b) discuss the theme and dramatic idea of the dance
   c) discuss required tempos, meters; determine the length of the dance and the music
   d) determine the type of ending for the music; a loud cadence, a soft, sustained ending, etc.
   e) determine types of instruments to be used

2) *compose the musical score first*
   a) create movement with or against the beat
   b) make sure pupils listen to recordings of the score many times, before composing the movement
   c) have discussions with the musician to determine the quality of work, length, mood, etc.
   d) blend dance with music—each should enhance the other.

Effective Ways to Use Music for Designing Dances

The following dance works have used music as the prime stimulus. In one case, the dance is choreographed by the teacher, in the other it is choreographed by pupils. These dances are presented in a graded progression:

1) *A Dance Composed by the Teacher—Main Theme—Movement in ¾ Time*

    Title: "Swings"

    Accompaniment: "Improvisations for Modern Dance" Series #1 by Sarah Malamet; Side #1—Band #5 (Time—1 ½ min.)

    Meter: ¾

    Theme: Experiences in moving to ¾ time (swings, triplets); Development of a sense of composition in terms of groups moving in unison and in opposition (as in a round or canon form).

Techniques: Axial—swings side to side, forward-upward, back-downward. Locomotor—triplet (modification of the walk; change of level; down, up, up)

Formation: Mass formation; four groups—1, 2, 3, 4, standing in alternate files: 2   3
                                                                                                                      1   4

Overall Pattern:

1. Swings—All Groups, Canon Form

2. Swings—All Groups, Unison Form

3. Triplets—Question/Answer Form

4. Swings—Culminating Movement, All Groups—Canon Form

Musical Introduction: 12 counts

Swing Movement Pattern—All Groups:

Starting position—legs in stride, arms down at sides; good posture should be stressed. Swing to right side, with arms moving parallel; body also tilts right, shift weight to right leg as you swing to the right, (3 counts).

Repeat the *swing* to the left side, (3 counts) swing *right* with a traveling step (step right—close left—step right); circle the arms as you move side, (6 counts).

Repeat the above 12-count phrase to the left side. (swing left, swing right, swing and travel left), (12 counts).

Swing to a forward-upward direction; arms move in a parallel fashion; body is in a high suspension, (3 counts). Swing to a backward-downward direction; arms move in the same way; the body is on a low level (hips tucked under), (3 counts).

Swing to a forward-upward direction and hold, (6 counts).

(Note: all swings should be performed with a quality of fall and recovery, or fall and suspension; the movement should be done in a smooth fashion with an accent on the first beat.)

1) *The Swing—Canon Form*

Group 1—Begin the movement after the 12-count introduction in the music and continue until the pattern is completed and hold.

Group 2—Begin the movement after Group 1 completes 12 counts of the movement phrase.

Group 3—Begin the movement after Group 2 completes 12 counts of the movement phrase.

Group 4—Begin the movement after Group 3 completes 12 counts of the movement phrase. (All groups are in a high suspension as Group 4 is the last to finish the phrase.)

2) *Swings—All Groups, Unison Form*

The opening swing pattern is repeated with a slight variation: Groups 1 and 2 swing to left, while Groups 3 and 4 swing right (groups swing toward each other), and then away from each other (6 counts). Then, all swing with the traveling step, making a quarter turn on the last step; Groups 1 and 2 turn left, Groups 3 and 4 turn right, groups end facing each other, (6 counts).

All groups swing forward-upward and backward-downward (6 counts); Groups 3 and 4 remain on a low level, while Groups 1 and 2 continue the phrase, ending in a forward-upward direction (6 counts).

3) *Triplets—Question/Answer Format*

Format

Groups 1 and 2 perform, while groups 3 and 4 hold;

Groups 3 and 4 perform, while groups 1 and 2 hold.

Then, all groups perform in unison.

Triplet Patterns

Triplets are performed in place and then traveling in different directions:

Triplets beginning on right foot (3 counts), repeat on left foot (3 counts).

Triplets facing back of gym—right (3), left (3).

Triplets; four times (12 counts) traveling, beginning on right foot.

Groups 3 and 4 repeat the same pattern, while groups 1 and 2 remain facing the back, (24 counts) All groups perform the triplets: one facing back (3), one facing the side (3), two facing front (6), then 4 triplets moving forward.

4) *Swings—Culminating Movement, All Groups, Canon Form Swing Pattern*

Swings forward-upward (3 counts),

backward-downward (3 counts),

forward-upward (3 counts),

hold (3 counts).

Canon Form—Swings

All groups move in a round form:

Group 1 begins the movement.

Group 2 begins after group 1 completes 3 counts of the movement phrase.

Group 3 begins after group 2 completes 3 counts of the movement phrase.

Group 4 begins after group 3 completes 3 counts of the movement phrase.

Lead-up activities might include:

1) discussion of the nature of the swing (rhythm, accent, quality)

2) exploration of how different parts of the body can perform a swinging action (head, arms, torso, legs)

3) perform arm swings (parallel and in opposition to each other)

4) add the tilt of body to arm swings

5) add traveling step and quarter turns

6) add a slight hop to the traveling step

7) practice leg swings (forward, back, forward-sideward)

8) perform walks and then vary them by changing level (low, high, high; high, low, low, etc.)

9) perform triplets (vary direction, tempo)

2) *An Exercise Dance Composed by Pupils and Teacher—Main Theme—Moving in ¼ Time*

This culminating activity involves pupil application of learned skills to a specific musical score. You can select music of a classical or popular nature, as long as it has a definite beat. This experience is highly motivating to pupils because it gives them the chance to really dance to music. Here are some preliminary steps to follow:

1) Listen to the music carefully.

2) Discuss the dynamic qualities of the music; moods, themes, etc.

3) Count out the beats of music; what is the meter?

4) Establish the length of the dance to be created.

5) Experiment working *on* the beat and *against* the beat.

6) Clap out the meter with the class.

7) Assign pupils to specific working groups; emphasize the need to work in silence, with pupils keeping the beat.

8) Use the rhythm machine to provide a backdrop.

9) Use the music selected when pupils are ready to perform their phrases.

The following outline represents a graded progression of learning how to create dance patterns in different count sequences:

1) Memory Game

2) Exercise dance created by teacher and students en masse

3) Exercise dance created by students in two groups

4) Methods for lengthening dances

5) Creating dances in smaller groups

   a) *The Memory Game:* see Chapter 2 for detailed description.

   b) *Exercise dance created by teacher and students, performed en masse.*

      Just as they have linked together movements in the Memory Game, they are now ready to link together exercises into a dance.

SAMPLE EXERCISE DANCE

The following is a short dance example, created by teacher and students to be performed by the entire class, en masse.

Starting Position—floor level—frog sit position

Actions

1) breathing—curl over 4 counts;

           3 straighten up 4 counts;

           repeat

2) bounce—16 counts

3) change legs to parallel position (4 counts)

4) breathing—curl over 4 counts;

           straighten up 4 counts;

           repeat

5) bounce—16 counts

6) change legs to stride position (4 counts)

7) breathing—curl over 4 counts;

           straighten up 4 counts;

           repeat

8) bounce—16 counts center

           8 counts over right leg

   8 counts over left leg

9) change legs to parallel position (4 counts)

10) flex feet and point feet—

   alternate flex and point 8 counts—2 counts for each movement.

   alternate flex and point 8 counts—1 count for each movement.

11) change to hook-sit position (4 counts)

12) roll down 8 counts, roll up 8 counts,

   roll down 4 counts, roll up 4 counts,

13) roll down 8 counts, chest arch 8 counts,

   roll down 4 counts, chest arch 4 counts,

14) coccyx balance 8 counts, rise up from knees to standing level (8 counts)

15) on standing level, rubber band stretch, stretch body and arms to ceiling, 4 counts

16) roll down torso, 4 counts

17) bounce rounded, 4 counts

18) roll up torso, 4 counts

19) body bounces:

side right, 4 counts; side left, 4 counts,

repeat using 2 counts, 1 count.

forward-rounded torso, 4 counts,

forward, straight torso, 4 counts,

repeat using 2 counts, 1 count.

20) arch backward, 4 counts,

forward-rounded torso, 4 counts,

repeat using 2 counts, 1 count.

21) plié-rélevé, first position, balance, hold.

3) *Exercise Dance Created by Students—Two Groups*

CLASS FORMATION

Divide class into 2 big groups; assign leaders to help supervise. Use drum to keep steady beat for class.

PRELIMINARY ACTIVITY

Have each group create 4 movements for the pattern using an exercise or an original idea. Students may use their own counts for each movement. Groups count aloud as they practice. Each group performs their pattern. Teacher helps groups smooth out their patterns.

SAMPLE SOLUTION

Group 1.

1) arms lift to side

2) plié and straighten in first position

3) rélevé and down

4) point right toe forward, close first

5) side lunge on right leg, focus eyes right, close. (repeat pattern two times and perform to music)

4) *Methods for Lengthening Dances*

    1) Group 1 teaches their pattern to group 2 and vice versa; now each group has 8 movements to perform.

    2) Perform the pattern backwards and link to original idea. For example, 8,7,6,5,4,3,2,1 or only partly backwards: 1,2,3,4,8,7,6,5.

    3) Add a series of movements already learned in class. For example, triplet, turn, arabesque.

5) *Creating Dances in Smaller Groups*

Pupils are now ready to accept more responsibility:

    1) Divide the class in small groups, maximum number of pupils:

    8 in each group. Assign leaders.

    2) Each pupil in the group devises a 4-count movement such as:

        a) an exercise learned in class

        b) an original idea

        c) a variation on an exercise

    3) Pupils teach their movements to members of their group; all practice in unison, linking one idea to another.

    4) Pupils can extend the pattern by performing in a round or canon form.

    5) Pupils create movements to enter and exit stage.

SUGGESTED DANCE ORGANIZATION FOR 3 PERFORMING GROUPS

Group 1 begins alone on stage and performs its exercise patterns in unison, then exits.

Group 2 enters on a definite visual cue from Group 1 and performs its pattern, then exits.

Group 3 enters on visual cue from Group 2, performs its pattern in a round and exits.

Ending: Representatives from Groups 1, 2 and 3 return, to perform portions of their patterns in unison. End on stage in static pose.

SUGGESTED DANCE ORGANIZATION FOR 4 PERFORMING GROUPS

1) Group 1 and 2 perform patterns on stage in unison (thus, you have 2 contrasting themes performed together)

2) Exit groups 1 and 2, enter group 3 alone, performs theme in a round

3) Exit group 3—enter group 4—perform pattern forward then backward, then finish the dance with a group design.

MUSICAL SELECTIONS

The following suggestions can be used interchangeably for the technique class, creative experiences and performance. Selections have been organized in terms of musical category and composer. This list is not an exhaustive one; it primarily represents selections we have used successfully with our pupils.

1) *Classical* (Renaissance, Baroque, Romantic, etc.)
   a) Bach
   b) Beethoven
   c) Handel
   d) Mozart
   e) Vivaldi
   f) Scarlatti
   g) Purcell

2) *Primitive and Medieval*
   a) Gregorian Chants
   b) Music from various ethnic groups (primitive)

3) *Contemporary*
   a) Percussion
      1) Carlos Chavez
      2) Edgar Varese
      3) William Kraft
   b) Electronic
      1) Helen El Dabb   3) Bulent Arel
      2) Tad Dockstader   4) Otto Luening

    5) Steve Reich   8) Milton Babbitt

    6) Morris Knight   9) Pauline Oliveros

    7) Richard Maxfield

c) *Modern*

    1) Aaron Copland   6) Alan Hovhaness

    2) Leonard Bernstein   7) Igor Stravinsky

    3) Bela Bartok   8) Karl Stockhausen

    4) Carl Orff

    5) John Cage

4) *Popular*

  a) *Jazz*

    1) Quincey Jones

    2) Scott Joplin

    3) Dave Brubeck

    4) Mose Allison

  b) *Novelty*

    1) silent movie music

    2) sound effects (Audio Fidelity Records—several volumes available, including sounds of animals, planes, cars, machines, etc.)

  c) *Gospel*

    1) Edwin Hawkins Singers

    2) Mahalia Jackson

    3) Voices of East Harlem

    4) Odetta

  d) *Country*

    1) Flatt and Scruggs (use country music popular in your area)

  e) *Moog*

    1) Walter Carlos

    2) Jacques Perrey

    3) Dick Hyman

  f) Social

    1) rock n' roll

    2) ballroom music
    (fox trot, lindy, etc.)

    3) latin american music
    (mambo, cha cha, etc.)

    4) novelty dance music
    (bunny hop, alley cat, etc.)

5) Dance Technique

  a) Modern Dance

    1) Bertram Ross (Graham)

    2) Carmen de Lavallade (Horten)

    3) Cameron Mc Cosh (Graham)

    4) Sarah Malamet (Humphrey-Weidman)

  b) Jazz

    1) Gwen Verdon

    2) Peter Genarro

    3) Gus Giordano

    4) Liz Williamson

  c) Ballet

    1) Hoctor records produces many albums for various technique levels and different ballet styles.

    2) Kimbo, S & R and Statler also produce similar recordings. Teachers should send for these catalogs for complete listings.

·→⊰ 8 ⊱←·

Sparking the Imagination through Creative Activities

This chapter provides a series of creative activities. The approaches are organized on a graded scale, from simple to complex. The learning that is achieved through one approach acts as a building block for future experiences.

Each approach includes discussion on class formations, suggested accompaniments, sample problems and solutions, and appropriate uses in the curriculum.

Why should we include creative activities in the dance curriculum? What are the objectives and merits of the program? What should the initial creative experiences consist of, and when should they be presented?

There are many important skills and psychological learnings developed from these creative approaches:

1) pupils expand their movement vocabularies through creative endeavors,

2) improve their performing abilities,

3) develop unique and original ways of moving,

4) develop problem solving and creative powers,

5) develop an appreciation and understanding of music,

6) psychologically, many students develop self-confidence and a more positive self image,

7) they learn the art of leading, as well as following,

8) many develop important skills of social interaction that are applicable beyond the realm of dance,

9) creative experiences provide the tools for independent thinking and problem solving needed for adulthood,

10) pupils extend their movement vocabulary to different dance styles, such as jazz, ballet, ethnic.

Use the three approaches presented in this chapter in chronological order. They are outgrowths of each other, and thereby provide a developmental flow of learning. Use the more advanced creative approaches discussed in the next chapter only after pupils have experienced the three basics that follow:

Summary of Three Creative Approaches

Approach 1) Developing Short Movement Sequences

Approach 2) Arranging Movement Sequences into a Dance

Approach 3) Performing Finished Dances in Different Moods and Qualities

DEVELOPING SHORT MOVEMENT SEQUENCES—APPROACH #1

In this approach, pupils in small groups utilize movements learned in the technique lesson, then arrange them into an interesting pattern. They are limited to specific and concrete movement problems and are constantly under teacher supervision.

SAMPLE PROBLEMS AND SOLUTIONS

PROBLEM I

Rearrange a given pattern into a new sequence, maintaining the same count sequence.

Sample Movements to be Used for the Problem

on floor level:

1) bounces over straight, parallel legs, 2 counts

2) bounces in frog-sit position, 2 counts

3) bounces in leg stride position, 2 counts

4) a roll down, 6 counts

5) a chest lift, 6 counts

6) point and flex toes, 4 counts

Sample Solution

1) starting position, legs stride position, 2 bounces center
2) legs to hook-sit position, roll down, 6 counts
3) chest lift, 6 counts
4) parallel legs, 2 bounces
5) flex and point toes (alternating feet) 4 counts
6) end position, frog sit, arms overhead, hold.

Preparing the Lesson

1) Pupils should practice movements in mass formation to make sure of technical accuracies, then break into small groups for creative problem solving.
2) Provide a visual demonstration of a possible solution to this problem (but make sure students don't use all your ideas; they have to be original in their sequences).
3) Help pupils create a smooth transition so that one step blends into the next.
4) Pupils determine beginning and ending positions (this is an excellent lead-up to future choreographic experiences requiring a beginning, middle and end).

VARIATIONS ON PROBLEM I

VARIATION #1—pupils may change the count sequences of given movements (Example: 4 bounces instead of 2 bounces, etc.)

VARIATION #2—class determines movements to be used for the pattern by selecting 3 or more from the technique lesson. Groups rearrange movement and determine count sequence.

Sample Solution on a Standing Level

1) plié in first position, 3 counts
2) straighten, 3 counts
3) point forward and close first; side point and close first
4) relevé, arms reach overhead, 6 counts

> VARIATION #3—class selects 3 movements from floor and 3 from standing level. Each group arranges the movements and determines their count sequence. The group should devise an original way of making level changes. For example, a kneeling motion, a crouch, a slow dissolve to the floor, a slow rise to stand, a sudden jump, etc.

Sample Solution Beginning on a Standing Level

1) plié, relevé, 12 counts
2) points forward and close, alternate right and left (2 times)
3) slow dissolve to floor, 12 counts

On Floor Level:

4) roll down, 6 counts
5) chest arch, 3 counts
6) stride sitting position, hold (arms to side)

PROBLEM II

Choose locomotor and standing movement techniques, such as: 2 triplets, 1 triplet turn, the swing series (sideward, forward and back) and arrange these movements in a phrase. Maintain count structure as given

Sample Solutions

turn, triplet, swing series, triplet

or

swing series, turn, triplet, triplet

or

triplet, turn, triplet, swing series

Preparing the Lesson

1) Review these movements en masse, accompany with a drum
2) Drill and practice in 2 or 3 groups to allow pupils to rest and observe each other
3) Organize them into small groups of 5 or 6 pupils

VARIATION

Groups can lengthen the pattern by using simple repetition, for example:

turn, turn, triplet, turn, swing
or
swing, triplet, triplet, triplet, turn

PROBLEM III

Choose 3 locomotor movements from a list on chalk board and arrange them into a pattern. Make these 3 movements add up to a particular number of counts established by the teacher. For example: 9 counts = 3 slides + 2 gallops + 4 walks or 12 counts = 4 slides + 3 gallops + 5 walks. Try to create an interesting floor pattern as you move through space (circle, square, figure 8, etc.).

Sample Solutions

Moving in a square formation; adding up to 15 counts

3 slides

3 slides   4 gallops

5 walks

Preparing the Lesson

1) Discuss locomotor movements learned in technique class, and list movements on chalk board.

2) Have class practice movements across the floor.

3) Organize class into groups.

PROBLEM IV

Add an original idea to the locomotor pattern devised in Problems II or III. An original idea can be limited to definite counts and body parts. For example, add a 6-count arm movement somewhere in the pattern; add a 12-count body movement; add a 3-count leg movement, etc.

Sample Solutions

triplet, triplet turn, leg lift in arabesque 6 counts
or
slide, gallop, arm lift to sky in one count, walk

PROBLEM V

Change appearance of locomotor movements with changes in direction, level and count sequences. For example:

1) perform movements in different directions and floor patterns

   forward, backward, sideways, etc.

   circle, figure 8, square, etc.

2) use any count sequence

3) add a level change somewhere in the pattern (any counts)
   Example: into the air, down to the floor, demi-plié, etc.

Sample Solution

 8 runs forward
 4 walks backward
 8 runs in a circle
 4 counts to crouch
 2 jumps upward
16 walks in a figure 8

PROBLEM VI

Devise your own movement response to each of the following actions: run, turn, slow fall, quick rise, balance, run. Use any direction, any body designs.

Sample Solution

run backwards in a line

skip turn (or triplet turn, or three-step turn, etc.)

slow fall to hook sit position with arms reaching to sky

quick rise to both knees (eyes focus upward)

stand to balance on one leg (arabesque)

run in circles

Preparing the lesson

1) Present general movement directions as pupils progress in learning.

2) Have groups devise their own counts.

3) Provide demonstration of possible solutions to help motivate your pupils.

VARIATIONS ON PROBLEM VI

VARIATION #1—using general movement directions, pupils structure movements into definite meters

Sample Problem

Choose from the following meters: 5/4; 4/4; 3/4

Arrange movements into a sequence from the following general directions: plié, run, lunge, slide

Sample Solution

In 5/4 meter, grande or demi-plié in first position (5 counts)

close and straighten up (5 counts)

5 runs forward

5 counts to lunge to side

5 slides in a circle

VARIATION #2—Alter the appearance of given movements by using varied energy qualities.

Sample Problem

1) list movements on a board such as: walk, run, skip.

2) create an original 16 count movement from one of the four energy qualities such as sustained, percussive, vibratory and swinging.

3) devise original corresponding arm motions and arrange the sequence in any order.

4) create an interesting floor pattern with these steps and let the floor pattern determine counts needed.

Sample Solution

1) walk in moderate speed in circle formation (arms move overhead and down as you walk)

2) run to different corners of the room in fast tempo (ending in center)

3) reach to the sky with a sustained, 16-count body movement, then curl over in contraction

4) exit with skips in figure-8 formation (swing arms freely)

ARRANGING MOVEMENT SEQUENCES INTO A DANCE— APPROACH #2

This approach is an expansion of the problems discussed in approach #1. Students will not only rearrange and create movements for a dance sequence, but can also perform them to music in finished dances.

An outstanding difference between approach #1 and #2 is that in approach #2, pupils must create longer patterns requiring greater memory resources. Through approach #2, pupils get firsthand knowledge of the choreographic tools necessary for arranging patterns into a finished dance.

SAMPLE PROBLEMS AND SOLUTIONS

ARRANGING MOVEMENT SEQUENCES INTO A DANCE— APPROACH #2.

PROBLEM I.

All groups arrange a longer dance linking 3 sections of movement sequences, A, B, C.

Section A.

Groups select 4 movements learned in technique class and arrange them into a sequence. For example, triplet, triplet turn, back fall, step-hop.

Section B.

1) Create an interesting floor pattern using one of the movements from Section A.

2) Create an original 16-count movement showing a level change.

Section C.

1) Create movements for the following action ideas: run, turn, fall.

2) Devise a shape for group representing the ideas of Night or Day.

Method for Arranging Group Choreography into a Finished Class Dance

1) Each group performs their choreography to determine their order in the class dance.

2) Visual cues are used to determine group entrances and exits.

3) Work with class to determine an ending for the dance. For example, all groups return and pose in unison, or one group returns and performs a final movement from its theme.

4) Add appropriate musical background.

PROBLEM II.

Groups devise 3 learned or original movements on one spatial level. Each movement is 8 counts, totalling 24 counts.

Preparing the Lesson

1) Organize the class into 4 groups

2) Assign each group a definite spatial level such as:

       group 1—floor

       group 2—standing

       group 3—floor

       group 4—standing

3) Each group creates 3 (8 count) movements on their spatial level (total-24 counts), then are assigned a second level to create 3 more movements (8 counts each, total 24 counts). For example:

       group 1—floor and standing

       group 2—standing and floor

group 3—floor and standing

group 4—standing and floor

4) Groups try to create a smooth transition from one level to the other.

5) To show contrast in movement and spatial level, groups 1 and 2 perform at the same time and groups 3 and 4 perform at the same time.

PROBLEM III.

Using 3 locomotor patterns, groups arrange them into an original sequence.

Sample Problem

Given 3 locomotor patterns, rearrange them using any number of counts.

1) slide, gallop, walk

2) triplet, turn, swing, skip

3) prance, jump, 8-count sustained movement

Sample Solution

1) 4 gallops, 4 slides, 6 walks

2) swing, 4 skips, 2 triplets, 2 turns

3) 4 jumps, 8-count sustained movement, 16 prances

Once groups rearrange movements into an original sequence they are ready to determine the order of the 3 patterns. For example: 123, 231, 321, etc.

Arrange group choreography into a dance by assigning numbers to groups: determine entrances and exits with visual cues: Voilá, a finished performance.

Note—visual cues involve selections of distinctive movements easily observed by pupils.

PROBLEM IV.

Groups are assigned 4 movements from a sequence of 8 movements. They must keep a set order, but create graceful transitions from one movement to the other.

Sample Movements to be Used for Problem

1) plié in second position, 4 counts
2) relevé, 4 counts
3) lunge to side, 2 counts
4) 2 jumps in place
5) side swing, right and left
6) lunge forward, 2 counts
7) spin turn in place, arms circling, 6 counts
8) arabesque, 4 counts

Preparing the Lesson

1) Divide the class into 4 groups
2) Group 1 does sequence 1—4
   Group 2 does sequence 5—8
   Group 3 does sequence 4—1
   Group 4 does sequence 8—5
3) The diagram reflects the given movements and how the groups will look as they perform with each other.

1 2 3 4	Group I	5 6 7 8	Group II
4 3 2 1	Group III	8 7 6 5	Group IV

METHOD FOR ARRANGING GROUP CHOREOGRAPHY INTO A FINISHED CLASS DANCE

Using the chart as your foundation, you can determine the order and arrangement of the groups for performance. For example, the following groups can perform at the same time:

groups 1 and 3

groups 2 and 4

groups 1 and 4

groups 2 and 3

PROBLEM V.

Using a chance format, each group determines the sequence of their movements.

Sample Problem

Given 5 movements such as:

1) back fall

2) walk

3) chest arch

4) body shape (letter)

5) step-hop arabesque

Each group puts 5 numbers corresponding to each movement into their own hat. Each group member randomly picks a number which determines the sequence of their movements.

Sample Chance Solutions
5,4,2,1,3; 1,3,4,5,2; 5,4,3,2,1.

PROBLEM VI.

This problem is like a dramatic script using movement rather than words. Groups must act out the given dance script.

Sample Dance Script

Section 1.   1) walk on stage (any number of counts; any
(assigned to   pattern)
Group 1.)

2) spell out the first letter of your first name (any number of counts)

3) spell out the word *LOVE* using different body parts and using 4 counts per letter

4) exit walking (any direction, any number of counts)

Section 2.   1) walk on stage in a floor pattern of the first letter
(assigned to   of your first name (any counts)
Group 2.)

　　　　　　　2) spell out word *LOVE,* 4 counts each
　　　　　　　3) do 4 quarter-turn jumps in place
　　　　　　　4) run and exit (any pattern, direction, counts)

Section 3.　1) run on stage (any formation, any number of
(assigned to　　counts)
Group 3.)　　2) suspend the body to the sky, sit, roll down, roll
　　　　　　　　up
　　　　　　　3) rise in 8 counts and make a letter E; then a letter
　　　　　　　　L in 4 counts
　　　　　　　4) exit with slides (any formation, any number of
　　　　　　　　counts)

Section 4.　1) skips (any formation, direction, counts)
(assigned to　2) spell out *LOVE* backwards *(EVOL),* 4 counts each
Group 4.)　　3) do swing series (sideward only, with travel step)
　　　　　　　4) exit with gallops (any formation, direction,
　　　　　　　　counts)

After the dance script is completed as given, you may vary the order of the script to 4,3,2,1 or 1,3,2,4.

　　Sample Endings for this dance:

　　1) only group 2 returns to the stage, spells out *LOVE* (4 counts per letter), and holds the final letter shape.

　　2) all groups return to perform the pattern of one of the groups in unison.

　　3) only groups 1 and 2 return, each pupil picks any letter from the word *LOVE* and spells it out in 4 counts, holding to the end.

PERFORMING FINISHED DANCES IN DIFFERENT MOODS AND QUALITIES—APPROACH #3

　　In this approach, students learn about choreographic design by performing model dances created by the teacher. Use the following elements to create the most successful dance works for your class:

　　1) select movements learned in technique class and add new
　　　movement ideas

2) add new ideas that provide changes in time, space, energy, and body design

3) devise interesting spatial and group formations

4) make sure the dance is appropriate to the ability level of your group

5) provide for the repetition of movements

6) keep counts simple and steady

7) choose music that supports the count structure

Although each dance will require a different formation, some general hints can be applied:

1) use mass formations to practice movements

2) divide into 2 or 3 groups for drill and rest

3) use 3 or 4 groups for the dance

Each dance provides suggested musical accompaniments; however, when dealing with music, remember to:

1) allow pupils to listen carefully, before moving

2) stress the quality of both the music and the movements

3) clap out rhythms and tempo

The following is a sampling of two dances that can be presented at various times in the dance unit. One is the modern dance mood "Games," the other in the jazz style, "Out a Space." Both are original dances and utilize skills learned in the dance class, and introduce new ideas. Use these dances as models for creating your own compositions.

With each dance, remember to present proper lead-up activities. For example for "Games" provide instruction and practice in swings in different tempos and directions, jumps in different directions, slides, prances, and skips across the floor.

MODERN DANCE STYLE

Title: "Games Children Play"

Accompaniment: "Arcadian Songs and Dances" by Virgil Thompson (or other appropriate background)

Time—1 ½ min.

Meter: ⁴⁄₄ and ³⁄₄

Techniques: Axial: swings forward, downward, sideward right and left; with a turn.

Locomotor: slides, step swings, hop-step-to-gether-step, jumps, prances, skips.

Theme: Experience in contrasting movement qualities; lively, bouncy, sustained, swinging.

Development of a sense of composition in terms of movement and spatial patterns.

Formation: Mass formation, three groups A, B, and C standing in alternate files; circle formation.

Musical Introduction: 16 counts

Groups A, B, and C move in a Canon form.

1. *Movement Pattern:* 4 slides right, 4 slides left, step right and brush left leg, step left and brush right leg, step right, step left, lunge forward right, 16 counts.

Group A—perform movement pattern and hold.

Group B—begin movement after 8 slides done by A and hold.

Group C—begin movement after 8 slides done by B and hold.

All groups—hop (left), step-together, step; repeat on right; repeat on left and again on right; step right and brush left leg forward, and to back diagonal, and toe touch; step left and brush right leg forward, to back diagonal, and lunge forward, 32 counts.

2. *Movement Pattern:* Jumps from two feet, leaning away from the direction of jump, arms bowed.

Groups A, B, and C move alternately and together.

Group A—3 jumps moving left and leaning right, hold.

Group C—3 jumps moving right and leaning left, hold.

Group B—3 jumps moving forward and leaning back, hold.

All groups—3 jumps moving backward and leaning forward (hold), 12 counts.

3. *Movement Pattern:* Swings forward, upward (arms forward, upward); swing forward, downward (arms forward, downward); swings forward middle (arms same); swing backward (arms same) to forward high position; swing arms right side; swing arms left side, swing side right with three step turn and end in preparation for prances (right leg flexed, toe touching, arms in second position); 27 counts (¾ meter).

All groups perform the movement at the same time.

4. *Movement Pattern:* Prances in place and then traveling to circle formation. Groups A, B, and C move alternately and together.

Group A—4 prances in place; on 4th count, change focus sharply to the left.

Group B—begin after 4 prances of A, same focus.

Group C—begin after 4 prances of B, same focus.

All groups—4 prances in place, together with focus front, 16 total counts.

All groups—16 prances travelling to circle formation, 3 separate circles are formed.

5. *Movement Pattern:* Slides: 4 right, 4 left, 4 right, 4 left, total 16 counts (dancers may hold hands); 4 skips traveling into the center of the circle (no hands); 4 skips traveling away from the center of the circle (back to center); swings forward, upward (4 counts): swing forward, downward; swing forward, middle; swing backward and to forward-high position, join hands high and face the center of the circle (4), 16 counts.

6. *Movement Pattern:* Release arms (4), skips (12) back to mass formation, 16 counts. All groups move at the same time.

7. *Movement Pattern:* Opening pattern: (4 slides right, 4 left; step right and brush left leg forward;

step left and brush right leg forward;
step right in place, step left in place;
lunge forward with right leg, hands on
waist) All groups move at same time.

JAZZ DANCE STYLE

Title: "Out-a-Space"

Accompaniment: "Out-a-Space" (45 rpm) by Billy Preston,
3½ min.

Meter: 4/4

Techniques: jazz walks, three step turn, isolations of body
parts (head, shoulders) lunges, rumba step, step-
kick, jazz contractions.

Theme: Experiences with jazz and modern dance movements;
moving in unison and in a round.

Formation: Mass formation (floor spots); eventually divide the
class into two groups.

Musical Introduction: 8 counts (counting 1, & 2, & etc.)

Movement Pattern #1—(8 counts)

a) Jazz walks in a forward direction (4 counts)

(step right (1), touch left (&)

step left (2), touch right (&)

step right (3), touch left (&)

step left (4), touch right (&)

(click fingers on (&) beat for emphasis)

b) Three step turn to right (step right, left, right, touch left) (5
& 6 &)

Three step turn to left (step left, right, left, touch right) (7 &
8 &)

(keep arms close to body on turn; open arms to second
position on touch)

Movement Pattern #2—(8 counts)

a) Circle head (4 counts) starting forward then to right, bring
arms and legs close together for balance.

b) Lunge with right leg to right side (5 &), also thrust right elbow outward toward right side

Return right leg to center closed position (6 &)

c) Circle right shoulder (7 &)

Circle left shoulder (8 &)

Movement Pattern #3—(8 counts)

a) Rumba step to right (2 counts)

step right to side (1), close left to right (&)

step right to side (2), touch left in place (&)

b) Rumba step to left (2 counts)

step left to side (3), close right to left (&)

step left to side (4), touch right in place (&)

c) Low lunge with right leg to right side (place left hand on floor between legs, focus downward) (5 &) (right arm is lifted overhead)

Straighten up to natural position (6 &)

d) Step on right foot and clap (lifting body upward) (7 &)

Step on left foot and clap (contracting body downward) (8 &)

Movement Pattern #4—(8 counts)

a) Step kicks in circle (around self) (4 counts)

step right (1), kick left leg (&)

step left (2), kick right leg (&)

step right (3), kick left leg (&)

step left (4), kick right leg (&)

(During kicks, imagine you are holding a cane (vaudeville style) and lean your body toward the leg that is kicked.)

b) Jazz Contractions suspend body upward to right (high release) (5)

Contract body sharply (&) shifting weight to the right

Repeat to left side (6 &)

Repeat the jazz contraction on both the right and left sides (7 &, 8 &)

During jazz contractions, lift arms overhead in rounded position on high release; bring arms sharply down and click fingers on contraction.)

ENDING THE DANCE

Give the class the freedom to "do their own thing" for 8 counts, to finish the dance. They must hold their final position.

PREPARING THE LESSON—GUIDELINES FOR TEACHING DANCES

1) Provide a model demonstration of the finished dance, preferably with musical accompaniment. Use talented pupils from advanced classes or a group of dance leaders to demonstrate.

2) Begin the instruction by having pupils listen to music before they dance. Clap out rhythms and tempo to get a feeling for the accompaniment.

3) Slowly and carefully, teach specific steps from the dance, giving verbal and physical cues. Pupils can maintain floor spots in mass formation.

4) Skill progression can involve:

   a) demonstration of the skill by the teacher or class leaders, to music

   b) pupil imitation of the skill in a slow tempo (mimetics)

   c) use of verbal cues with the physical demonstration to heighten learning

   d) exploration of the skill in a faster tempo

   e) practice of the skill with frequent repetitions (drill, no music yet; a dance drum can be used to maintain a steady beat)

   f) performance to music by the entire group in unison; they later perform in two groups to provide an opportunity for other students to rest and view their classmates' performances.

5) Performance opportunities should be provided as culminating activities. Informal performances for gym classes can be scheduled. Performances can be developed for classes in different subject areas. For example, history

classes might enjoy a performance of an ethnic dance related to their studies, while a music class might enjoy a jazz presentation or novelty dance.

TEACHER HINT

Vary your position during skill instruction. For example:

a) Face pupils and work in opposition (mirror-image style).

b) Turn back to pupils while analyzing a skill.

c) Assign dance leaders to various places in the gym to aid pupil learning.

d) Vary the positions of pupils; allow them to work in front, back or middle lines.

EXPANDING YOUR STUDENTS' KNOWLEDGE OF FINISHED DANCES

1) In your dance curriculum, include the use of bulletin boards to show items relevant to dances studied, such as pictures of unusual or abstract movements, group formations, etc.

2) Films or video tapes of dances can be shown to enhance learning.

3) Visits can be made to places of interest in the community. For example, jazz and novelty patterns may be seen at *Radio City Music Hall* in New York City; examples of modern jazz and modern ballet can be found in a Broadway musical comedy; examples of ballet and modern dance and ethnic dance can be seen at dance concerts, night clubs, discos.

4) Watch certain television programs to observe dance styles in action.

5) If ethnic dances are being studied, assign reports on topics such as the culture of the people, the costumes worn for dances, the geographic and climatic conditions, and how these factors affect the kinds of dances produced.

EVALUATIVE PROCEDURES

To evaluate your groups, use various criteria. Appraise their technical and creative output. In addition, use your pupils to assist in the evaluative process. It helps them gain insight into movement and gives them an important sense of responsibility. The following plan can be used for evaluating group output in creative approaches 1, 2 and 3.

1) Use a grading scale of 1 through 10 points, in which 10 represents a perfect score (100), 9 is a 90, etc. Discuss with the class your evaluative criteria; tell them what you are looking for.

2) Break down creative projects into many skills; score each skill separately, then add them up. For example, with approach #1, the teacher asks:

   a) Were the requirements of the problem met? Did the group solve the problem, using steps given?

   b) Do they project? Are movements accurately performed? Is the group keeping time to the music? Is there a demonstration of postural awareness?

   c) Is the solution to problem interesting? Is there some originality?

9

Designing Dances for the Advanced Student

This chapter presents a variety of different stimuli for creating movement patterns. We have included images and ideas that are stimulating and motivating for the dance pupil.

There are five approaches that can be applied at different times throughout the dance unit.

Approach #1. Improvisations based on:

    I. Problems in the craft of movement (time, space, energy and body shape).

    II. Developing a creative response using emotions, dramatic themes, and sensory stimuli.

    III. Creating a unique movement vocabulary through explorations of sport, play, work, animals, and everyday motions.

Approach #2 Inventing dances through the field dance or chance dance.

Approach #3. Creating movement variations on dance themes.

Approach #4. Exploring movement based on visual and performing art stimuli such as music, drama, painting, and sculpture.

Approach #5. Designing dances based on historical periods.

APPROACH # 1. IMPROVISATIONS

In this activity, pupils are given creative problems to solve using various types of imagery. Improvisations can involve the following stimuli:

CATEGORIES FOR IMPROVISATION

I. *Exploring the Craft of Movement*
Warming up the imagination with short studies in:
A) Time   B) Space   C) Energy   D) Body Shape
II. *Stimulating a Creative Response with:*
A) Emotions
B) Dramatic Themes
C) Sensory Stimuli (sight, sound, taste, touch, smell)
III. *Developing a Unique Movement Vocabulary*
A) Sport
B) Work
C) Play
D) Everyday Activities
E) Animal Imagery

The improvisational approach should be reserved for more advanced pupils because they have a more extensive movement vocabulary and therefore more self-confidence for experimentation.

Problems involving creative imagery should be analyzed prior to actually dancing. It is important for the class to realize the many responses possible and that there is often no right or wrong answer.

In addition to developing creative powers, these improvisations also help to improve technical skills. You can use them to provide opportunities for social development, and to motivate improved pupil performance.

PREPARING FOR THE LESSON

Each problem will dictate a particular class format. However, some general rules can be followed:

1) Hold an informal discussion about the image or problem to be solved.
2) Use the friendlier and more intimate circle formation for discussions and analysis of problems.

3) Assign pupils to partnerships or small groups for problem solving.

4) Provide opportunities for informal performance by the groups.

ACCOMPANIMENT

1) Use appropriate sounds.

2) Select music that supports problem.

3) Be imaginative in your selections.

IMPROVISATIONS BASED ON SAMPLE MOVEMENT PROBLEMS AND SOLUTIONS

I. EXPLORING THE CRAFT OF MOVEMENT

These short improvisational studies deal with the elements of time, space, energy and body shape. The following are sample problems which can be adjusted to your particular needs. Pupils can work alone, with a partner or in small groups.

A) *TIME:* Explorations in tempo, rhythm, meter, and accent.

1) *Tempo*
   Create a dance phrase based on the following imagery. *Make believe you are:*

   in a slow motion movie

   in a speeded-up movie

   a feather floating in the breeze

   an astronaut in space

   a bullet shot from a gun

Perform movements in different tempos. For example:

   a) triplet, triplet, side swing in fast motion.

   b) triplet, plus a 12 count original idea fast and in slow motion.

   c) walk, run, skip, plus your own axial movement for 16 counts in a tempo that accelerates, then decelerates.

   d) create a 32 count phrase using one axial and one locomotor movement and perform in slow motion.

e) move on the floor for 16 counts in fast motion.

f) use isolated body parts such as an arm, leg, head, chest. Perform movements in a fast, percussive manner.

2) *Rhythm*

Given a rhythmic pattern, clap it out, then dance it out. For example:

Let class make up their own dance phrase to this rhythmic pattern or give them a finished phrase, such as:

a) 4 walks forward

b) sustained body contraction

c) lunge right and left side

d) run with arms reaching; finish in pose

3) *Meter*

Students compose movements based on different meters. Have several pupils write out their note values and rhythmic patterns, and present them to the class, or have class members attempt to notate the rhythmic pattern and meter by observing the pattern. Work with simple meters (²/₄, ⁴/₄, ³/₄, ⁶/₈), and use mixed meter (create a pattern of notes that constantly change meter).

4) *Accent*

Give the class a definite pattern; let them add accents and then dance it out; or, give the accent pattern, with pupils creating dance movements around this pattern. To emphasize accents ask pupils to move certain body parts on each accent.

B) *SPACE:* Explorations with props, real and imaginary spaces

1) *Props:* Students develop dances based on the shape, texture and motion of a variety of props. Types of props to explore include: umbrellas, boxes, fabric, chairs, ropes, hoops, plastic tables, etc.

Preparing the Lesson

a) organize class into small groups of pupils or use solo studies

b) distribute props and analyze shapes, structures or movable parts.

c) distribute different numbers of props to pupils. For example: 2 chairs for 3 pupils; one umbrella for 2 pupils; one table for 4 pupils, a large piece of plastic for one pupil, etc.

d) avoid artificial exploration of props: a) encourage pupils to make contact with the prop; b) translate the motion of the prop through different body movements; c) use the prop as a connection between other pupils.

e) perform dances with or without musical accompaniment

f) create your own props out of different materials and create dances based on their shape, texture and movement.

2) *Real Space*

a) the classroom itself (doors, walls, etc.)

b) the hallway (explore the length, width and height of space)

c) the gymnasium, the staircase, a closet

d) other spaces such as, the park, street or museum.

SAMPLE MOVEMENT PROBLEMS IN REAL SPACE

a) Explore the area of the gymnasium—create big axial and locomotor movements in a wide spatial range.

b) Explore the way you can move up and down a staircase; create interesting movements and rhythms

c) Given the emotion, Fear, create a short study using a corner of the room reflecting this emotion

3) *Imaginary Space*

Pupils create dances based on imaginary space. a) Pupils *make believe* they are: in a box, a field, a closet, under a table, etc. b) Pupils develop movements that reflect their space. For example, constricted movements in a closet, big, open leaps and runs for a field, etc. c) Pupils create a dramatic idea around their space. For example: You are in a box that is tall and narrow; you cannot escape. You are locked in and can only move in a vertical dimension—suddenly you are able to escape; crawl out from the box and run for your life.

4) Use paths in space to create dance studies. Use small groups as soloists.

SAMPLE SHAPES IN SPACE

a) move your body in place and reflect the spatial pattern through axial movements

b) move your body through space, creating floor plan based on the given drawing

c) devise a dramatic idea based on the drawing

d) use solo or group studies

C) *ENERGY*

See Chapter 1 for interesting movement problems to solve using the Mirror Image format.

D) *BODY SHAPE AND DESIGN*—Explorations with letters and geometric designs

SAMPLE MOVEMENT PROBLEMS

1) Body Shape

Using *letters* as stimuli:

a) Choose a letter and make the shape with your body, in a static pose (students enjoy trying to guess your letter).

b) Spell out different words by linking one shape to the other.

c) Trace a letter by walking its shape in a floor pattern.

d) Take a partner and create letter shapes connecting different body parts.

e) Spell out words by writing letter shapes in space with an arm or leg.

f) Use letter shapes created by group members and link these together in a cluster design.

SAMPLE MOVEMENT PROBLEMS

Using *geometric designs* as stimuli:

a) Work with square, rectangular or triangular shapes individually, and create body shapes and movements that reflect their design.

b) Pick objects with different shapes and create movements reflecting the line, volume and weight of these shapes. For example: a lamp, a table, a chair, a piece of sculpture, etc.

c) Use photos of different shapes and have each pupil create dances based on pictures. For example, look through a book of ballet poses; assign pupils to different groups, connect the shapes into a dance phrase, add music, and you have a finished dance study!

d) Use different images in nature to evoke shapes. For example: climate, seasons, rocks, leaves, trees or clouds.

Sample problem using seasons:

1) Create a design in space that is expressive of some feature of one of the four seasons.

2) Interpret an outstanding quality of the season, such as its climate (summer heat), prevalent shapes (ice of winter), dominant colors (green and yellow—summer; orange and brown—fall), mood (awakening in spring; barrenness of winter).

II. DEVELOPING A CREATIVE RESPONSE

The following approach involves the creation of movements based on emotional, dramatic and sensory stimuli. Use your imagination to extend and vary the sample problems described below:

A) EMOTIONS

1) Preparing the lesson for Sample Problem 1. List different emotions on the chalkboard, such as: fear, jealousy, love or anger. Students work solo or in groups.

Sample Problem 1.

1) Each group of dancers selects an emotion and translates it into a dance pattern.

2) The class observes the performance of each group and attempts to guess the emotion being expressed.

Preparing the lesson for Sample Problem 2.

1) Discuss with the class the different life situations and emotions involved.

2) List dramatic situations that reflect different emotions, such as: going to school for the first time, a first date, a fight with parents, or being followed by a stranger.

Sample Problem 2.

1) Groups act out situations and the class tries to guess the theme being expressed.

2) Music can be used for background.

Sample Problem 3.

Use photos of different scenes brought in by the students (or you) which show various emotions, such as: a fight scene, a mother caring for her child, a young child crying over a broken toy, or a family gathering.

B) DRAMATIC THEMES

Sample Problem 1

Act out key scenes from plays or movies, showing dramatic and emotional contrasts. Sources can be obtained from:

Hamlet, Our Town, West Side Story, The Crucible, A Hatful of Rain.

Sample Problem 2.

2) Act out simple and short situations, such as: a crowded train, a rocking boat, being locked in a closet, or enjoying nature in an open field

Sample Problem 3.

3) Select certain *action words* for the class to interpret through dance. Use such words as flop, jump, kick, slide, fall, jerk, run, pop, sputter or leap. Give these words a dramatic impetus. For example, fall like a drunk or a new baby, run from a stranger, leap through a field with joy, or kick imaginary insects.

C) SENSORY STIMULI Sample movement problems using: texture, smell, taste, sight and sound.

1) an ice cube melting, a feather floating in the breeze.

2) the color red, black, yellow.

3) the textures of velvet, sandpaper, stretch nylon, water.

4) the smell of perfume, gas, polluted air.

5) sweet or sour taste.

6) the sound of trains, silence, a screeching violin.

7) the texture of pieces of material or other objects from home.

III. Improvisations based on Creating a Unique Movement Vocabulary

Using the following categories as a source of movement development, alter the appearance of the activity by dancing. For example, disguise a basketball lay-up shot by turning it into a series of running and hopping motions; develop a leap from the action of putting on stockings; create body swings from a swimming stroke, etc.

Sample Movement Categories

A) *Sports*—pitching and batting a ball, tennis and golf swings, swimming strokes, or basketball moves, such as dribbling, lay-ups, etc.

B) *Work*—actions such as drilling, shoveling, raking leaves, hammering a nail, or painting a wall.

C) *Play*—actions such as children's games, like hopscotch, London Bridges, Ring-A-Round the Rosie, or jump-rope.

D) *Everyday Activities* such as combing your hair, brushing your teeth, making a bed, getting dressed, or running for the bus.

E) *Animal Imagery* such as interpreting the shapes, qualities and motions of insects, animals in the zoo, or house pets, such as canaries, cats or dogs.

Sample Solutions

After students choose a category, they can create interesting patterns by varying the time, space, and energy of their action. For example:

a) *TIME*—perform an action in a normal speed, very slowly, very quickly; create a rhythmic pattern. For example, combing hair slowly, then quickly; batting a ball in slow motion; jumping rope in quick-time, etc.

b) *SPACE*—perform actions in different directions, levels and ranges; vary the focus of motion; create an interesting spatial design; perform the action with a prop, such as a fabric, rope, pole, box, chair, scarf or umbrella. For example, hammering a nail using different spatial ranges from small to large, and on different spatial levels (from the floor to the air).

c) *ENERGY*—perform action in a sustained and smooth fashion; sharply, in a vibratory way with a swinging quality. For example, jump rope in slow motion.

d) *BODY SHAPE*—perform the actions using different parts of the body: comb your hair with your leg, brush your teeth with your elbow, or swing a bat with your leg.

A dance pattern can be developed by connecting different actions.

For example: Comb your hair slowly, put on stockings quickly, perform a shoulder pass quickly, imitate a cat moving, paint a wall with your knee, etc. Actions can also be varied by placing them on a moving or traveling base. Thus, a locomotor action can be developed. For example, using the original action, place it on a moving base across the floor and exaggerate the action so that it can be easily observed as a dance motion.

SAMPLE SOLUTIONS

Create a leap from the everyday action of putting on stockings

Create a pattern of runs and step-hops with the basketball dribble and lay-up shot.

Create a swinging phrase, using various tennis strokes.

EVALUATIVE PROCEDURES

Remember that many possible answers exist to the same problem, so grade your pupils on the following basis:

1) Are pupils on right track; are they solving problem?

2) Are they performing movements accurately?

3) Are solutions imaginative and creative?

4) What was the original action (sport, work or play)?

5) Was the variation in time, space and energy successfully performed?

6) Is the sequence of action interesting and does it have a pleasant flow?

7) Does the pupil perform the actions in the proper style, technique and mood?

8) How can the student improve the pattern?

The following problems can be presented to your classes as *Quickie Improvisations*. In each problem, there is a definite goal to be achieved. Select various problems related to your specific needs.

Before you present a problem, ask pupils to think about it, then *Go* and solve it. Pupils can work alone or in groups.

SAMPLE—QUICKIE IMPROVISATIONS

PROBLEM	GOAL
MAKE BELIEVE YOU ARE:	
1) a broken mirror crashing to the ground	energy
2) a bouncing ball	unusual movement
3) a strange insect	body shape
4) locked in a closet	dramatic situation
5) a washing machine	comic action

APPROACH #2. INVENTING DANCES THROUGH THE FIELD DANCE OR CHANCE DANCE

The field or chance dance was originally developed by Merce Cunningham during the 1960s. It involves solo improvisation within a group framework. Dancers improvise, with certain guidelines in mind, to create an open-ended, and spontaneous composition. Field dances are exciting and unpredictable to watch and perform. The choreography is not planned, so there is an element of unpredictability because one dancer never knows what the other is going to do!

HOW THE FIELD DANCE WORKS

In the field dance, perfomers are provided with a series of movements that are performed in different patterns and at different times. Throughout the length of the dance, the decisions to move or not to move, to enter or to exit, belong to the dancers.

GENERAL FIELD DANCE PROCEDURES

A) Preparing the Lesson

1) Organize groups in mass formation to practice movements to be used in the dance.

2) Provide movements previously learned in techniques class or introduce new movement ideas.

3) Choose movements appropriate to the ability level of your pupils.

4) Select movement ideas with potential for variation in time, space and energy.

SAMPLE FIELD DANCE #1.

1) practice en masse a stiff-legged walk; use a mysterious quality, as though being drawn by an invisible force;

arm position; side-shoulder level

eyes focused forward

feet move carefully, as though on a tight rope

move in different directions as you walk

2) perform a swing forward and backward (see exercise Chapter 4 for description)

3) skip with arms moving freely; move in different directions; make sure you keep the skip simple—alternating from one foot to the the other

4) you can add other ideas:

    a) add a body shape in the form of a letter or number

    b) call out a name in a loving or hateful manner

    c) strike a frozen pose and hold it for 8 counts

B) Preparing the Lesson

    1) After sufficient practice of steps, organize pupils into small groups of 6-8 students.

    2) Discuss with groups the *rules* of the field dance For Example:

        a) individual students can arrange movements in any sequence as they perform

        b) all students must perform all movements and enter and exit at least two times

        c) students can perform their movements in different count sequences; no preplanning is required

        d) groups decide the beginning and ending of their dance from several options. For example:

            begin with an empty stage

            begin with a solo dancer in a pose

            begin with a large group on stage

            end with an empty stage

            end with a group shape

            end with performers moving in different directions

Teacher Hints

1) Set a time limit for the dance, especially if you are teaching a 30-minute class. For example, provide each group with at least five minutes to explore and perform their dances.

2) Remind pupils to be sensitive and aware of each others' space. Even though they are performing as soloists, they are still in a group.

3) Encourage student awareness of group design and stage balance as they make their entrances and exits.

4) Add the Mirror Image device to expand the field dance; pupils may decide when they wish to imitate the movements of another dancer.

5) Add the Shadow technique to expand the field dance. Beautiful designs can develop as 1,2,3 or more dancers begin to imitate each other's movement patterns. The Shadow and Mirror Image techniques are based on follow the leader.

GUIDELINES FOR DEVELOPING FIELD DANCE THEMES

1) fun Field Dance movements to use:
   a) prances in all directions
   b) jumps and turns
   c) collapsing in fast and slow motion
   d) a funny walk

2) lyrical Field Dance movements suggested:
   a) a triplet, a triplet turn
   b) a side fall
   c) swings
   d) sustained movements in 8 and 16 counts developed by pupils

3) using general movement directions to compose a Field Dance:
   a) a traveling step
   b) a level change
   c) a body shape
   d) a frozen position
   e) a sudden dynamic change

SUGGESTED FIELD DANCE ACCOMPANIMENT

Use music to stimulate pupil imagination and motivate performance. Musical selections can be determined by you or your pupils. Electronic music is an excellent accompaniment for the beginning field dance. It provides a free meter and tempo and is less distracting to pupils. Later, use classical, popular, rock or ethnic music.

EVALUATION

After a field dance experience is concluded, find time to evaluate pupil responses. For example:

1) How did you feel making decisions on the spur of the moment?

2) Were you aware of other pupils while you were dancing?

3) Did the music help or hinder you?

4) Did you observe interesting designs and patterns throughout the dance? Can you describe some?

5) Did any interesting surprises occur while you were performing?

APPROACH #3. CREATING MOVEMENT VARIATIONS ON DANCE THEMES

In this approach, pupils create dances based on movement themes and variations. The teacher devises a short movement theme for the class (class theme), with a specific count structure.

Preparing the Lesson

1) Teach and practice the class theme in mass formation. The theme can consist of new or familiar movements.

2) Organize the class into small groups.

3) Have groups create variations on the class theme. For example:

   a) vary the direction of a step

   b) change the level of a given step, its range, its dynamics.

   c) repeat one movement exactly as given

4) Have groups rearrange their pattern into an interesting sequence and perform it in unison.

5) Have each group practice the original class theme, as well as their own variation.

SAMPLE PROBLEM THEME AND VARIATIONS BASED ON SPECIFIC COUNT STRUCTURE

Class Theme

1) walk 8 counts
2) arabesque 4 counts
3) three triplets (9 counts)
4) a lunge
5) plié (two times)
6) back fall and rise (16 counts)

Group Variation

1) walks in circle
2) arabesque on knee
3) triplet turns
4) lunge
5) plié and relevé
6) back fall and rise in 8 counts

GROUP VARIATION AND REARRANGEMENT OF STEPS

walk in a circle
plié and relevé
back fall
arabesque on the knee
rise
three triplet turns
lunge repeated twice

A PROCEDURE FOR PERFORMING A DANCE IN THEME AND VARIATION

Assign groups to corners of the room as shown.

Section 1

groups 1 and 3 perform the class theme in unison

groups 2 and 4 perform their group variation in unison

Section 2

group 1 performs their variation

group 2 performs class theme in a round (one part of group begins the theme 4 counts before the other)

group 3 performs their variation

group 4 performs the class theme in a round

IDEAS FOR ENDING THE DANCE

Section 3)

a) all groups perform the class theme in unison

b) all groups perform their variations

c) groups 1 and 2, 3, or 4, perform the class theme in a round

d) representatives from groups perform the class theme in round, then in unison

e) pick one movement from each group variation and create a new pattern.

THEME AND VARIATIONS BASED ON GENERAL DIRECTIONS

After creating the class theme with counts from general directions, the groups compose their own variations and rearrange the movements into an interesting pattern.

SAMPLE CLASS THEME BASED ON GENERAL DIRECTIONS

a) a group sculptural effect, create a pose without touching body parts

b) a vibratory motion; pick any body part to vibrate

c) a roll (side or forward)

d) a slide-jump-skip pattern

e) a mirror image idea

f) an unusual shape (by contacting different body parts)

g) funny walks in all directions

ACCOMPANIMENT

1) Select music that supports your theme in terms of count structure and tempo.

2) The class theme can be performed to a free-metered (electronic) piece giving pupils more freedom in their performance.

APPROACH # 4. EXPLORING MOVEMENT BASED ON VISUAL AND PERFORMING ART STIMULI

Art stimuli provide an unlimited resource for dance exploration and invention. Teachers can stress various aspects of each art form. The following ideas are suggested for your dance units:
VISUAL ARTS

1) *Painting*—explore a particular work of art; study the line, design, color, texture and theme of the work; students can bring in their own pictures or the teacher can organize a trip to the museum or art gallery.

2) *Sculpture*—have pupils bring in objects from home or nature; discuss and analyze the shape, texture, line, weight, and design of object; attempt to translate them into dance movement; also study sculptures created in school art classes, and in museums.

3) *Architecture*—take walking tours of your community and study line, contours and shapes of buildings.

4) *Photography*—capture themes, shapes and designs from photos in magazines; assign different photos to different groups.

PERFORMING ARTS-DRAMA

The following studies involve greater pupil preparation and development.

1) *Mime*—perform short studies using movement and gesture, to tell a story or express a mood.

2) *Plays*—choose outstanding scenes and re-enact them in dance; assign various characters to dancers; act out different emotions expressed in the play.

3) *Poetry*—read and analyze various poems of interest to the class; assign one line of poetry to different groups and interpret them in movement; have students recite poetry and then dance, or recite and dance simultaneously. Take the meter and rhythm of a poetic line and interpret it in movement.

MUSIC

1) *Songs*—select from classical opera to popular; analyze the lyrics and interpret them in dance.

2) *Instrumental music*—study the various instruments and interpret their tonal qualities in movement; create an orchestra of dancers; also study the shapes of instruments, as well as how they are played.

3) *Classical music*—interpret melodies, rhythms and moods through movement; design dances through musical structures, such as: ABA, theme and variations, rondo, canon, or fugue.

4) *Popular music*—create dances based on themes, instruments, rhythm of music.

WRITING AN ART REPORT AS A CULMINATING ACTIVITY

The following outline can be used as a guide for writing an art report on a live concert in any style of dance. Teachers should analyze and discuss what is expected from pupil reports.

PERFORMANCE REPORT

Title page includes:

Name of performing dance company

Date seen

Your name

Official class

Dance class

Name of dance teacher

The report is to be written in composition form. It should include the following for each dance:

Title of dance

Choreographer

Type of music used

(e.g., folk-classical-jazz-modern)

Reasons for your emotional response

(e.g., like it or not and why)

Description of costumes

give reasons why a particular costume is worn

Description of lighting

give reasons why a particular color or colors are used: if a spot light
is used—describe its function.
The dance itself

1. Describe any floor patterns (lines, circles, etc.)
2. Numbers of dancers on stage (soloist, duets, etc.)
3. Tell the story only if it is relevant to specific movements
   (African, folk, etc.)
4. Describe any quality of movements that affect the mood
   of the dance (percussive, smooth, etc.)

What steps or movements did you see that we do in class? Any
personal or additional comments about the dance?

APPROACH #5. DESIGNING DANCES BASED ON HISTORICAL PERIODS

In this approach, pupils actively learn how dance developed
from earliest times to the present day, and create dances in
different moods, styles and periods. Historical periods are studied
in terms of:

a) geography and climate of the country

b) economic, political and social aspects

c) the general mood of the times

d) the arts (music, painting, sculpture, etc.)

e) dance developments

The suggested textbook to be used is *History of Dance,* by Richard
Kraus. Use films, bulletin boards, trips to museums, libraries and
concert halls to illustrate ideas. A suggested time graph for study
is:

Primitive Period

Pre-Christian (B.C.)—Egypt, Hebrew, Greek, Roman

Middle Ages (4th—14th century)

Renaissance (15th—18th century)

Romantic Period (19th century)

Modern Period (20th century)

The following is a description of class projects related to each
historical period. The purpose is to make history come alive

through dance. When possible, use music to help illustrate ideas. Small groups of students function well together, with leaders appointed to supervise. Each project could last three to five days. The final day should involve a performance with class evaluation and discussion.

SUGGESTED PROCEDURES AND ACTIVITIES IN THE HISTORY OF DANCE

1. PRIMITIVE PERIOD

a) Organize the class into small groups.

b) Pick a primitive dance theme (death, war, fertility, etc.).

c) Create a dance using primitive dance steps demonstrated by the teacher, with a primitive dance theme as the foundation.

d) Use primitive dance music for accompaniment.

e) Present pupils with varied art experiences (music, art, drama) reflecting the primitive period.

2. PRE-CHRISTIAN PERIOD

EGYPT

a) Look at an example of Egyptian sculpture or painting.

b) Analyze the art object in terms of shape, color and theme.

c) Groups create movements reflecting Egyptian art objects.

d) Use various Egyptian dance movements, such as: somersault, bridge, hip rotations. Include them in group dances.

HEBREWS

a) Practice Hebraic folk-dance steps, such as the mayim, hora, grapevine, etc.

b) Pupils rearrange the steps in a pattern and perform them in groups to Hebrew music.

c) Use the field dance approach as a device for choreographing these dances.

GREEKS

a) Using the Greek Pyrrhic (war) dances as a theme, pupils create a story about war through movements, such as marching, climbing, rolling, etc.

b) Modern music can be used for accompaniment (electronic, percussive etc.).

ROMANS

a) Use the art of pantomime as an example of the Roman contribution to the development of dance.

b) Study the elements of pantomime with the class organized into groups.

c) Groups select from the following list of sketches, then create a group pantomime: a date, a party, at home, in the classroom. Use silent movie music as background.

3. MIDDLE AGES

a) Reflect the mood or quality of the Dark Ages by creating a religious dance.

b) Use paintings of the Middle Ages as sources for dance ideas and movements. Study color, line, design and the theme of the paintings.

c) Use music, such as the Gregorian Chants, for accompaniment.

4. RENAISSANCE

a) Learn examples of court dance steps through the technique of mirror image (teacher demonstrates actions and pupils imitate).

b) Choose from the "magic envelope" whether to create a *basse* dance, such as the Pavanne, or an *haute* dance, such as the Galliard.

c) Use music of the Renaissance to accompany the dances.

d) Give pupils several lessons in ballet technique to expose them to the vocabulary.

5. ROMANTIC PERIOD

a) Class choose a fairy tale such as Cinderella, and re-enact it with romantic movements of the period.

b) Use the music of the time period.

c) Study and analyze the changes in the ballet costumes.

6. BALLET TODAY

a) Study the jazz ballet style.

b) Recreate a dance from "West Side Story."

c) Study the dance of George Ballanchine.

d) Recreate an abstract ballet in the style of Ballanchine.

7. SOCIAL DANCE IN THE UNITED STATES (EARLY FORMS)

Study and practice movements from:

a)square dances (e.g., Cumberland Eight)

b)round dances (e.g., Jessie Polka)

c)contra dances (e.g., Virginia Reel)

d)waltz

e)polka

8. TAP DANCE

a) Study several tap dance steps and learn a short routine to music.

b) Invite a guest artist to demonstrate several finished tap routines or show a film on tap dancing.

9. MODERN DANCE

PAST

Study contributions of dance pioneers such as:

a) *Isadora Duncan*—listen to music she used for dances; study her style of dancing. Pupils create a short work to her music, utilizing a dramatic theme such as war.

b) *Martha Graham*—provide pupils with several lessons in Graham technique; show films of the Graham company, such as "Dancer's World" or "Appalchian Spring"; create a short dance reflecting her movement style, music and use of props.

PRESENT

Study contributions of various choreographers such as:

a) *Merce Cunningham*—study avant-garde styles and have pupils recreate "chance dances" to John Cage music.

b) *Alwin Nikolais*—study the multi-media dance.

10. MODERN JAZZ

a) Study the various techniques of modern jazz dancing.

b) Teach pupils a short and simple routine to music.

11. SOCIAL DANCE TODAY

Study various styles of social dancing such as: disco (hustle, twist, bump, etc.); fox trot, lindy, Latin American dances, novelty dances (Alley Cat, Hokey-Pokey). Students can choose from dances and perform them for the class.

12. OTHER FOLK AND ETHNIC DANCES

Study dances from different lands such as: Africa, East India, Hawaii, Russia, or Israel.

Index